# TEAM MATES

I felt a pair of hands come right down on my shoulders, give a squeeze. That took me by surprise; I didn't have a shoulder-squeezing-level friend at Raycroft, yet. My first thought: maybe Harlan. But JC's all were under-age for Emil's.

I let my head loll back, the way you do. It brushed against a soft and scented shirt-front, but she didn't move. Kelly.

I straightened up and turned. Okay-sure, I gulped. She wore a different name tag. It said: "Clumsy Carp."

"Hey, Red," she said, maybe not as loud as last night. "As of this afternoon, I got to be a Red myself. What say we take a little walk and talk about color?"

"Now?" I said. Yes, I was stalling, trying to get my stuff together. She nodded. "Sure. O.K.," I said, while getting up. Obviously, the guys were watching me, and they were strangers. Randy Duke would say: "If you'll excuse me, gentlemen." I did. Everyone had sure shut up.

*Other Avon Flare Books by*
**Julian F. Thompson**

THE GROUNDING OF GROUP 6

# FACING IT

JULIAN F. THOMPSON

FACING IT is an original publication of Avon Books. This work has never before appeared in book form.

AVON BOOKS
A division of
The Hearst Corporation
1790 Broadway
New York, New York 10019


Published by arrangement with the author
Library of Congress Catalog Card Number: 83-11885
ISBN: 0-380-84491-5



**Library of Congress Cataloging in Publication Data**

Thompson, Julian F.
Facing it.

(An Avon/Flare book)
Summary: Assuming a new name for a summer job as a camp counselor in order to put his problems behind him, a college student finds that decision regrettably complicated his relationship with a girl who has a secret of her own.
[1. Camp counselors—Fiction] I. Title.
PZ7.T371596Fac 1983 [Fic] 83-11885
ISBN 0-380-84491-5

First Flare Printing, September, 1983

FLARE TRADEMARK REG. U. S. PAT. OFF. AND IN OTHER COUNTRIES, MARCA REGISTRADA, HECHO EN U.S.A.

Printed in the U. S. A.

WFH 10 9 8 7 6 5 4 3 2 1

For the people in the living room at Lower,
the kitchen in the tiny Inc., and the back
room at the Airport Inn: the best of times,
the best of friends, the best of teachers.

# CHAPTER 1

Later on, this afternoon and evening, I'm going to say to lots of strangers, ''Hi, I'm Randy Duke.'' Which almost surely is a lie, and certainly is not a thing I've ever said before, except to ''Fisher'' Fleer.

I'll bet there're lots of people who would like to try some different names on their pianolas.

That's a thing my father says, from time to time: ''Try this-or-that on your pianola.'' I asked him what one was, when I was little, and he just laughed and said what did it sound like, silly? I said what you'd expect, and he said, ''Close enough.''

Close enough. Which is the way we've always been, I guess. There's no such thing as a pianola, nowadays.

I've wished a lot of times he *was* my father, in more than legal fact. The same thing with my mother. But if they were, of course, I wouldn't be the way I am. I wouldn't look the same, or think the same, or act the same. I never would have had The Arm. I might not even want them as my parents. That's the way it works, a lot, as possibly you've noticed.

''And vice-ho-ho-versa,'' my father'd be inclined to add.

It isn't easy to adopt a child; you really have to measure up. My parents aren't perfect—*I* can tell you that—but here's the way they come across: friendly—check; cleanly—check; respectable—check-check; intelligent—sufficiently; popular—for sure; affluent—increasingly.

Was I a match for them? I like to think so: an alert Caucasian foundling baby boy, well-dressed, with no apparent scars or shortages. Lying in a crib (the way I must have been), I'm sure I didn't even show I was a southpaw. *Was* a southpaw is, unfortunately, the tense (the lad says, with a tinge of bitterness, you'll note).

But anyway—today, and for the next eight weeks, three days, I am, and will be, Randy Duke. Of course I chose the name myself; isn't it a dandy? When they adopted me, my parents put me in the record books as Jonathan, and their last name, which I won't even mention. It isn't relevant, so why get them involved? Once, when I was twelve, I think, I drove myself a little coo-coo trying to guess (remember?) what my *real* name was. It's sort of funny now to know. It *could* be Randy Duke (I guess it also could be Jonathan ________________), but that's not the reason that I chose it.

I chose it just because it sounds the way I'd like to be. The name has a certain *panache*, if you can stand that word. I wouldn't say I'm all that randy ("lecherous"; "sexy"—*Webster's New Collegiate*). Actually, my best guess is I'm only slightly over-sexed. I think I always have been. I was humping the mattress all through my latency period, if you're familiar with Freud's theories at all. Pre-adolescents aren't supposed to be all that genital-centered, but I was. I didn't know what was up, of course, aside from the obvious. My parents dealt with things more or less after the fact; they didn't anticipate much. So, as a kid, I experienced a lot before I'd heard of it, if that makes any sense to you. In some ways, I bet I enjoyed sex most before I knew too much about it, when it was just me and those fantasies and feelings that I had. I didn't have to think at all—except to make sure that nobody caught me. At my present age, I still have to think about that, plus all this other garbage. Blah-blah: birth-control and do-I-really-want-to-say-exactly-that? and am-I-being-fair? and is-it-any-good-for-her? and on-and-on-etcetera-amen. Sometimes I wonder if anybody else's mind can speed as much as mine. On nothing. Nothing seems to help. I'm getting off the point.

So—"Randy Duke" is not a joke, or code, like crossword-puzzle-ese for "horny nobleman." I'm not into making up those kinds of games and symbols; life does well enough at that without my help. As I was saying, I just like the sound of both those names. Together, they sound cool and carefree, but also solid and dependable. Yes, they are a little jockish, but certainly intelligent, would you agree? Which makes them perfect for my purposes. Randy Duke is going to be my name at Camp Raycroft, the summer camp I'm going to work at for the next eight weeks, three days, starting later on this afternoon.

Dunbar Dibble, my roommate down at college, is responsible. He has gone to Raycroft every summer since the age of seven; six years as a camper, then two as Helper in the Dining Hall (HDH), another two as Junior Counsellor (JC) and finally, ever since he started college, as a full-fledged counsellor. It's like a second summer home to him. His father worked there also, all through college, and still goes to alumni parties in New York; he was a founding-year counsellor (FYC, I guess).

Well, this year, Dunny came to realize, about the first of May, that he would like to go to Europe with his girl friend, The Irrepressible Irene. And so, with my connivance, he wrote the camp Director, Fisher Fleer, a letter, asking for a year's sabbatical, unpaid, and saying he had just the perfect fill-in, namely me. His father wrote another letter, saying much the same, and Fisher Fleer agreed it was a "great" idea. Our interview was merely a formality, I'd say.

It's possible you wonder why in hell I would agree to such a scheme—and then adopt (get this) a *nom d'été*, as well. I hardly blame you.

When first suggested, a summer spent in working/living with a bunch of kids (say, ten, eleven years of age) struck me as a great deal less than dreamy. But Dunbar Dibble has a way with words. Dibble=Lawyer, as long as there's been sin in Cincinnati.

"Jon," he said, "a summer up at camp is like a magic time. It's time that doesn't count—no carry-overs, no one keeping score. Rake-off isn't *like* the world, it isn't meant to be. It's *fun*. The kids are *great*, the guys who work there are *fantastic*." And, of course, he switched to the stupid

French-type accent that he does: "For *Monsieur's* after-dark delight, we have our sister (heh-heh) Camp Raylene."

I made the skeptic's smirk, around a rude suggestion. I was being cool, of course, and Dunny was a sly one. After the accident, my dating life had . . . undergone (that's good) some changes. I still liked the idea of girls a lot, the way they're put together, how they are, and all that jazz. I just hadn't felt like hanging around any of them, at school. I didn't want them feeling sorry for me. That's what I kept telling myself, anyway.

"Besides," he pressed, "you haven't got a goddam thing to do this summer. And if you stay at home, you'll feel so goddam sorry for yourself, you'll melt."

That stuck it to me, right between the blades. Ever since The Accident, now seven months ago, I *hadn't* had a thing to do this summer, or the next, or next, or next—or any of the ten or fifteen after that, according to my former plans. Until the thing that happened happened, I'd planned to, basically, pitch baseball every summer—after college, in the major leagues.

And now I'll have to tell about The Accident. I always seem to have to end up telling people all about it, even when I swear I won't, ahead of time. I never will forget the thing, that's obvious, and anyone who sees me when I haven't got a baseball glove on it, would want to know just how the hell . . . ? , though ninety-nine percent will look away real quick, as if they didn't notice. I'm apt to tell them anyway. I can tell it short, or middle-sized, or long, depending on the audience.

The story's never much like the experience, even in the longest form, with every tiny detail put in place. I remember everything. The sound, for instance. You wouldn't think I'd hear a thing, except that noisy little motor. But yes, I did, and I can tell you what it sounded like, as just another part of everything. That doesn't make the story real, though. It's still blah-blah, a pleading bunch of words that just add up to "Pity me," or "Don't you think I'm interesting?" or "How cool can I be?" or "Let me gross you out."

Talking's mostly tricks like that. Once a thing is done, it's dead, but people learn to copy it, in words, and use it as a tool to get their way a lot. To call it bullshit is to oversimplify the matter.

But anyway, I'm going to tell this story now, and every time I tell it, I have to see how hopeless-goddam-*dumb* the whole thing was, so unbe-fucking-lievably *unnecessary*. I am meant to be intelligent. Just ask the NMSQT/PSAT; just ask the SATs and the Achievement Tests. Wanna know my GPA? But I will tell you something not-so-very secret: the kind of dumb I am will probably be fatal.

As long as I remember, I've O.D.ed on activity. My parents turned me on to it: busy, busy, busy. No idle hands around the ______________ house. My mother zipped herself and us from lessons to appointments to committees to rehearsals to the games; my father always "found the time" for one more worthwhile task/responsibility. Up till seven months ago, I thought of that as life.

So here's the scene. It's Christmas break from college; I'm at my parents' summer/winter hideaway, near Brandon, in Vermont: a family vacation. We're splitting firewood, my sister, Tish, and I; I'm in a rush to finish up and meet some kids at Pico while there's still good light. Of course I *would* ski, wouldn't I? My father's rented a gasoline-powered wood splitter from the local hardware store, and I am picking up the heavy sections of some big old maple trunks, and dropping them in the proper place, while sister Tish young-womans the controls.

You may not know the way a splitter works. It doesn't strike a blow, it pushes. At one end there's the motor, set above a pair of eight-inch wheels, so you can move the thing around. The motor activates the pushing force; the principle involved is called hydraulics. What you see is this: from out a two-foot cylinder there comes a heavy stainless pipe, with a flat piece on the end of it. That is the ram, the force. Running from the motor's base, below the ram, there is a heavy rail, a great deal like a piece of railroad track, and maybe five feet long. Attached to the end of it, and sticking up, so as to face the ram, there is a big steel wedge, perhaps ten inches high. You take your piece of log and lay it on the rail, down on its side, with one end near the wedge, or even touching it. Then you push a lever down, and the thing begins to work. The force of the damned thing is merely awesome. Slowly, slowly, slowly, this ram untelescopes itself. It snakes up to the log end, pushes it against the wedge, and into it. That sharp and shiny, dented, nicked-up wedge just knifes into the log as if the log were cheese, or meatloaf. The log lets out some cracks and groans, but also splits, sometimes all at once and sometimes bit by bit. Dealers challenge you to bring on in a log that they can't split; some of them will bet you fifty bucks on it.

So there we were, my sister, Tish, who's ten, and me, a college junior and possessor of "the most active left-handed fastball I have ever seen, including Koufax" (that was in a letter to his front office from Pete Mulcahey, thirty-five years a scout, Philadelphia Phillies organization), splitting log-wood with a rented Vann machine. The system was, I'd take a log and lay it down in place. When I'd done that, I'd nod at Tish and shout, "Okay"; she'd push the lever down and make the splitter do its number. Once it had, I'd yell, "Okay" again; she'd pull the lever up and make the ram retreat, retract, slide home. Then I'd take a *half* a log and set *it*, split side down, and we'd split that in twos and threes. I'd toss these final pieces into piles; later on, my dad would stack them, just the way he liked to have it done, of course.

It isn't really heavy work, but, boy, it gets your back, even if you're in the sort of shape I guess I always used to be in. The bending is a bitch.

"Bend your back, kid, bend your back." My coach said that to me in high school all the time. You have to bend your back to throw a fastball. But then you get to straighten right back up again. That makes a difference.

And I was also bored. More bored than tired, probably. But the pile of unsplit maple chunks was getting small, and so my mind was halfway out of there already, and onto what came next: what trails I'd want to ski, and what we might do after. My best laid plans, you might say. Can't you feel the *dumbness* dripping off this scene?

I still can see the log. The thing about it was, it wasn't nice and round and perfect. It was a knotty bastard: a piece of trunk that once had three good branches growing out of it, in one way or another. Whoever chain-sawed off those branches left a little stub of each, the way you almost have to. And that meant the log was kind of tipsy when I dropped it on the rail. One end of it was fairly near the ram, the other four or five inches from the wedge. I could have shoved it right up by the wedge, but then I thought, oh, what the hell, why bother? Let the ram just push it. I nodded to my sister Tish and yelled, "Okay."

The ram came up against the log so gently: such a neutral, harmless act. It persevered, and pushed it. For, perhaps, the fifty-thousandth time, the dumb machine performed as it was made to: half its total repertoire. It wasn't bored or tired, wasn't in the past or future. I had a hand placed firmly on the log, to rest my back and sort of steady it. But just before the log made contact with the wedge, it bucked and rolled. The branch-stub it was riding on had fallen part-way off the rail. And when that happened, my left hand was jarred from off the top end of the log. Because I had my weight on it (ah, yes, my aching back!) it dropped right down between the log and wedge.

I wasn't wearing gloves. I'm sure that I said, "Hey!" or made some noise like that, but even as I said it, I heard and saw my little finger fall. My little *finger!* And then there came into my mind this one big thought? "You've really done it this time. *You've really done it this time!*"

The next thing that I think I said was, "Stop, stop, stop, stop, stop," but if you want to know the truth, there wasn't any point in doing that, or anything at all. Because, by then, I could and did stand up, and almost all my ring and middle fingers, slightly curled, were lying on the slushy, muddy ground quite near the little one.

Tish had stopped—reversed—the thing as quick as anybody could. I *know* that's so. Sitting on a stump to work the lever, she couldn't even see what happened, which is one good thing. But she had to see my face when I stood up. I'd cupped my other hand around . . . the bad part. I didn't want to look at it. My head was full of screams. This couldn't be happening to me—I thought that, over and over. Like they always say, it didn't hurt a real lot then.

"Tell Dad there's been an accident," I said to Tish deliberately. I didn't look at her, and I could feel my face was stiff and drawn, as if the skin had got too tight for it. "Run to the house and tell him. Or Mom, if he's not there." I wondered what would happen when I tried to walk. "Tell them to get out the car." I felt I must pronounce each word as clearly as I could; it wouldn't do for her to have to ask a question.

I waited. Nothing happened, so I turned and faced her. Her eyes and mouth got huge. She turned and sprinted toward the house, and halfway there she started in to scream. "Mommie! Mommie! *Mommie!*"

And in my head there was the echo of her screams, and how it sounded when the wedge took off my fingers.

There weren't ever any hopes of miracles. The microsurgical variety, I mean. Of course my father picked the fingers up and put them in a sandwich baggie, and drove them to the Rutland Hospital with me. The doctors promised us there wasn't *anything* that *anyone* could do with them, given all the damage to the bones (mashed and cracked and split as well as cut in half) and to the tendons, nerves, and veins etcetera. They even called up Boston to make sure. So what they did was knock me out and kind of finish off a sloppy job, leaving me with quite a neat two-fingered hand, complete with palm. I looked like a sign that showed you where the washroom was.

The days that I was there, the hand all swathed in bandages, the doctors and the nurses told me lots of times how lucky (yes) it was I had "apposable" fingers still, to wit: the thumb and forefinger. With those, they said, I could "perform" (their language) *vir-tu-ally* all the "functions" that I could with five. One doctor even winked, as if this was a dirty joke, or some big secret that we shared.

Of course they would be right; I could do almost everything. Except for little things like pitching baseballs. Which I could not "perform" at all.

My parents knew, as best two people could if they were middle-aged, completely unathletic, and largely unimaginative (check and check and double-check), exactly what that meant to me. And so they chose to also dwell on my good fortune: how wonderful it was, they said, that I was so peculiarly (but luckily) arranged as to be quite close to ambidextrous. After a few weeks of that, I could have "performed" the "strangulation function" on them, using either hand.

It was quite true, however, that I am weird, in terms of dominance. I should probably stutter, and drool, and part my hair from ear to ear, and drive on the shoulder of the road. Up until The Accident, I'd always thrown a ball and eaten left, but golfed and written and played tennis right. Can you believe it? I also seemed to have more power batting right, but switched to left because that put my right shoulder toward the pitcher, and I didn't want to get hit on The Arm.

In basketball, I'd heave a pass downcourt left-handed, but liked to shoot my jumper right.

So the sum of all this is: I can throw a baseball pretty well with my right hand, probably as well or better than ninety percent of the right-handed males in North Dakota, say. But I can't *pitch* one, that's the difference. No amount of practice can give me a major-league fastball. I'm afraid not. I'm afraid it's a matter of kinesiology, English translation: you either got it or you ain't. Like a knockout punch for a boxer, it's not a matter of muscle, solely. It's all in the computer, babe.

I started to throw in April; my left hand wore the glove now, and of course it hurt, but not unbearably. Athletes are used to pain. By late May, I was pitching batting practice for my college team. And naturally everyone said I'd be back in the starting rotation by next spring, and didn't it feel great to throw like normal people? "The Comeback Kid," they called me. But Salty Barnum (coach and former Red Sox infielder) had tears in his eyes when he said it, and scout Pete

Mulcahey could only shake his head, after he shook my hand. I told him I was sorry. He could have taken his wife to Hawaii, if he'd signed me. And got his name in *TSN*, as well.

So, "Randy Duke" *could* do the job as Head of Baseball at Dunny Dibble's second summer home, Camp Raycroft, just as well as Dunny (not a bad switch-hitter) could have done it, maybe. He thought my putting on an alias was funny, also "neat"; he said the name was like a person in a story in *Boys' Life*. I suspect he told his father that I was still upset about the accident and that the funny name was just a part of my psychological adjustment to not being Jonathan ______________, the best young left-hander in the country, anymore. In any case, his father wrote letters to both the owner and the Director of the camp, recommending Randy Duke "confidently and enthusiastically." As I said, my interview with the Director, Fisher Fleer, was more of a formality than anything.

SAMPLE QUESTION (FLEER): "What position do you play, Randy?"
SAMPLE ANSWER (ME): "Pitcher."
FLEER: "Hey, that's great!" [Which is what he almost always said wherever you or I might say "Uh, huh."]

I didn't hide my hand, exactly, when I talked to Fleer, but I didn't flaunt it either. I figured I'd be spending most of the summer with a fielder's glove on the darned thing, which'd make me look as normal as the next guy.

Driving northward in my calm and rusty Squareback, I'd have to say that I was nervous and excited. Once again I was a basket case, an unknown quantity, a cipher. It struck me, when I had the accident, that lots of what I "was" had nothing much to do with *me*. In my early life, and even later on, somewhat, I'd floated on my father's name. Being Weldon ______________'s boy—which, of course, I wasn't, really—meant that I was treated in a friendly way by almost everyone. It also meant that I ate well, had straightened teeth, a ten-speed bike, and "tastes" that helped me into college. On top of that there was The Arm, again a thing I didn't work for—as much a piece of luck as my last name. The Arm meant I was automatically a standout: chosen first (or, more likely, chooser), looked up to by the boys and girls alike. High school mirrors life in this regard, at least: people get respect for the wrong reasons. Making me a class officer because I could throw a baseball hard and accurately makes as much sense as electing someone mayor because he's sold a lot of Cadillacs. But those things happen, don't they?

Now, this summer, I wouldn't have the name, the record, or The Arm. I'd just be Randy Duke, an unknown quantity with kids, with summer camps, etcetera. A stranger in a strange land, spotting all the natives three left fingers. You wonder that my stomach rumbled on the way?

As I got closer to the camps, I more or less relaxed a bit. The town of Sandgrove, in Vermont, is pretty soothing real estate: wooded hills and brooks and narrow roads, some dairy farms, three tiny settlements, with churches. And somewhere in those hills, camps Raycroft and Raylene.

Here are background facts(?) supplied by Dunbar Dibble.

Martin Raycroft, president of Martin Raycroft Funerals, Incorporated, was the number one mortician(!) in New York (forty-six locations in the state). In 1949, when he was forty-two, he realized he was sick of death and sadness all the time. He'd never seen a summer camp, but he assumed that they were full of life and happiness, and warm and active bodies, so he started two, and names himself "Coach" Raycroft. He never tried to coach, or even referee; he didn't know the rules of (even) run-sheep-run. All he did was toddle here and there, in his tubby little t-shirts and his turned-down sailor hats, and smile and pay top salaries for first-rate personnel.

Dunny said he also used to go from bunk to bunk at bedtime, and say goodnight to everyone, but now he used the camp P.A.

"Good night, boys," he would say, as soon as taps was done.

"Good *night,* Coach," everyone would holler in the dark.

His wife, Raylene, was younger by at least ten years, or maybe even twenty. Her parents both were bakers (Dunny Dibble said); from them, presumably, she got her face, which looked (more Dunny D.) like a soft roll, a Parker House, he thought. By making brother-sister camps and putting her in charge of that which bore her name, Martin Raycroft got her off his back, somewhat, and guaranteed his quiet little summers, getting off on life, etcetera.

And one more thing. Food at both the camps was ordered/supervised/prepared by Jean-François Fasson, chef at La Brouillac in New York City. Coach always ate at La Brouillac on Thursday nights in winter, and didn't like to change his diet altogether.

"I'm sure I won't eat half as well in Paris," Dunny Dibble moaned.

# CHAPTER 2

The private gravel road that leads to both the camps comes off Clinch Hollow Road, a public gravel road that runs for fifteen miles or so off 315, the blacktop road from Newell Creek, New York, to Wellington, Vermont. For reasons of security, I guess, there aren't any normal signs to point the way, but all along Clinch Hollow Road, at every place you *can* go wrong, there is a red, wood, running *R* nailed to a tree—a tree a short ways up the road you want to take. That's right, a big capital letter *R*, but with both its legs bent at the knees, and little feet. Just a *hair* grade-schoolish, you might say. But that's the camps' official monogram: the running *R*. All the camp awards—the pin, the patch, the banner—have the running *R* on them. It's also on the t-shirts (just like Coach's) you can sign for at the All-Camps Store. Raylene Raycroft has it on her writing paper, Dunny told me. He said he'd give me three to guess who thought it up. The camps' own private road does have a sign: "PRIVATE ROAD," it simply says, but both the *R*'s are running.

This road wanders through some woods for a half a mile or more, and reaches this enormous blacktopped parking lot. A really huge expanse. And right there, there's *this* sign:

**PLEASE**

No cars allowed beyond this point, except to drop or pick up campers and their gear. Trucks making deliveries (9 to 5 on weekdays *only*) must register at the Gatehouse, straight ahead.

Do *not* ask the Gateman On Duty to make exceptions to these rules. He's just doing his job and has *no* authority whatsoever.

A big steel chain that stretched between two heavy concrete posts on either side of the road appeared to be the Gate. I drove to it and stopped.

The Gatehouse had what's called a cottage door, I think—the kind that's cut in half so you can open just the top and get some air, but keep the sheep inside. This one had the bottom open, but the top part shut, making, like, a cave effect. A guy sat in this open space, leaning up against a doorjamb. He had on shorts and a t-shirt, a balding head of rusty-colored hair, trimmed short, and quite a major sunburn. He was either asleep, meditating, passed-out, or dead.

I guess he heard the car. In any case, his eyes snapped open.

"Ho!" he said, and smiled. "I was trying to put a little alpha on this burn."

"Hi," I said, and I could feel the butterflies. Now I'd have to say my name to someone on the scene—no turning back. "I've got a job at Raycroft, here. The camp? My name is . . ."

"Randy Duke," he said before I could, and scrambled to his feet and offered me a hand. He was short and getting wide around the hips, and soft, but with the calves he had, he could have been a sprinter once. I guessed his age as twenty-eight or thirty. Turned out that he was twenty-five. "And I'm Bill George," he added.

"I'm glad . . ." I started in again.

"So little Dunny Ding-Dong's gone to Europe," he went on. "It seems like only yesterday he couldn't even pass the swim test."

"Uh-huh," I said. I didn't realize yet that everyone at Raycroft seemed to talk just slightly odd, more or less like Dunny, actually. "Just out of curiosity," I said, "how come you—"

"Had your name just hanging on my lips? Well, there isn't any mystery at all." He opened up the top half of the door and reached around inside. "You only could have been two people, and the other one's already here: Howard "Hillside" Hildebrand. As everyone in Dallas knows, he's also six foot six, two-sixty." He offered me a stack of name tags, the kind you take the paper off the back of and stick them to your clothes. These had running *R*'s on them and "HI, I'M" at the top.

I took the cards and made a face. "Gee," I said, "if there's only *two* of us, I'll bet that we could *memorize* each other's names in no time. And you make *three,* and I know you're Bill George already. See how quick I am?" Of course, he had a name tag on himself. It said he was "BILL G."

"Bilgy," he corrected, nodding, pleased with me, it seemed. "All one word. What I meant is you're the only two *new* guys. The rest of us have been around forever. Rake-off's just like gum drops or salt peanuts. You'll see." He smiled again. "And anyway, you peeked. At my ID. Of course it's idiotic wearing them, but Coach insists. It's only for the first few days. And what you have to write on them is your first name and last initial: Randy D. Like in the second grade. If I didn't know he was so totally unfunny, I'd think it was a joke. Let's see," he said, "you're in Cabin Two, in Bucks. Boys are grouped in three divisions: Bobcats, Bucks, and Bears. Bucks are ten, eleven, up to younger twelves. Your JC's in already. Harlan Klein. He's a fantastic kid. What else? Dinner bell at six, okay? All-staff meeting in the theater, seven-thirty." An old red Saab pulled up behind my back and honked. "Think of any other thing you need to know?"

"Well, yes," I said. "I know that you have no authority, but . . ."

He yanked the chain, and it flopped down and lay along the ground. "Fuck that," he said. "People drive in all the time, unless Raylene's around. When you see the lake, bear right. Then take your second little left. That semicircle's Bucks. Yours is second from the end." The car behind was driven by a girl, and had a plastic rose on its antenna.

I waved and pulled ahead.

I drove on through a grove of pines, tall ones with no lower branches, and lots of needles under them. The lake was straight ahead; I guess it was a mile or so across—I stink at distances. Its shape was something like a human heart—the real one in your chest, not Valentines—with the wide part at the other end. On the nearby right-hand shore, there were some docks, and sailboats and canoes; a float was being moored by two tall guys in trunks with swimmers' builds. Way up at the other end, I saw another bunch of docks and floats and boats: the girls' camp waterfront.

The road split into two in front of me. The left-hand fork soon disappeared into some woods; in time, I learned that's where the stables were, and archery, and the rifle range—places that I'd go to only out of curiosity, I thought. The right-hand fork, the one I followed, gave me my first view of good Camp Raycroft.

Here's the way it looks—and when you know the way it looks, you'll know how Camp Raylene looks, too. They are identical, down to the last toilet seat, one camp at this end of the right-hand side of the lake, and one at the other.

All along the right-hand shore, the ground stays rather flat for quite a ways; that's where the buildings of the camps are set. Then there's a slope, which flattens out again, and that's where all the fields are. Clear?

Okay. Well, down below, each camp consists of one main lodge (with dining hall), three sets of cabins (six in a semicircle), each with its own washhouse. There's one arts and crafts building, various storage sheds, asphalt courts with lights for basketball and volleyball, and lots of open spaces big enough for frisbees, mini-games of this and that, and even modest fungo-hitting. More big pines are spotted here and there for shade and aromatic values; cinder paths go everywhere that you would want them to.

The very biggest building/complex in the camps is just *exactly* halfway in between the two main lodges. It is the Fossel Fine Arts Building, the space for theater, movies, dance, and music. Attached to it, and going up the slope, there is an outdoor amphitheater. Underneath it is the All-Camps Store and junk-food center. Right beside it, nearer to the lake, there squats the Coach House where (surprise!) the Coach himself resides with fair Raylene. This complex is a buffer zone, a Switzerland, where all may intermingle freely (*sic*) regardless of . . . whatever. At certain most explicit hours, anyway.

Architecture-wise, the camps are rich-folk rustic: wide board, rough exteriors in mellow dark-brown stains, with shutters. Fieldstone fireplaces everywhere, cedar shingles; major buildings have their dormers and their little outside balconies. Yodel City on the Allagash.

The fields above are just what you'd expect. Boys have baseball, soccer, and lacrosse, a tartan track, and jumping pits; girls have softball, soccer, and lacrosse, plus field hockey and their own track and pits. In between these vast expanses there is another (sort of) co-ed zone, the tennis courts: sixteen, green, all-weather.

Perhaps to make up for the girls getting an extra field, the boys have a cement-block building, small and white. Inside are lots of barbell weights and mirrors—Iron City. Even little kids are lifting nowadays, if they are "serious." But not if they are female, says Raylene. Girls are not the same as boys, she says.

One last thing. The road that I was on goes by the boys' camp buildings (with little blacktop branches reaching in behind them), and then right up and all around the fields. Finally, it comes down again and goes behind the girls' camp buildings. Got it? Spaced along the road are structures called "the Cottages." These are home for older, married personnel and former waterfront directors and etcetera who couldn't bear to cut the cord to "camp." Others serve as housing for parent or alumni guests.

And there you have the setup. Of course it took me time to get it all down. At first glance what I saw was just "a summer camp." I took the second left (as Bilgy said) and drove behind the cabins where the Bucks lived, pulling up beside the second from the end.

I took a breath, arranged my features in a cool/sincere/reserved/delighted fan-tas-ti-cally friendly smile, and left my Squareback carapace to go into the land of Camp.

* * *

By ten o'clock that evening, I was on familiar ground (in a generic sense) again: a table in the "banquet" room at Emil's Rustic Inn, which is a bar. At my left was Howard "Hillside" Hildebrand, the other new boy on the block; on my right was bald Bill George, "Uncle Bilgy" to his many old campadres. Opposite were people by the name tags of Bob T., Amos S., Roger R., and Running Bear—Roger R. being black and Running Bear being guess what? Farther down the table there were others, and at the table next to it.

Across the room—at first I wondered why—there were two tablefuls of girls who also had on name tags. They were, at least in that sense, ours.

And behind me (speaking time, not space) was a string of fresh encounters with the natives of this place, beginning with the one inside my cabin. Harlan Klein had been there. Fantastic kid, as Uncle Bilgy said.

"Don't worry, I'm going to shave it off," were the first words he addressed to me.

"It," I had to guess, referred collectively to all the wispy dark blond hairs that sprouted here and there on Harlan's face, rather than the thicker, longer blond stuff on his head.

"Fisher said I had to. And also get a trim. I never saw that side of him before. That kind of blind conventionality—is that the word? Conventionalism? It's not conventioneering, is it? *You* know what I mean. But look, I'm being selfish. And possibly unfair. That's kind of hard to know about, sometimes." He paused. "But honest. I'm telling you the truth about my feelings. Anyway"—at last he smiled and offered me his hand—"I'm Harlan Klein. You must be Randy Duke."

Harlan Klein was seventeen; he would be a high-school senior in the fall. Up until the March just past he'd been, he told me, "just another preppy Scarsdale jock." But over his spring holidays he'd met a girl, at Hobe Sound—had I heard of it, in Florida?—and she had changed his life. . . . We sat down on our bunks.

Two hours later, we heard the dinner bell, got up, and

headed down to (Harlan's word, now) "chow." In those two hours, I:

—Learned that I would be living with a person who had made an "absolute commitment" to a life of honesty and selflessness. And also purity and love.
—found out more about a girl named Mary Jean than even her parents knew, I'll bet. Or at least her father.
—discovered that I, too, felt that Harlan was sort of a fantastic kid—modest, sincere, and even funny—at least when he wasn't hinting around that I, too, might want to experience the "incredible rush" that comes from telling someone else my darkest secrets.

"All right," I said to him at one point. "I'll take you to the bottom of my bag: I'm not *really* Randy Duke."

But he just laughed and waved his hand at me.

"Chow" was pretty much what you'd expect on first-night-back-at-camp, with the exception of the food, of course. There were lots of whoops and laughter and "All *Right!*"s. Eighteen cabins equalled eighteen cabin counsellors, and all but two had "been around forever." Ditto with the Harlan Klein equivalents; most of them had risen through the system. Then there were the older guys who lived up in the Cottages, like Captain Larkspur, who taught riding, and "Boats" McKendrick, Waterfront Director, and Hyacinth Fossel, Maestro/Donor of the fine arts building. In all, a merry group of friends.

The food—Harlan said you always had a choice of hot or cold—was either steak *tartare* or *suprêmes de volaille* ("chicken cutlets" in the words of Hillside H.).

Harlan took me over to the head table and introduced me to Coach Raycroft: "This is Randy Duke."

"How nice," the little man replied. "I hope you like capers as much as I do."

I suppose I stood and stared, the perfect yokel (at *that* time, I hasten to append; now I know the names of all the stuff I shove off to one side). The fact is that I thought I might be being propositioned.

"I don't think I really . . .," I began.

"That's too bad." He popped his fork into his mouth and murmured, "Yum."

"Well, good to meet you," was my exit line.

By seven-thirty, we were all together in the theater of the Fossel Fine Arts Building, our numbers swelled (or, rather, curved—heh-heh) by sister staffers from Raylene. As in the dining hall, there were reunions: screams and smiles and simpers, and even some embraces of the good-old-brother-sister sort. I got the feeling, watching them, that there were two or three real "couples" in our midst; I guess I envied them the setup. Bilgy said five women on the Raylene staff were virgins; I asked him how he possibly knew that. He looked at me as if I was out of that bar in *Star Wars*, but then he chuckled, shook his head, and said, "Haven't been to *camp* before, that means."

"Of *course,*" I said, and then went back to staring. I was feeling rather virginal myself.

That might have been the trigger, my feeling kind of off-to-one-side of everything. Or maybe, somewhere in the old subconscious, I (whoever that is) had more or less decided that "Randy Duke" could try to find a girl up there. That certainly made sense. "Randy Duke" had never had The Arm. There wasn't any need for anyone to feel that sorry for him. Oh, sure, he'd lost some fingers on his hand, but everybody said it didn't look real gross or anything. He was just another average guy, and when your average guy is put around a bunch of girls, he looks for one for him. Right? Sure.

Or maybe I/he/we got blown away by someone.

It had happened twice before, to what's-his-name, both times sort of unexpectedly. One time in the gym, at registration; the other time—will you believe this?—on a train. He'd just looked up, and *wham!* A someone.

The only quality that both those someones had in common, Dunny said, was that they looked like trouble. If you added this one, that made three.

I must agree with Dunny? there's no trouble *type*. Like, smart, or short, or dark green eyes. It's more a quality a person has. Cassius, in *Julius Caesar*, had it, I suppose. Though I doubt that I'd have tried to hang around with him.

This girl looked as if she didn't give a shit, but in the sort of way that laughs and makes a joke of it, instead of being bitter. Her hair was brown and wound up on her head in back, and she had bangs, light-colored eyes, and a mouth so big and active, wet and wonderful that . . . well, if I were back in junior high, I'd have hidden it from my mother. She was wearing a leotard that looked as if it had a lot of faded colors stirred into it, and a black skirt wrapped around her waist. When she sat down, she hooked her legs over the seat in front of her, the way that ushers hate you to; she was barefoot, and her legs looked smooth and strong. When Martin Raycroft shuffled to the microphone, she swung them back to the floor in front of her. She did that with a smooth and easy quickness that took me by surprise. I figured she'd leave them where they were.

The meeting started with a welcome by the Coach, who told us that the camps began in 1950 and had, year-in year-out, given beautiful children the best of summer fun. He wanted us to know that he considered this year's staff the most gifted and committed, and this year's children the most beautiful, in the entire history of the camps.

"Coach says the same thing every year," Bilgy whispered in my ear. "Don't he have a way with words?"

The ones he used to close his little talk were by way of introduction, ". . . Directress of the camp that bears her name, my dear Raylene." We all struck palms together.

I don't mean to be cruel, or a wise guy, but if there is any sort of society around that protects the good name and reputation of Parker House rolls, Dunny Dibble may be in for a lawsuit. Not that I couldn't see what he meant, concerning Raylene Raycroft's looks. A bulging forehead and her fat pinked cheeks made slits of little pig eyes, and kind of folded down into her mouth and lower jaw and what, if she were a cow, would be her dewlap. It was a two-tiered face, I'm trying to say, and topped by carrot-colored Brillo hair. Of course she had a pants suit on, and naturally you guessed the color.

"Good evening, all," she cried. "I know you're *itching* to get going!"

And then she told us, unspecifically but unmistakably, the sort of going that she hoped we weren't itching to get, and neither must the campers. (Remember, they were ripe old eight to lecherous thirteen.) But Raylene Raycroft had one of those minds. She told us that the camps were, as we knew, quite "liberal." Boys and girls could do a lot of healthy things together: theater, dance (and dances), music, tennis, waterfront (at times), and eating junk food (her word: "snacks"). But, as Raylene reminded us, we knew what things like that could lead to.

"Good Lord." I whispered this to Bilgy. "Are taco chips an aphrodisiac?"

"We've never had an accident, thank God"—Raylene dropped her eyes, in deference or modesty, I wot not—"and one could be our ruination. We know full well our girls are little ladies, but we need cooperation from you men. You all were boys yourselves, and so I know you know the way boys are. *Program* is your answer: Schedule! Keep them romping all day long, just like the little puppies that they are! At supper, if we've done the job, their heads should all be nodding in their soup. Which means they'll have a good, clean, healthy summer!" ("Providing that they're served clear soup," said Bilgy *sotto voce*.) Raylene raised her fist, more like a cheerleader than a militant, I had to feel.

"Good camping, all!" she cried, and took her seat to moderate, but sustained, applause.

"Is she insane?" I queried Bilgy later.

"Oh, no," he said, "not certifiably. Actually, she's quite a sharp old gal, in lots of ways. And energetic—phew! Her trouble is she reads too many nurse novels: they're always full of accidents, I think. What you have to do, when she gets onto sex, is think of something else. Last year, I started through the alphabet making up big-league baseball teams out of players whose last names start with the same letter. Modern day—my era. I kind of liked the *C*'s, except for their pitching. Pretty nice little letter. Let's see, my infield, it was Cey, Concepcion, Carew, and Chambliss, was it? Anyway, Running Bear told me he just goes with the flow and thinks about sex—I guess your aborigines are really into that. Last year, he imagined he got the job of Sex Play Counsellor—Head of Sex Play, actually—and it was his job to set up a good sex play program for the kids. He said that really passed the time."

But back to the meeting. When Raylene was finished, Fisher Fleer went front and center, to blab about the program for a while. Fisher seemed like just a guy: a small, well-organized, enthusiastic man of forty-five or so, who, they told me, liked to fish for bass and play the alto sax, and hated all the unexpected or unscheduled things that have a way of cropping up in camps, or life. He ran us through the dos and don'ts of Parents and Arrival and First-Nights-Away-From-Home, and had us out of there by nine.

Most of us were happily ensconced in Emil's Rustic Inn before it struck half past. I learned the banquet room was where we sat—locals in the bar—and I felt that Emil's "Good-to-see-you-back"'s were right up with the heartiest I'd heard all day.

I like a drink, and handle it okay to good. Among the bits of good advice my father laid on me were these: liquor doesn't mix with sweets and chemicals like quinine any more than it does with driving; the better stuff is better; vodka produces less formaldehyde in the human system than other liquors, hence, also, fewer hangovers. It's thanks to him (and his money), then, that my drinks are J&B with water, and vodka-lime-and-soda. This night it was the J&B.

Hillside stuck with Coors and drank it from the bottle, both of which I said were a cliche. He said that he agreed, but that Fisher put it in his contract. He also said he had to call someone a "good old boy" at least six times a day and exclaim "Golly *Dawg!*", in tones of great delight, at meals and all camp movies.

And anyway, he told me, I should look to my own "cleetches." Look what I was drinking, would you? And how about that yaller shetland sweater and them funny shoes with white bottoms and no socks on?

I raised my glass to him. "Tootch," I said.

"And that's *another* one," said Hillside.

As you'd imagine, I was drawn to the guy immediately. Coupla rookies, feeling just a little bit outside. Huge men seem to come in two quite different models. Some of them are born with exclamation points inside them; they make a big thing out of being big. They slap their hands on tabletops, and people's backs, and laugh much louder than they have to. A sub-group of this species also wears a huge and delicately balanced shoulder-chip. They seem to think that somebody's looking at them "like that" a lot, which calls for laying on of hands.

Hillside was the other model: diffident and gentle. When I got to know him better, he told me that he doesn't like "ol' eighty-four," his number in the films. "I *hate* to watch my game films, Randy. I see a killer out there. And here's the coaches clappin' hands and tellin' everyone 'See that?' I hate it, I'm not foolin'." He paused and scratched his curly head. "But I must like it when I'm doin' it. I have to say, those games are purely fun."

The other guys at Emil's also seemed okay, as seen through a glass, lightly. Randy Duke was fitting in, I guessed. Mostly he just stayed laid-back and listened, heard about the characters and carryings-on of many summers past. I could see what kept them coming back. No one talked about the "other" world except in passing: you didn't hear, for instance, what they did at school, or what they thought about the President, or what they might be doing when or if they ever got too old for camp. Part of me thought that was great; Dunny'd recommended it: "a magic time." The funny part was, if I'd still been who I used to be, and knew that I'd be throwing baseballs for a while, for megabucks (enough, let's face it, to retire on by thirty, with salary deferred for fifty years), well, then I could've just hung out, enjoyed it absolutely, altogether. But now that I was Randy Duke—yes, *really*—there were problems. What the hell *was* I going to do—this ordinary guy that I'd become? When I left college, just eleven months from now, I'd say good-bye to the last little remnants of the guy I was, the guy I'd been for maybe half my life. What once had been my game plan had been . . . not *postponed*, called off. For good, or anyway, forever. Did all these guys up here have it all worked out, or what? They sure as hell were pretty damned relaxed. Once, while getting refilled at the bar, I heard the guy I'd guessed was Emil ask the guy called Amos S. ("Heinous Anus," sometimes) if he thought that maybe Congress would revive the draft.

"Oh, Jesus, don't ask me," said Amos, "the only draft I like to think about is Genesee's. Make it a pitcher, will you, Emil?" Amos was going to start at Georgetown Law School in the fall. Bilgy mentioned that one time, by accident, I guess.

As time slid by, guys began to migrate to the tables that the girls were at, dragging chairs behind them. This was tribal ritual, I learned. People drove to Emil's in a same-sex group, and sat at same-sex tables for a while, hashing over soccer games, or incidents on overnights, and different campers' craziness or warmup suits or jump shots. Very in-group stuff, it was, with lots of hadda-be-there jokes and kidding.

Then, more or less around ten-thirty, people who were into getting racked that night would drink up, leave, and head for bed. The ones who stayed beyond that time were (mostly) game for something else. Raylene could tell you what, I guess.

On this first night, though, a lot of people stayed around and talked. Bilgy said, "Come on and meet some people," so we two rookies went with him, and sat, and met such female veterans as Christine G. ("Tina Tutu"), Sherry L. ("Sack" or "Dry Sack"), Debbie S. ("Blondie"), Wendy R. ("Bendy"), and others. They were all extremely loose and easy with and around the guys, I thought, as if they'd all grown up and taken baths together, which of course they kind of had. No one seemed to expect anything of anybody else, so I didn't seem to be hearing judgments all the time. But new cars don't have dents, either.

While I was sitting where I was, I kept on sneaking little looks over to the table next to ours. I sort of hate to tell you that; it makes me sound so childish, or perverted, or something. But you have to remember: I hadn't been doing this kind of thing for a while. She was getting quite hysterical with laughter, and her hair was starting to unravel. Wendy R. told Amos S. that her name was Kelly C., for Carnevale, and she "did dance" and was "a real rare stamp." She was drinking Old Mr. Boston Ginger-Flavored Brandy and skimmed milk, Wendy said. She'd brought her own, figuring correctly that Emil wouldn't stock them, and given them to him so she could buy them back, a drink at a time, the way Vermont law said she had to. My father would have said that it wasn't any wonder her hair was starting to unravel.

I eavesdropped on the conversation she was in. Jokes and kidding, telling that-reminds-me stories. Kelly seemed to know a lot of comic-strip characters. For instance:

"Well, who should walk in but Michael Doonesbury, the second . . ." and, ". . . just looked at her and said, 'You jam it, Mary Worth,' . . ." and ". . . talk about your Jugheads . . ."

Not the sort of stuff to set your heart to pounding, right? But yet, my heart was pounding. And when I got up next, and headed for the men's, I swerved on by her table.

I leaned my hand and two-fifths on the back of an empty chair where she'd be sure to notice them, I guess, and looked at her, and smiled. Her name tag said "The Wizard of Id." I started in on my familiar "Hi, I'm . . ."

"Hey," she said, "Red Ryder!" She quickly lifted up a hand and aimed the forefinger at me; her thumb pumped one, two, three. "You're slowing down, Red, baby," she proclaimed. "Gotcha three right through the gizzard."

I simply turned and walked on past the men's room, out the door, and over to my Squareback. I drove it steadily to camp and got into my sleeping bag without a light. A little wind was in the pines, and Harlan Klein breathed easily.

It wasn't Randy Duke who felt the way I did.

# CHAPTER 3

Sometimes—sure, you've noticed this—you wake up in the morning and you can't believe the way you felt the night before. It isn't that you don't remember it. But what it doesn't make is sense. You smile and shake your head and feel intensely glad that it's today. The past has let you go and you are light and hungry.

The present is a present is the present. I offer you this morning-mantra, wishing it were mine.

Because there's also other kinds of waking up. You take one blink, and then—oh, no!—you're right back struggling in quick-shit, just the place you were the night before.

This day was that, the other kind. I felt like getting up, and folding up my sleeping bag, and simply heading out of there for good. But also, maybe not so much inside my head as somewhere else, I knew I wasn't likely to do that. I made up reasons, because that's the thing to do: (1) I didn't have a place to go that wouldn't mean a thousand questions; (2) I wouldn't want to let down Dunny Dibble, my best friend; (3) leaving didn't seem the sort of thing that Randy Duke would do. Forget Jonathan ______________.

"You're over-reacting." So I told myself, or him—whomever. For this deep bruise to my emotions, ego, confidence, I prescribed not whirlpool or massage, but ultrasound: the sound of my own mind as it churned out the words, those little jabberers, explainers—liars, oftentimes. "Your problem," I told myself, "is, ever since the accident, you have been spoiled. Everywhere you've been, the people there have known about what happened, and The

Arm and all, and they've been super-sensitive and nice. But that can't last—and shouldn't. There is a whole wide world of folks that don't know and aren't interested. You'd better just get used to that, big boy."

Not a word, so far, about the fact that Kelly was a girl, the first one I'd approached in months and months.

"And besides," my busy babbler went on, "check out the situation. 'Consider the source,' as your father always says." My God, quoting my father now, was it? "Here's this sort of nutty girl who's had a lot to drink and thinks she's being funny. And you, you've had a few yourself—which, face it, makes a person touchy sometimes—and on top of all that, you didn't sleep a lot the night before, and you had a long drive, and a new situation can be kind of upsetting anyway." Sometimes it sounded more like my mother than my mind.

And I still sort of felt like crying.

"Hey, Randy? You awake?"

I opened up my eyes a second time, and focused. Harlan Klein was sitting on his bunk in striped pajama bottoms, knees up, back against the wall. He had a clipboard on his thighs.

"I'm writing Mary Jean," he said, and smiled.

"You shaved," I said.

"Yeah." He ran a hand around his face. It couldn't have felt much different. "Last night. I really didn't want to. It made me feel like such a *kid,* being told to do something personal like that. You know what I mean? And this morning, Oscar—he's the salad chef, a real neat guy—he's giving me a ride to Wellington to get a haircut." He shook his head. "But Randy . . ."

"Yeah?" I said.

"I'm writing Mary Jean—I write her every day—and telling her . . . oh, everything. You know. All about you, and how we talked and stuff. I was wondering if you'd mind if I asked you something. Something kind of personal." The atmosphere of the cabin began to tingle with "absolute honesty," or the anticipation of same.

I suppose I nodded; I hope I didn't roll my eyes.

"Whatever happened to your *hand?*" he said.

By the time I'd finished telling him, I *knew* that I was staying. Really.

Other camps may do it differently, for all I know, but up at Rake-off and Raylene you spend the day before the campers come at meetings, mostly.

That morning I met twice with Fleer. He had an office in the basement of our camp's main lodge; sometimes he would play his saxophone down there: "Summertime," and "Caravan," and "Come Back to Sorrento." Fisher was a wailer, man. This was strictly talk, though, and I was present as the—harumph—Head of Baseball, with his staff.

Almost everyone was Head of something, it turned out, and Assistant in something else. Baseball was a major, meaning that a lot of campers took it, so I had two assistants: the elegant and charming Amos Satterthwaite, the perfect Head of Sailing ("Too bad we can't have yachting," he once said to me), and swarthy, pigeon-toed Running Bear, who was Head of Nature and Canoeing. At first, I was surprised and, to be honest, Harlan, a little discomforted by the idea of having the only Native American in the place as my assistant. To a certain extent, it was a matter of appearances: Running Bear seemed to only wear a shirt on two occasions: at meals in camp, and in bars at night. He also wore his hair in two long braids, most often with a head band, and sometimes with a turkey feather, too. I mean, he just didn't look like peanuts and Crackerjack and getting two the hard way. I guess I was afraid he'd think that hitting fungoes or working on the squeeze with kids was . . . well, *frivolous*. You know, compared to basics like survival skills, and talking to the trees. I also was a little put off by Running Bear's initial reaction to *me*. He wasn't overtly hostile or anything; I didn't find a broken arrow in my toilet kit, or a baby porcupine stuffed inside a sneaker. What he was was more withdrawn. Not inclined to look at me a lot, or say much. Sort of defensive, almost. As if he were expecting me to suddenly come on with some tribal slur, or try to steal some land of his or something. Running Bear had only been at camp for just a year, so maybe it was insecurity, who knows?

After Amos, Running Bear, and I got through the meeting that we had with Fleer (safety, promptness, yawn, etcetera), we went up to the fields to check out our equipment in the storage shack. The stuff was all grade-A, as Dunny'd said it would be, and Amos and the Bear seemed pleased to hear my practice plans. I'd thought about them off and on, for weeks, and I was organized. Baseball practice can be boring, but it needn't be. For my part, I was glad they seemed to know some things about the game but didn't try to dazzle me. Running Bear had caught, and Amos was a shortstop, so we had balance on the staff. Amos had played a year of college ball, before he started sailing in the spring. Because he didn't mention it at all, I got the feeling Running Bear had never gone to college. It appeared they got along, and that was good.

When we were walking back on down the hill, Amos said, "Say, Randy?"

And I said, "Yeah?"

"Uh, look—I hope you don't mind," he said, "but—would you tell us about your hand? I think it's amazing you're still playing—I mean, it's wonderful. But, it's fairly recent, isn't it?" I nodded. "Can you still swing a bat all right? Was it, like, in a factory or something?"

I smiled. Real casual. "I didn't actually *play* this year," I said. "Just threw a little batting practice. I did it with a log-splitter over Christmas. As far as hitting's concerned, I never was that big of a threat."

Running Bear was looking at me hard; I thought that maybe he was going to ask me how in hell I could have been so clumsy, or tell me that's what happens when you trust the white man's magic.

"I love the game," I said, "but I'm no Hillside, no big-league prospect or anything. I just throw junk. I'm going to try to add a decent knuckle ball this summer."

Amos nodded, and we kept on walking down.

This was going to be it from now on: me acting as if the

loss of those three fingers was just sort of a minor inconvenience. That's the way it *was*—for Randy Duke.

Which made me feel like screaming, if you want to know the truth.

The next meeting I had was in my role as Assistant in Basketball, another major activity. The Head was Roger Redmond, who was known as Rodge-Podge, or a lot of other names. Before long, I realized that he liked to refer to himself as "Brother-in-Residence" and "Coach's Token Schoolyard," as if he hadn't come to camp as many years as anyone, or started in the Amherst front court, fresh from Lawrenceville. He also liked to jive about his game, as in, "You guys' job will be to teach the sweaty, humble little things, like playing D and passing off and blocking out and that. My spesh-ee-al-itay is Shoot the Basketball. My teammates, on the other hand, are specialists in feeding me. At college I am known as 'Red-the-Fed.' "

The "you guys" he addressed were me and Hillside Hildebrand—who was also Head of Football, need I add? After we had talked to Fleer, Roger took us to the court, where we played Horse for half an hour. You know that playground game: you have to make the shot the guy who goes before you makes, exactly as he made it; miss it and you get the letter "H," miss again and you're "H-O," and so on. If the guy before you hasn't made a shot, you get to shoot whatever shot you want, whatever is *your* spesh-ee-al-itay. Roger beat Mt. Hildebrand and me for seven Cokes apiece, although I thought we both did pretty well, considering an unfamiliar rim outdoors.

"Man," said Red to me, as we sat on benches just outside the All-Camps Store and dripped, "you got a pretty little jumper there, for a *base*ball player. Your hand don't seem to bother you with that at all. I'd guess the hardest thing is goin' to your left. How'd you ever do that, anyway?"

He was stretching his legs and looking down at his toes while he was asking me that question; he had the best looking legs I'd ever seen on a guy. At times, I've thought I'd like to have a black guy's body, but I'd settle for a few left fingers.

Anyway, I told my little tale again, but just about The Accident; baseball wasn't mentioned. Roger'd never seen a splitter in his life, so he had lots of questions. Hillside shook his head and clucked his tongue. He really seemed to get upset. Later on, at lunch, he stirred his *ratatouille* around his plate and said, "Say, Randy. Is it okay if I say something? Well, I don't think your injury is anybody's business except for yours. It seemed to me, like Roger, he was out of line to ask you all that stuff. If it was me, I'd just as soon not have to talk about it much." He shook his head. "But seeing that he brought it up, I just wanted to tell you how goldang *sorry* I am. Seems like it was just an awful goldang piece of luck. Makes me mad that that should happen to a person, let along an athalete." He put down his fork and made a fist, which he used to grind around a water mark his glass had made. "I mean, where's the sense of it? There ought to be some way things like that don't happen." Hillside shook his curly head from side to side again and sighed.

I didn't say a thing. If Hillside thought he felt bad, knowing the little bit he did, he should have tried out the whole scenario. To tell you the truth, I was halfway tempted to tell him, partly because he was the only person up there who could possibly have the slightest idea of what it'd be like to be in my shoes. And partly because then *he* could tell everybody in the whole *camp*, and it'd be just like being back in college!

Was this what it was going to be like for the entire rest of my life? I wondered. Of course I didn't tell him.

After lunch came something that they called The Draft; it happened, also, at the same time, at the girls' camp.

The Draft was how the kids and counsellors and kitchen boys and girls were split up for the summer into Reds and Blues. Everyone, excepting Coach and Fisher and Raylene and Jean-François Fasson (and others in the kitchen or in maintenance) was either Red or Blue, and the summer was an almost-eight-week color war. The color that won would have a giant banquet at the end of camp. The losers didn't do too badly, either, I was told. They sent out for pizza and meatball sandwiches and soda, which came in this huge truck from down in Bennington, for Christ's sake. They ate it outside, and whatever they didn't finish, they threw at each other. The idea was, they were meant to act like a bunch of losers; some people said it was better than the banquet.

Starting in the second week at both the camps, every day had lots of competition: the Reds against the Blues in everything from archery to water sports. And I mean everything.

Point awards were complicated, based on things like camper interest and involvement, as well as which side "won." Fisher and Raylene (alone) computed and announced the totals. The color race was always very close, they told me.

There were a lot of special rules, concerning playing time and stuff, that I needn't fill your mind with—other than to say you quickly learned them all or perished. Strategy, it seemed, was half the fun. Coaching Reds and Blues was no game for beginners, or the faint of heart.

The Draft was held in both main lodges, according to the same procedures. In ours, Fisher Fleer sat behind a small table, with his back to the enormous fieldstone fireplace. On the table were the necessary clipboards, and an all-sports time clock, and a backup stopwatch, along with freshly sharpened pencils and a gum eraser. Of course he had his whistle on the lanyard round his neck.

Larger tables stood to either side of Fisher. Each of them was covered with a solid-colored flag: one a bright, emphatic red, the other one a deep, majestic blue. There were three folding chairs behind each of those tables, but only two of the six were occupied. Back of the Blue table sat Bob Tracey, Head of Tennis, often known as "Trace-the Face," and also as "Big Dick." I would have to say he had the widest, friendliest, sincerest smile I'd ever seen. It was the sort of smile that would almost certainly have been on the cover of the catalogue of whatever eastern prep school he almost certainly would have gone to, along with the kid from East

Harlem, who would also have been laughing. Trace's teeth would have been just a hair whiter.

Behind the Red table was Uncle Bilgy, Head of Soccer. He was the other captain for this year. Behind each captain's table, there were large, portable bulletin boards, empty except for a lot of thumb tacks. The blue thumb tacks were in neat little rows, but Bilge had arranged his to read "Chew Blue," in big script letters.

On the left-hand wall of the room, there were huge permanent bulletin boards, and on them were tacked more than a hundred and fifty three-by-five index cards, each with a name printed on it in large capital letters. One of them, I just happened to notice, was RANDY DUKE.

Some fifty to sixty folding chairs were more or less in rows, facing the three tables in front of the fireplace. These soon filled with cabin counsellors, JCs, and Heads of this and that from up the hill, the Cottages. And also Helpers in the Dining Hall. Would you believe me if I called the atmosphere "electric"? Well, it really was, no kidding. Of course you can also produce electricity by shuffling your feet on a wool carpet, or rubbing a rubber comb with a piece of velvet.

Fisher Fleer blew one short beep for order, and everyone sat quiet. "Before we toss the coin," he said, "does anyone have anything to say?"

That was the cue for pandemonium. Did you ever see those TV films of trading in commodities, like gold? Lots of people jumping up and down and screaming, pointing, waving arms above their heads, etcetera? Well, that's what this was like.

Lots of guys were yelling, "Choose me, choose me, choose me, Uncle Bilgy" (or "Traceykins," depending). Others screamed, "I've got to be a Blue; I've always been a Blue; I promised mother. Better dead than Red." And "If I'm not a Red this year, I'll kill myself, you'll see. And then you'll wish you'd listened. Then you'll be real sorry, won't you?"

Some people stuck to simple cries for recognition: "Mr. *Chair*man! Mr. *Chair*man!" Then, of course, there were the threats: "If you don't choose me, Bilgy-Bottom or Big Dick you'll never have another one of my cookies, ride in my Jeep, date with my sister, tip from my broker, decent night's sleep in your entire life."

One frenzied kitchen boy just kept shouting, "You like ground glass, Tracey? You really like ground glass?"

Fisher Fleer had painted on his good sport's smile, and simply sat and waited till the chant of "Toss! Toss! Toss!" began. When almost everyone was screaming that, he blew his whistle one more time, and silence reigned again.

"This is," he said, in solemn tones of revelation, "an even-numbered year, which means that Blue will call the coin. Will you do the honors, Coach?"

Martin Raycroft rose and shuffled forward, to applause. He looked surprised and pleased. Fleer handed him a silver dollar, the Eisenhower kind.

"All ready, Bobby," Martin Raycroft said, and Trace-the-Face got up and stood beside him. With a little grunt of effort, Martin Raycroft tossed the coin toward the rustic rafters; Tracey shouted, "Tails!" and caught it neatly when it fell. Then he flipped it over onto the back of Martin Raycroft's patient, blue-veined hand.

"And heads it is!" the old man solemnly proclaimed. And then, more softly, "I'm very, very sorry, Bobby."

"That's all right, Coach," said Tracey with a searchlight of a smile. "It was a helluva beautiful toss anyway." And he patted Martin Raycroft gently on the back. The old man tottered to his seat, smiling merrily, and apparently delighted with his big athletic moment of the summer. Everyone clapped like mad again.

"All right," said Fisher Fleer, "we now begin round one of the counsellors' draft. Picking first will be the Red team, represented by its captain, Mr. George. You have two minutes to make your selection." He reached for the timer.

Uncle Bilgy rose at once. "I am ready, Mr. Chairman," he said solemnly. "Red's first choice is . . ." Of course he paused to let the tension build, and, much to my amazement, even I could feel it. ". . . the immortal Hyacinth Fossel!"

A large black-bearded man got slowly to his feet. He spread his arms out wide: a blessing, an embrace. If Gregory Rasputin had lived in a trailer in Port Ste. Lucie, Florida, instead of at the Tsar's palace, or wherever, he probably would have looked something like this guy: flowered shirt with sunglasses hooked in the breast pocket and white wash-and-wear slacks held up by an old striped necktie.

"A *magnificent* choice," he informed us all, turning slightly to the left and right. He pointed at his captain. "Ball-bag, I congratulate you. 'That which ordinary men are fit for, I am qualified in, and the best of me is diligence.' *Lear*, Act I, Scene whatchacallit." With which he strode over to the main bulletin board, detached the card that bore his name, and carried it to the Red bulletin board, behind his captain's seat. He tacked it up and then sat down on Bilgy's right and began to whisper in his ear in fine conspiratorial style. The room seethed with excited conversation.

"*Very* shrewd of Bilgy," Amos said behind me. "The points are in the arts these days. Their signups seem to set a record every year."

"Plus," said Roger Redmond back to him, "if I know my uncle, and I do, he'll work on Hy to teach the little Reds some acting tricks you don't see on the stage. Like drawing fouls in basketball."

"Who'd you take if you were Tracey?" Amos asked.

"I'd either go for Boats, to get some strength down on the waterfront, or maybe pick up Red-nose so's to keep Bilgy from a sweep in the Center. Hyacinth counts a lot on Rudy—my chico-bro-in-residence. I'm not sure," said Roger. "It's a tough one."

"One minute Mr. Tracey," Fisher said.

"Blue is ready, Mr. Chairman," said Trace-the-Face with his disarming smile, "and pleased that it can call on Mr. Ralph McC. McKendrick as its preeminent selection."

A ruddy man wearing a yachting cap and following what my father would have called "a good front porch" rose and trotted forward. The audience made noises more or less like foghorns in his honor; Boats McKendrick had the face of a man who'd be hard to dislike, full of smile and weather lines. As he passed the Red table, he playfully emptied the bowl of his stubby meerschaum on Uncle Bilgy's most official clipboard. Naturally, the latter rose in fury, but Fossel held him back; his whispered "Easy, Bag, not now" was audible throughout the room.

"Bag?" I turned and asked of Amos.

He nodded. "Bilgy-poo's initials. Bill A. George. BAG. Or WAG. Or, sometimes, Ball-bag; that's from this huge canvas sack of soccer balls he lugs around. Or sometimes Wilgy, Bulgy, Ballsy, Bugsy. Take your choice or use your own. He'll answer to almost anything by now."

I nodded back. Me, plain and simple Randy Duke. How boring can you be?

The Draft continued. Bilgy, now with Fossel as his conferee and first co-captain, caused another stir by picking Running Bear. That, said Roger, lessened Boats' importance and gave the Red a lock on nature and survival skills, which Bilgy'd guessed could be the sleeper of the summer.

Tracey took his whole two minutes whispering with Boats. And then he said that Blue was taking Howard "Hillside" Hildebrand.

That really got a buzz, all through the room. Face man gambles on unknown.

"Bold," said Roger Redmond. "*Really* bold." He patted Hillside on the back and told him he should go and get his card and take it up and sit alongside Trace and Boats. He was alternate co-captain.

"Trace has figured Hillside for a super-draw," said Amos. "He may be right at that. Interesting—two sleepers in round two."

"And with Hy and Bear on Red, Trace could use some color . . . get my meaning?" Roger Redmond said. "Look for him to go for Coach's Token Schoolyard—that's *if* I'm still available. Bet a dollar Red-the-Fed is gonna be a Blue."

The color Red's third choice was Rudy Red-nose, Rodolfo Caceres, Head of Boys' Music, and Assistant in Drama and Dance. He'd had Broadway credits by the age of twelve and was about to be a senior at Carnegie-Mellon. Bill George was going for that sweep in the arts.

Rodge-Podge was right. He was chosen third by Blue. Two big glamor sports for Tracey.

The fourth round was announced and, yes, I'd noticed that I wasn't chosen yet. Two of us new guys, and Hillside chosen on the second round, an alternate co-captain. Even though he didn't know the first thing about the strategy of Reds and Blues, or who among the kids and staff they ought to pick. Of course, I told myself, there were good reasons he was chosen. First of all, as the All-American Attraction, he'd make kids glad to be a Blue, like him. And then, on top of that, he was the Head of Football; teams he coached could win a lot of points, if lots of kids signed up, which, naturally, they would. Because—here's number three—he was a real good guy.

Now, had *I* still been Supersonic Jon ______________, and had I worn a Phillies warmup jacket everywhere and talked about my bonus possibilities, well, maybe then I would have been safely Red or Blue already, too. But I wasn't and hadn't and didn't. I was Randy Duke, some kind of mediocrity, a middle-round selection, *maybe*. Better get used to it. It was just a lucky thing that I was Head of Baseball, thanks to Dunny Dibble. I braced myself to be about a number ten.

Bilgy picked me fourth. I suppose he had to have major sport to counter Trace's taking Rodge and Hillside. I was glad to be on Uncle's team, but sorry not to be with Hillside. Reds and Blues was like the Civil War, in the pitting-brother-against-brother department.

Running Bear surprised me by putting out a palm to be slapped, when I took my card up.

"Hey, Red-man!" he exclaimed, with maybe half a smile.

The campers' draft was a bore of humungous proportions; it had all the excitement of a reading at New England Telephone, for me. Everyone else, of course, was going crazy—well, except for Hillside, who had no more idea than I did whether nine-year-old Richmond "Mighty Mo" Morabito was a spaz or a superstar. Nicknames didn't tell you anything at Rake-off, the camp where irony was mined as greedily as gold. At least Hillside had something to do; as alternate co-captain, he got to make lists on a clipboard.

When they started to draft the new campers, the colors had nothing to go on but the application heights and weights, most of them some six to eight months old. Would Michael "Mickey" Gallagher, at five foot four, one-twenty, turn out to be a pillow or a fire plug? And how about young Willis Lippincott, a lad of five foot seven, but only one-oh-five? Was he a slender, graceful reed who'd dominate the boards in Bucks—or a birdie-legged baby with bad hands? It seemed to me that Tracey always took a "Mickey," rather than a "Willis," which figured for a face man.

In any case, by supper it was over. Basically, the sides were drawn. That evening, Fisher would assign the kids to cabins, making sure that each was more or less half Red, half Blue. In the morning we'd get cards from him at breakfast, with names and home addresses. And shortly after that, the kids to match the names would start to dribble in.

After supper there were "unit meetings," which meant that all the counsellors and JCs in Bucks sat around in Barney Rothman's cabin and heard the word on such arcana as letters-home-on-Sunday, laundry-pick-up-and-return, inspection-of-the-cabins-that-included-clotheslines, and what-nurses-would-and-wouldn't-do-for-staff. Barney owned a white '57 T-bird and was our Unit Head, it seemed, which gave him such awesome responsibilities as scheduling unit campfires, coordinating cabin overnights, and collecting the reports we'd have to write on every kid, both midway through the eight-week season and at the end of it.

"For Chrissake look up words you don't know how to spell. Or ask one of your campers. You'll probably have one or two who've finished up sixth grade already. Just to get you off on the right foot, I'll tell you now that 'delightful,' 'helpful,' and 'wonderful' all have only one *l* on the end," Barney told us. He was a handsome guy who was meant to play outstanding lacrosse. He seemed to specialize in insults, criticisms, and complaints that appeared to bother no one.

Amos raised his hand. "Is pain-in-the-ass hyphenated?" he asked our leader. "I can never seem to get that straight."

"Yes, dear Anus, it is," said Barney, "and here's a good way to remember it. Just look in the mirror. What you will see is a fuck-off, which is also hyphenated, and that will remind you of the correct usage."

"Thank you, Bonny Boom-Boom," Amos said. "If I ever get it wrong again, I'll write it on your car a hundred times, in orange Day-Glo Magic Marker. And speaking of your car, what say you we get in it and drive to someplace where we can soak up inspiration for the morrow?"

"Good idea," said Barney, getting up. "Emil's anyone?"

I said I'd be along a little later, which was a semi-lie, because at that point I just didn't know exactly what I planned to do. But more or less to look as if I had some things in mind, I bustled straight across the campus, past the main lodge porch and up behind the arts and crafts, leaving Bobcat cabins on my right. Ahead of me, and winding upward through the trees, was the path that went up to the fields. I took it. What better place to be alone, I asked myself, than on a diamond after dusk?

It was nice up there? a big empty space edged by trees and smelling of grass and dust and, very faintly, pines. You could hear some bits of sound from down below: a radio, a car door slamming shut, a voice that called for "Snake-eyes." I sat on the mound a little while. It had a new white pitcher's plate, and I parked my ass on it and hugged my knees, and smiled when it occurred to me that I was committing a balk.

You know what a balk is, in baseball. There are a lot of sections in the balk rule, but basically a balk is something fake a pitcher does. And it's a no-no. A pitcher can't *pretend* he's going to throw to the plate, or over to first, to catch a man off base. He's got to either do it or not—no tricks.

The balk I was committing right then wasn't covered by

the rule book, but it was a balk anyway. I was sitting on the pitcher's rubber, pretending that maybe I was going to check out a bar in Wellington or Newell Creek. I knew I wasn't going to do that. I was going to go to Emil's. I had to; I knew that.

I was absolutely not going to be kept out of Emil's by the fact that I might see Kelly Carnevale there. Fuck *her*. Emil's was a big part of the relaxation scene at this camp; Dunny had told me that, originally, and now I'd seen that for myself. I didn't have to have anything to do with Kelly Carnevale or any of the other girls, if I didn't want to. I'd been getting along all right without women. What I couldn't get along without was what you might call a regular life: doing the sorts of things the average guy would do. That had nothing to do with being an All-American, or a big-league prospect, or any stuff like that. Anyone could have a few drinks with the guys, on a nice summer evening down at Emil's.

I got up and stretched, and wandered through the outfield, then turned left and passed beside the little weight house, heading toward the tennis courts. I skirted them and saw another path that started down the slope. In less than fifty steps, it brought me to the very upper back of what I guess is called the Fossel Outdoor Amphitheater. It was an impressive place, row after row of curving seats, with aisles of smaller steps between them. I took Classical Drama in college, so I can tell you that in a well-constructed ancient amphitheater you could hear an actor *whisper* from the very top-most row. I didn't hear anyone whispering in this empty place, thank goodness. I'd heard enough from myself, as usual. I got back on the path and headed down.

When I walked in to Emil's, the voices and the laughter coming from the banquet room just kind of stopped me for a second. Did you ever have that feeling, getting to a party, maybe slightly late? And thinking you don't want to make the effort, sort of? What's going on seems full, complete, without you. I wished that I could either leave or simply be there, without ever having to come in.

I stopped at the bar and bought a vodka-lime-and-soda. In

the box, Hawkeye Pierce was letting a little more hot air out of Charles Emerson Winchester's sails. I wondered what Alan Alda would do if he were in my shoes. Of course, to make that a completely fair comparison, it'd have to be an Alan Alda who had lost his quick wit and sense of humor, somehow. I headed to the banquet room.

No one seemed to notice my arrival much. They were arguing about The Draft. Roger took his Pumas off a chair so I could sit. She wasn't in the room, in case you happened to be wondering.

"I think you blew it in the early rounds," Rodge was telling Bilgy. "What I'd have done, if I were you, was try to counter coaching with ability. For instance. You had a chance to pick up Alec Middleton. You know Alec is going to dominate Bear basketball, unless he's broke his leg. The kid is pure franchise; he was as a Buck, he was as a Bobcat. But no, you let Trace have him, which means Blue has both the best bench coach"—hoots from all around—"and the best player, too."

Bilgy's head was starting to peel already. He shook it hard. "If you are ever captain, Fed, just make me one promise, okay? Don't draft me."

"What I want with you, dumb Bag? I'm not that crazy, man."

"The thing about you is that you've got tunnel vision. You can't see outside your own sport. Of course Alec will dominate Bear basketball—probably. And he'll do a lot in track and tennis. But in track he can only enter three events each meet. In tennis he can win at number one, but how about the other fourteen matches? And that is all he really does, you know that. The kid's as bad as you are. Freddy Agostino, who we took on that round if you remember, will also win in tennis, at maybe number five or six. He's top three in canoeing and nature lore, right, Bear? He's a bonanza in the arts building, and a good little second baseman. He scores in soccer, size or no size, and he's a terrific kid on a team. Now, tell me the truth—who'd you rather have in your cabin, an Alec Middleton or a Freddy Agostino?"

"Oh, man," Roger sighed. "Forget *cabin*. We're talking

Red and Blue. Now you tell *me* something. Which is going to do more for the morale of a color: seeing Alec Middleton score his thirty on the *main* court by the *main* lodge with everyone in camp watching, or having Freddy win some points for bringing back a fox feces?"

"The thing I'm wonderin'," Hillside said, "is how the new kids figure in. Not so much Randy and me. I mean, you can count on us for perfect. But campers. What I hear is maybe three or four kids out of every ten in Bucks and Bears are new, and maybe six or seven in ten in Bobcats. Can't they tilt the whole thing out of whack? I mean, suppose some sucker comes along who stuffs ol' Alec Middleton good, and rolls in thirty-five himself?"

"Hillside, you astound me," Bilgy said. "Second night in camp and you see the whole thing clearer than the Prince of Driveways here, who's been playing Reds and Blues for years. Exactly. The Alec Middletons *can* get stuffed, but not your Freddy Agostinos. Fox shit is fox shit, and there's no way Freddy's going to miss it."

Roger Redmond slapped his cheek and rolled his eyes. "Oh, man," he said, "now all I'm going to hear is fox shit, all this season. What happens is"—he turned to Hillside—"you got the trading time to even up. Before the competitions start, we coaches kind of grade the new ones out. And then we get together and make trades. To try to get the competition even. No one wants to see a lot of routs. Excepting some nasty old Ball-bags I can think of."

"But, fool," said Uncle Bilgy, "no one evens up by putting new-kid Doctor-Dunk *with* Alec Middleton, do they? He can still . . ."

I felt a pair of hands come right down on my shoulders, give a squeeze. That took me by surprise; I didn't have a shoulder-squeezing-level friend at Raycroft yet. My first thought: maybe Harlan. But JCs all were under-age for Emil's.

I let my head loll back, the way you do. It brushed against a soft and scented shirt-front, but she didn't move. Kelly.

I straightened up and turned. Okay-shit-sure, I gulped. She wore a different name tag. It said, "Clumsy Carp."

"Hey, Red," she said, maybe not as loud as last night. "As of this afternoon, I got to be a Red myself. What say we take a little walk and talk about our color?"

"Now?" I said. Yes, I was stalling, trying to get my stuff together. She nodded. "Sure. Okay," I said, while getting up. Obviously, the guys were watching me, and they were strangers. Randy Duke would say, "If you'll excuse me, gentlemen." I did. Everyone had sure shut up.

"Well, seeing she's a *Red,*" said Uncle Bilgy.

Kelly led me to the parking lot.

"I guess you've got your car," she said. I nodded.

"Well, so do I," she said. "If you don't mind, I'd rather sit in mine. I'd like to tell you something."

I bobbed my head again. "Okay. That's fine." Hers was the red Saab. She got into the driver's seat; I circled and got in beside her. Randy Duke, I kept saying to myself, Randy Duke.

"Officially, I got to be a Red today," she said to me. "But my face sure qualified last night. I'm really, really sorry. Sometimes I try to be funny and end up just a fool, but last night must have been the record. How could I be so insensitive? That's what I've been asking myself all day. You must have thought I was the All-Camps Asshole. Maybe I am. But as soon as I said that—did that—thing last night, I was sorry. I wanted everything back. And I didn't even have the guts to get up and go after you. I've been telling myself that *that* was because I was new to all this"—she made a little circle wave beside her head—"but I don't know." She was staring at her steering wheel, a little bit bent over. "I don't know why that should have anything to do with it, but I think it did. And now I want you to forgive me, to tell me it's all right. Can you do that for me?"

She turned and looked at me as she said that, but still bent over, more or less as if she had a pain. She wore a little painted, pleading smile, and her eyes glistened.

"Oh, sure," I said, and I was pretty close to tears myself. And not because of me, exactly—this one time. "Listen, forget it. I mean it. It's okay." I was borrowing my former poise. "I was in a real weird mood myself. I know what you mean about being new up here. I feel the same way." I laughed. Now it sounded forced and nervous. "So, anyway. Where were we? I'm Randy Duke, did I say that? I know your name is Kelly, right? Are you really a Red?"

She leaned back in her seat and closed her eyes for just a flash. "Thanks," she said. She reached into her pocket, took out cigarettes. "You want one? No?" She picked one out and struck a match for it, then blew the smoke toward her window.

"I feel a whole lot better," she said. "And, yes, my name is Kelly. And Jesus Christ, I guess I *am* a Red. Did you ever get involved in anything so idiotic in your entire life?"

The atmosphere had changed. She was actually able to do that.

"Oh, I don't know," I said. "I think it's pretty funny. I mean, the guys seem to be taking it all so seriously, and then you realize that it's also . . . almost like a takeoff on itself or something. As if it is, but it isn't. Real, I mean."

She nodded, sucked, and blew out smoke. It curled toward me; she waved at it. "Sorry. Yeah. It's the same over at our place I guess. And the funny part's okay. I kind of like the people I've met. But the thought of giving points for Red and Blue in *dance,* for Christ's sake! That's so ridiculous. If there's one thing that ruins dancing for a lot of kids, it's when they make it like a fucking *competition!* Have kids walking around asking each other what they got in *arabesque?* I can just see it. And of course there'd have to be marks for guts and pride and character and *love,* seeing as *they're* all part of dancing, too."

"That does sound pretty absurd," I said. I had to say one thing for Kelly: whatever the subject was, it got her total attention. "Maybe if you feel all that strongly about it, you can talk to—"

"Fossel, sure!" she finished for me, with a joyful laugh. "Believe me, I have. I *screamed* at him. I told him he could stick it. I asked him what the hell he'd gotten me into, anyway. He must have thought I'd gone nuts." She laughed again, at my expression this time, probably. I'd been going to suggest Raylene, or Fisher Fleer. "Well, I have," she went on, "but I do love Hy, and I know what sort of artist he is, and he knows I know. Who the hell doesn't? Anyway, I'm not going to hand out any stupid points, I don't think. Are you?"

"Well, I shouldn't really have to," I said. "What I'm doing is baseball and basketball. The games pretty much decide the points, the way I understand it. It's all on the scoreboard."

"Look," she said. She really fixed her eyes on me, and moved her lips around and smiled. That mouth. I was looking, I guarantee you. "I just got through apologizing for last night, so the last thing I want to do is piss you off again. All right? But, look, I've got to ask you this. This is, like, a *thing* with me. Doesn't a lot of other stuff . . . well, happen in a game, besides whatever crap you put up on a scoreboard? Runs or goals or whatever the hell it is."

"Well, sure," I said. "Of course. And I agree with you. The old intangibles. How you play the game, character, all that jive. But still, a scoreboard tells you something, doesn't it? What goes down there is how you did that day—you and your team in that one game, compared to someone else. You can't avoid comparisons. The score just formalizes them." That sounded moderate and mature. We were having a conversation; I was enjoying it. Hell, I was starting to feel relaxed. Randy Duke had stuff to say.

She put a hand down on the handle of her door. Uh-oh. "Formalizes or maximizes?" she asked. "See? I'm really a fanatic. Why compare so much? It becomes a kid's whole life. Before the little thing is even born, its parents start telling each other how great it's going to be. Compared to all the other kids, of course. And then—of course—they get real pissed or disappointed when it isn't. The kid grows up surrounded by this great huge wall of rotten expectations. Everybody gets into it: the parents and the teachers and the coaches and the boy friends. And she gets points or bucks or strokes for this and that, but hardly ever feels she's *satisfied* someone. Everyone compares her grades, her tits, the way she keeps her room, her attitudes—to someone else's that they think are better. Fuck that. It stinks. Myself, I'm sick of being judged that way. Down there"—she pointed down the highway—"it never lets up. I thought that if I came up here, I could maybe get away from it. Just hang out and dance and have some fun with kids. The last thing I'm going to do is make them sad, or make them think they're not as good as Joe, or Josie."

"You're right," I said. "And you don't have to, do you?" What she'd just said made a lot more sense to me as Randy Duke than it would have to old Jon. Did that mean big J was an asshole, or that Randy was a wimp?

"I'm not planning to," I said. "My college roommate got me the job—he'd been coming up for years and years—and he said it wasn't like that other world. It's just us and the kids; the parents aren't in it. We'll be the parents, in a way. What I am is curious—how will I make out? Everybody says that kids can really spot a phony. Am *I* going to get along? Maybe I'll find out that the last thing I ever want to do is have a kid."

She opened the car door and got out fast. She seemed to talk, move—everything—on the same setting: floored, flat-out. The ember of her cigarette arced through the air. She went and put a sandaled foot on it and ground it into the gravel.

"Raylene said some of us would get the jitters. I think that's me, too," she said. She shook her head and kept on turning her toe. "I'm sorry. I'm sure you'll do a good job—treat your kids right. I get a little crazy on that comparison thing." She waved a hand. "It goes way back, with me."

I said, "Maybe with me, too. My *real* parents put me in a basket and left me at a foundling home."

I felt my face get red. Maybe not so much because I'd said it, but because I was *using* it. I wanted her attention. More of her attention.

She'd started walking toward the door, but stopped, and halfway turned around. "You're kidding," she said.

I shook my head, and smiled a half a one. "Uh-uh," I said. "Just like you read about, outside the door. It was probably the luckiest thing that ever happened to me. The people who adopted me are fine. Even sort of rich. No one knows who my real parents are. I'd kind of like to, I guess."

She thought. "I can see that," she said. And she smiled a real one. "Though you'd probably end up comparing them with the people who adopted you."

"Yeah," I said. I shook my head. "I don't know why I brought that up. I don't very often. It's no big deal. I'm afraid it sort of slipped out. Talk about dumb."

"Okay," she said, and she touched me on the wrist. Her shirt was real light blue, that sort of misty cotton kind that you can see through; underneath, she wore another leotard, a black one, and the minimum. And jeans. She had some faded jeans on, too.

"Kelly?" Seemed like the thing to say.

"Yes?" she said.

"Could we go out to dinner sometime? I don't know how the days off work, exactly . . ." I hadn't been looking at her when I started saying that, but when I did, I stopped. Her face had sort of stiffened and closed up.

"Well," she said, "actually . . . you see . . . the thing is I'm not into dating much. At all. These days." She gave a little shrug, and made a sort of laughing sound.

I nodded, feeling like the winner of the super-jerks. Turn-down number one—looking good, Randy. Was she telling me that she was gay, or was it just yours-oh-so-truly? Maybe she was grossed out by my hand. It seemed like she was the first person all day who hadn't asked me how I did it.

"Jesus, don't look at me like that," she said. "It isn't *you.*" And then the sound she made was a real laugh. "You don't know how well off you are, Red Ryder. And, anyway, you appear to be the sort of lad who takes a glass from time to time." She cocked a thumb at Emil's place. "*Believe* me, you will see me here. And also here and there around the campus. We can *compare* . . . notes." She winked and turned.

We reached the tavern door. I opened it and watched her ass go in in front of me. I really thought that she was beautiful.

* * *

My return to the table was celebrated in about the same way as my original arrival. Roger took his feet down off the chair again and kept on telling Bilgy he was crazy. But this time, funnily, I felt a little bit at home.

# CHAPTER 4

The first day of anything just has to be exciting. I don't care if it's the world, school, jail, a job, marriage, summer camp, or afterlife, the first day's apt to have you speeding. When I woke up, the first official day of camp, my heart got out the jump rope.

Oh-oh, this is it, I thought, the kids get here today. And then I thought of Kelly and the night before. I wiggled in my bunk, hoping Harlan wasn't watching me. They'd played the NCAA tournament in Omaha my freshman year, and the way I'd felt before I went out to pitch against Southern Cal was more or less the way I was feeling now. Scared to death and wild-eyed-crazy to get started, try my luck.

There are probably pitchers—guys—who've never been afraid, at least as far as they can tell. I'm not one of those. I've always been afraid—and then I've gone and tried. It's seemed to me that admitting to my fear has helped me, rather than the opposite; it's part of my adrenaline, my concentration. I know I'm going to fight, not flee; approach and not avoid. That's the way it was for me in baseball.

Now there was this thing with Kelly. And in my bunk that morning, there in Cabin 2, in Bucks, I faced the fact I was afraid. I was afraid of not just Kelly but of girls, of girl friends, of having a relationship. The way it looked to me, there wasn't much about me that a woman would be drawn to—not the sort of woman I wanted, anyway. When I went out to face Southern Cal, I was afraid I'd get murdered, because I'd never pitched against a team that had that kind of batting order. I wasn't used to going against the Fred Lynns of this world, for God's sake. But at least I knew that against the people I *had* gone against, I'd been overpoweringly successful. There was a chance . . . if I just did my best, my best would be enough, and I'd survive. And maybe even win. I knew that this was possible. But now, in this situation, I didn't even have any offset to the fear. Sure, I'd done well with girls before, in other places, other leagues—but that was him, not me. That guy had been a prize, way up there on the charts. Randy Duke was a new release, not even apt to get reviewed. I realized that on one level I was kind of glad that Kelly wasn't dating. Maybe if I hung around her some at Emil's, saw the kind of pitch she liked to hit—high, low, in, out, soft, hard, breaking stuff or straight—well then, I might become a welcome sight to her, a somebody. She was a *some body* to me already, all right.

What an MCP you are, I thought: you, Randy Duke, you.

But first: the kids, the parents. Oh, my God, the parents! How would they like Randy Duke, the handy-dandy parent substitute? And how would he like them? In certain ways, I wanted them to treat me as an equal—in fact, they better had. But yet, I also didn't want to see myself as one of them.

You say that isn't fair? Well, I'm no longer bound by fairness rules these days. I've got me an exemption, you might say.

Fisher handed out the cabin cards at breakfast, the one meal of the day that more or less approximated home. Jean-François Fasson had this in common with my mother: they both believed that any fool can pour, boil, fry, or scramble, and that the hour between seven and eight A.M. is best given over to sleep. So I was contentedly involved with a bowl of Special K and coffee, when the Director perched his presence on the next seat down from me.

"Here's your roster, Randy." He pressed a small stack of cards into my hand. "I think it's a terrific mix of kids. Five old, three new; four Red, four Blue. You'll have three boys on scholarship. Jimmy Gummage—his dad's a minister, worked here for years himself—and Gerry Ramos are both old campers. David Taliaferro is new. He's on the Cathedral

Scholarship. Coach has an—er—*establishment* right next to the Cathedral in New York, and for years he's had a scholarship that's set up for a choirboy from there. David's this year's winner. Apparently, he's something rather special, as a singer. Coach tells me he's the best they've ever had." He beamed at me.

"Uh-huh," I said. I'd never been exactly what you'd call a real boy's choir fan. To understate the case a little. "Sounds interesting. I'll go through all the names with Harlan, maybe, after breakfast."

"Hey, that's *great!*" Fisher said, while getting up. "You won't forget that they'll be having swimming tests down at the docks, from nine to eleven and one to five? *Great* if they can get that done today!"

I snapped him off a half-salute and reached to pour myself another coffee. I think I'd been told eight times about those swimming tests, so far.

When I got back to Cabin 2, with camper cards in hand, Harlan spotted them at once. I thought he might jump up and lick my face. With his new haircut and his clean, but faded, running-*R* t-shirt, he looked a little cover-boyish, I might add.

Shuffle, shuffle, shuffle; he went through the cards, glanced up, and smiled. A winning hand.

"Just great," he said. "Terrific cabin, Randy. Fisher sure was more than fair to us."

Of course I wondered why, thinking that if I were Fisher, I'd give the better kids to weaker staff. But then I thought, to hell with that: I'd like a real good cabin. Have a great career, one-time big-timer Randy Duke! Then, too—I asked myself—would honest Harlan ever call a cabin crappy?

"Great." I found that I was picking up the local dialect right smartly. "Maybe you could brief me, one by one?"

We were sitting in our cabin on the two green, sturdy, straight-backed chairs that every cabin had, in addition to a small, green, sturdy, square-topped table about the size of a card table. The perfect setup for a nice long letter home, eh, campers? Those three items were the only furniture that moved; all the rest was built in to the cabin. Along the wall that faced the door, there were three sets of double-decker bunks, with built-in wooden lockers flanking each of them. At one end of every bunk, there was a little shelf, the size for toilet articles and flashlights and retainers, and also just the perfect height and solidity to produce contusions on the head of any person dumb enough to plant a pillow under it and try to get up fast. On each end of the cabin was another set of double-deckers and more lockers. Against the near wall, to the right, a built-in window seat, quite near the fieldstone fireplace. All the woodwork was a soft and lustrous brown; the mattresses had clean white covers.

I'd taken the middle bunk, directly opposite the cabin door, and Harlan had the lower on the right-hand side, closest to the fireplace. He told me kids preferred the uppers, as a rule, and asked me how I'd bruised my forehead.

"All right," he cackled, armored by the wisdom of his vast experience, "let's see. Okay. We might as well take these together. 'Cause that's the way they'll be, most of the time." He showed me "Trevor Bain, Larchmont, N.Y." and "Mitchell Woodman, South Orange, N.J."

"Uh-huh," I said. A real high-verbal reaction. The first one sounded like a British movie star and the other like a high-school principal.

"Trevor Bain, called 'Tiny' or 'T.B.,' is what you'd call a real neat little kid," my wing commander briefed me. "Always the big smile, always into everything. Well coordinated but small, you know? Him and Mitchell are best friends. Mitch is built, but still has baby fat. Terrific sense of humor. Not a great athlete on account of being heavy, but he can hit a ball a mile. And he loves to play. His nickname for himself is 'Wood the Good.' The two of them are great kids to have in a cabin. Oh—and Mitch's parents are good friends of mine. My parents, I mean. They met one another up here."

My God, I thought, even the parents. . . . "Sounds great so far," I said.

"Okay," he said, and showed me "Jimmy Gummage, Painted Post, N.Y." "Jimmy's a good little guy, too. Not as small as Tiny, but short and kind of stocky. Not a leader''—Harlan shook his head emphatically, and I imagined Jimmy Gummage plodding stockily along behind a bunch of other kids—''but solid on a team. He does a lot of stuff with Running Bear, I think, like nature and canoeing.'' I nodded, seeing a canoe a ways behind the others, with a sturdy little paddler.

''Okay,'' I said, ''now how about a . . .''—reading off the card— ''Simon King, of Cedarhurst, New York?''

''Superstar,'' said Harlan quickly. ''*Excellent* athlete, real leader. What you'd call a great all-rounder. The Kings are a big Raycroft family. Simon had two older brothers here. One of them's my age; he's the JC in Rudy's cabin, down in Bobcats. Fantastic guy, too. We're really lucky to get Si.''

I wondered if, some day, my Harlan would the Red team captain be. You never know, I guess. It could be he'd be Blue.

''All right,'' I said, ''so the last of the old campers is 'Gerry Ramos, New York, New York.' What do we know about him?''

''That's Heraldo,'' Harlan said, ''Gerry *or* Heraldo. He's a character. Absolutely baseball-crazy—that's all he wants to do in life, play second base. He may just drive you nuts. 'Wanna heet a copple, Randy?' I swear, if he could pick up grounders all day long, he would. He'll be so happy he's a Red like you.'' Harlan shook his head. It seemed that baseball-crazy wasn't Harlan's favorite form of lunacy. ''I think his folks are Puerto Rican. Let's see. I'm pretty sure he'll come up on the bus. Most years, the camps will charter two or three, to come up from New York.''

''Makes sense,'' I said. ''You'd think that with the price of gas and all, almost everyone'd—''

''Well''—Harlan shook his head again—''the thing is that a lot of parents make the trip to camp as part of their vacation. I know my parents wouldn't miss a stop up here. They get to see some different friends and stuff.'' He paused. ''I guess I didn't used to like them coming all that much, but now . . . it's cool.''

I was glad my parents weren't coming. Nothing against them, or the Dukes either, but there are times when it is best to be alone.

"So that leaves just the new ones." I fanned the three cards out so he could see. I read the names aloud: "David Taliaferro, New York, New York; Reynolds Watson, Far Hills, New Jersey; Edward Larrabee, Redding, Connecticut. Fisher said that David Taliaferro got the scholarship from the Cathedral choir or something?" I imagined a cherubic-looking fat kid in a surplice, natch.

"That's right," Harlan said. "There's one from there who comes up every year. Really fantastic singers, too." He looked down at the cabin floor and said, "Uh, Randy?"

"Yes," I said, and braced myself for revelation.

"I think that name of David's—his last name—is pronounced like, 'Tolliver.' "

I said, "Come on, you're joking. That's not what Fisher said."

And he said, "No. No, really. Could be he doesn't know himself. What I *mean* is Fisher may not know. But, the thing is, when I was in the eighth grade, there was this kid who came to school. And *his* last name was spelled like that, and he said 'Tolliver.' He said that that's the way the English people say it. You know, like they say 'Gloster,' when it's spelled like 'Glow-ses-ter.' "

"Huh," I said. "Well, that's amazing. Boy, I'll bet he'll be surprised when we both say his name right."

"Yeah," said Harlan, smiling broadly. "That kid will just be blown away by all the smarts in good old Cabin Two!" He held out both his palms for slapping; I obliged as best I could. Harlan had a way of making me feel good, I swear.

"Let's see," he said, and pointed. "Fisher's put an *R* or *B* on every card—see here? So that makes Tiny, David, Si, and Gerry Reds; the rest of them are Blues. Wow—that means Mitch and Tiny won't be teammates; that'll be a riot." Harlan laughed and shook his head, and then stood up. "Well, it's me for the washhouse, Randy. Feels like I had butterflies for breakfast."

I nodded back at him and crossed the fingers on the hand that could. I couldn't cross my fingers on my left hand anymore, and that knowledge, that awareness, made me think of Kelly. She wasn't dating, but it wasn't me—or so she'd said. It wasn't me *specifically*, did that mean? She could still be gay, and I wouldn't be, *specifically*, the reason she wasn't dating men. Maybe the reason she hadn't asked about my hand was that she was so grossed out by it she couldn't even stand to call attention to it. I'd heard that sometimes people responded to physical deformities that way. In fact, you read about some people who are turned on by deformities, but those are the sickies. Normal people would probably just as soon not get too intimately involved with your average amputation. Thinking that, I looked at my left hand and then, very deliberately crossed the thumb and forefinger. There, Kelly Carnevale, I thought, that one's for you.

Simon King, superstar—of course he was the first to get to Cabin 2. Maybe thirty seconds after Harlan left. Simon put me at my ease immediately, absurd as that may sound.

Compare (oh, oops, beg pardon, Kel) your twelve-year-old to this: slender-strong with dark blond hair in bangs that just lay smooth and perfect on his head, and clear blue eyes that smiled right into yours while shaking hands, yes, firmly. Blue and white striped rugby shirt with blue athletic shorts, both clean, and white Adidases that matched his teeth for brightness.

The block he was a chip right off wore white Lacoste with khaki pants and Tretorns. "Randy, Hi!" said Mr. K., his eyes upon my name tag in a flash. "I'm Durwood King. It's awfully good to see you. You've met the number three son. Good. Sorry it's the crack of dawn, but Si insisted that we come on up the day before and spend the night in Wellington. I know that you've a million things to do, so I'll just help him get his gear unloaded and get out from under foot, okay?"

That may not be verbatim, but it's close enough. In less than five, a foot locker, duffel bag, and tennis racquet were out of the Volvo wagon and into the cabin, and Mr. K. was shaking hands with me and, without embarrassment to either one, hug-and-kissing Simon. And then he simply left, saying he'd see both of us around.

Si took a breath or two and then began to ask me questions—all about the cabin and his color and the sports I'd coach. He said he couldn't wait. When Harlan eased back in, and saw the kid, he hollered, "Simple!" to which Si responded, "Har-de-har-har!" which set off hand slaps and "All *right*"s awhile. I was relieved. When your center fielder's new, you always want to see him go and get one in a game. Practices don't count.

So, having Simon come in first was good. He and Harlan gave old Randy confidence, a false and unearned confidence, for sure, but you can warm yourself in a manure pile. I chatted with the two of them awhile, and watched the kid unpack the things he'd keep up on his shelf (at the *foot* of his bunk, of course) and in his locker. Then I wandered out and circulated some, saying "Hi!" to half a dozen early kids and parents, who belonged to other cabins even. I reminded everyone I saw about the swimming test, and threw a Frisbee for a while with Barney Rothman. All of that made me feel very campish, very poised. Randy Duke was looking pretty good, I thought.

Well before the luncheon bell, the Bains arrived, followed minutes later by the Larrabees. Trevor "Tiny" Bain had wavy hair and freckles, and big ears, and looked like a kid in a cartoon. His parents were older, the father a doctor, small and round and bald, and out of it. The mother was that birdy sort of little woman who has big glasses and thin ankles and lot of plumps between. She hoped that I'd remember Trevor's vitamins.

"He"—she jerked a thumb at the physician—"says I'm full of flapjacks, but ever since he started taking them, he's grown an inch and hasn't had a cold. Trevor, that is. Talk about your stubborn mules. The doctor, that is."

I told her that I'd do my best; my mother was a true believer, too, I said. Then I excused myself and moved on to the Larrabees. They had that "where-are-all-the-sales-clerks?" look.

"Hi," I said, all slick with confidence and affability, "I'm Randy Duke, and I'll be Eddie's counsellor." They didn't look as if they shook with members of my caste, and so I sought their offspring's eyes and offered *him* a hand. "Hi, Ed, I'm Randy," I blabbed on.

He just put fingers in my palm and pulled them out again. "Hi," he said. "Which bed do I get?" He looked like he'd be fun to poke; he wasn't fat, exactly, just a little soft. His hair was on the long side—mine was, too—but styled, and *he* had one wet mouth, with braces.

"Well," I said, "I guess that's pretty much up—"

"We'll take this one," said his mother. She had a shiny, wrinkled tan and lots of rings. She pointed to the lower on the cabin's left, across the room from Harlan's and the fireplace. ("Will that be cash or charge?" I felt like asking.)

The Larrabees had lots and lots of questions, too. They hit me questions that I couldn't find the handle on, questions that ran up my arms and through my legs. Of course I got some, too, and threw the runner out at first, but by and large, I was no Golden Glover. Try these on your own pianolas: Where was the nearest telephone, and when would it be free, and when could campers call their parents? Did the camp have outboard motors for the rowboats; would there be objections if a camper brought his own? Could they see, and copy down, the list of Edward's cabin mates? Supposing Edward made some better friends than those lodged in this cabin—would he then be free to move? Was I related to the Dukes who lived in Asheville? Who were my parents, then? What was my experience with "youngsters" Edward's age? Could Edward compete with older boys if he proved to be too outstanding an athlete for his age group? Would I be sure he sent his laundry home each week? Who would help their boy achieve an even higher level of self-discipline? And motivation? A little "killer instinct," did I understand? Apparently he was "too nice a guy," at times. Where would he sit at meals? Did he have to? When was bedtime? What did that mean? And etcetera.

Mother Larrabee helped Edward unpack, and Father Larrabee made sure I was impressed by his son's baseball glove, and fishing rod, and radio. And, believe me, I was. With the sort of stuff Edward was accustomed to, Randy Duke was quite a comedown, clearly. He should have had, say, Norman Vincent Peale for cabin counsellor, with Roger Tory Peterson for JC, and maybe George Herman Ruth for baseball. Randy Nothing Duke would never do.

The Larrabees announced that they were taking Edward out for lunch, so he could have a good "last meal."

"If I know camps, the food will be nutritious, but nothing to write home about," said Mr. Larrabee in a confidential bellow. "So don't you bother, Eddie." He wore a lime-green shirt and patchwork pants and two-tone shoes with little tassels on the laces. I figured that the *maître d'* at La Brouillac would seat him by the kitchen door, if he was lucky.

I explained that by the time they got back, Eddie's "guide" would doubtless be here. That was another camp tradition that I didn't mention yet. It amounted to a kind of buddy system for the first two days. Every kid who hadn't been to camp before would have, as guide, a kid who had. The guide would take him everywhere and show him everything and answer all his questions and introduce him all around, to everyone. In Bobcats, a guide would often have to take two new ones with him, but in the older units it was one-on-one. Jimmy Gummage would be guide for Eddie Larrabee.

"Gummage? Gummage?" shouted Mr. L. "And where might he be from, pray tell?"

I had to get the cards in order to pray-tell him.

"Painted *Post*, New York?" he said. "Sounds more like something in Alaska! Or Totem Pole, Saskatchewan." He chortled at his geographic humor.

"I think it's west a ways," I said, "sort of near Elmira, maybe. Jimmy's father is a minister."

"A minister," he said, and sobered. "I see. Well, be sure you watch your language, son." He laughed again. "I guess we'll see you later," meaning me, "uh, *Sandy*, is it?"

"Randy," I replied.

"Oh, yes, yes, *Randy*. Yes, of course," he said, then flicked his wrist toward me and mounted his Mercedes.

I turned to find that Harlan had observed the scene, and now was trying different ways to curl a lip. "Nothing against Edward," Harlan said, "but that Mr. and Mrs. Larrabee seem like a couple of *phonies.*" He changed his face to sorrow, or compassion maybe. "Oh, well"—he popped a smile—"three down and five to go," he said.

After lunch, there was a mild stampede: Mitchell Woodman (South Orange, N.J.), Jimmy Gummage (Painted Post, N.Y.), and Reynolds Watson (Far Hills, N.J.) all came during what would soon be known as Rest-Hour-Thank-God.

The Woodmans were down home: warm but not wornout, and only slightly over-stuffed.

"Les and Laurie," they insisted, handing me an open box of chocolate Malomars. "You finish them. And these are Pam and Wendy, who get to come to camp next year. The other one, up there"—a hand tossed up the lake—"though if they had their choice . . ."—eyes rolled around. Pam and Wendy had a twin-sized crush on Trevor Bain.

"Hey, T.B.," was Mitchell's first hello to his best buddy. "How are you, you small disease?"

"Oh, gross," cried Trevor Bain, "it's The Inedible Bulk. Quick, someone, get the door. And better widen it."

"Tiny, Tiny," chanted both the girls. "Take us for a sailboat ride?"

"*Harlan*. Wonderful to see you," Les and Laurie said to my JC. "We tried to get your parents just before we left. We heard about a place in Manchester . . ." Once more eyes were rolled, and this time lips were smacked.

"Hi, Mr. and Mrs. Woodman," Harlan said. "They wanted me to tell you they'd call you, like next week or something. And see if they could meet you sometime later on. Dad had to go to Cincinnati this last week."

Randy Duke stood back and beamed. How cleverly he'd planned the guest list, at good old Cabin 2, in Bucks.

The Gummages arrived just then, so I left Harlan with the

Woodmans and went back to work. "Bill" Gummage had a beard and wore a velour pullover: a Schlitz and sex and sit-in kind of minister. They had one down at college. His wife, "Marge," looked as if she might prefer a covered-dish supper to an encounter group, but was going to make the best of things. Jimmy was a lot like Harlan said, a chunky little guy, a trifle on the shy side, but glad to be at camp. He told me he'd do his swimming test first thing, so he could spend the afternoon with Eddie Larrabee. The nature-nurture question crossed my mind.

Harlan got the Watsons started while I finished off the Gummages. He learned to his relief that Reynolds was called Rennie. I arrived to learn he was a sports nut, apparently of macadamian proportions. Names, statistics, and cliches came flying from his lips; I loved it. He didn't concentrate on all the standard winners, either. He liked guys like young Buck Williams, rookie forward on the Nets ("He'll be *awesome*, wait and see"), and the other Palmer, on the Expos (". . . knock on wood his knee'll be all right"). It was weird to realize he might have heard of me, this eager, skinny kid from not-too-far-from-where-I-lived-Hills, New Jersey. He seemed to pay close, almost fanatical attention to everything I said to him. I attributed that to intelligence, but it could have been just nerves. His parents were very good-looking and young; they never could have gotten jobs as parents in commercials on TV. She was going to hate to say good-bye, I had the feeling; she was taking lots of time with the unpacking.

While that was going on, Mr. Watson crossed behind the two of them and headed toward the door. On the way, he paused and looked at me, and jerked his head and raised his eyebrows. I followed him outside. He waited for me by the cabin steps, and then he started walking toward the lake. A confidential chat was clearly on his program.

"My name's Bob Ingalls, Randy," was his first surprise. "Buzz, that's Rennie's dad, and I were roommates once. He and Laney, Rennie's mother, are going to be divorced. We intend to marry, when the dust has settled."

I nodded, feeling one of them, but also wary. This was

heavy stuff: the counsellor as confidant. "I see," I sagely said. At college, people switched their roommates, too.

"I'd very much appreciate," Bob Ingalls said, "anything you could do for Rennie. As you can see, he is a high-strung little guy. I'm afraid all this has been quite rough on him. In fact, that's why he's here. To give him a nice unpressured summer." He had a low, slow, charming way of speaking. "To get him out from under."

I wondered what he meant by that exactly.

"If anything comes up—and mind you, I don't think it will—it might be best if you would call me first." He reached onto his hip, slid out a very thin black wallet. From it he removed a business card that had a paper clip attached to it. "My office number's right on here," he said.

"Anything comes up?" I parroted. Was this my normal tone of voice? "Like what, I'm not sure. . . ."

"Oh, I don't know," he said. "I suppose it's barely possible that Buzz—that's Rennie's father, right?—might . . . well, show up. And want to take the boy away from camp with him. He's not a . . . *stable* man. That shouldn't be allowed to happen. Laney doesn't want that. Not at all. Now, I happen to be an attorney"—he smiled—". . . yes, *her* attorney, too, so I can set your mind at rest as far as your position is concerned. Rennie's *mother* put the boy in camp; she signed the papers, pays the bills. You are, in a strictly legal sense, her agent, as his counsellor. She asked if I would pass along her wishes on this thing." He handed me the card.

I took the thing. There was a folded piece of paper clipped behind it; I turned the card to look at it. Yes, it was crisp and green and had "100" in the corners.

"What's this?" I said, and threw him the half-smile Jon used to use on hitters sometimes. "Look, I can call collect." I felt a little pump of energy, adrenaline, like three and two, the tying run on third.

He laughed. "No, that's for you. Rennie needs a friend right now. I think you'll be a good one to him. We're giving you some extra problems, beyond the everyday concerns of camping, and we're grateful."

I slid the bill from under the paper clip and pushed it back toward him. "I hope I can be Rennie's friend," said Randy Cleancut Duke. "But this won't help to make that happen, Mr. Ingalls. If anything, the opposite." I cranked up and challenged him to hit my junk. "Mrs. Watson's bought the best that I can do already. I'll try to carry out her wishes when it comes to Mr. Watson. But I don't take tips."

He took the hundred back and shrugged. "That makes you pretty rare," he said, and smiled. "I hope you're not offended. It was my idea." He slipped the money in his trouser pocket, the very one in which I keep loose change. "Laney's number's up in Rennie's file. Call her if you have to. I imagine she'll tell you to call me." He hadn't hit my pitch, exactly; I'd say he'd fouled it off and stayed alive.

He turned and headed back toward Bucks. "What a gorgeous setting. . . ." he began.

And that left two to go, or still to come, depending on the way you want to say it. Harlan thought that Gerry Ramos always took the bus. David Taliaferro might; I thought he would. Chances were his parents didn't have a car, living in New York and him on scholarship. The buses always came in middle afternoon.

By three o'clock, the Larrabees had gone, thank God, and Jimmy Gummage had a lock on Ed, giving him a tour of such extraordinary distinction that it even had a swimming test (oh, yay!) built into it. Mitch and Tiny sandwiched Rennie Watson and wandered him around to "see the sights and meet a few celebrities," as Mitchell put it. I played a little Horse with Simon King and Harlan, this time coming out ahead two Mountain Dews and a Fudgesicle. I felt that I was speeding slightly, but in a happy, mellow way. Randy Duke was getting by on change-ups and a nickel curve and lots of good control when he threw straight ones. He didn't have a fastball, just a straight one.

It was almost four before the buses came, two big Greyhound charters, honking horns that sounded strange beside the shore of Beaver Lake. Harlan, Si, and I went up to meet them.

Gerry was among the first ones out. He was a black-eyed

little dude whose shiny hair was mostly covered by an NY cap, a little bit off center. He also wore a dark and limber fielder's glove, a t-shirt, jeans, and sneakers, and he let out piercing whistles through his teeth as he got off. Harlan told him the good news about his cabin, and that I was Randy Duke, the Head of Baseball, Dunny Dibble's friend, and his own cabin counsellor.

"Eh, Randy," Gerry said, and smiled the biggest one I'd seen all day. "Head of Baseball, eh? Fantastic! Dunny's a good guy. You play on the same team with him? Hey, Si, how's it goin'? Eh, man"—he rolled his eyes— "I jus' met the cutes' girl. I can' believe it. I got to sit with her from Albany to here."

"Oh-oh," said Harlan. "Here it comes. The ballplayer's plague: more catching than the common cold and deadlier than cancer. Women! When a guy starts chasing bimbos instead of fungos, that's-all-she-wrote for him, Heraldo."

"Oh, Harlan, man, don' be so stupid." He pounded a fist into the pocket of his glove. "Girls are jus' for—you know—recreation." He laughed. "And anyway, you know that ol' Raylene. She ain' gonna let me get too close to Angela too often."

"*Angela!*" said Harlan. "Wow. Another dark-eyed Latin beauty, sounds like. Maybe next year I'll just take the bus. I mean, if a little nerdy second baseman does that good, Heraldo, a handsome, suave, young *college* guy like me should just about—"

"Listen. Randy." Gerry turned to me, ignoring Harlan. It was pretty clear that *he* had been to camp before. "Tell Fisher that he better put some barf-bags on that bus, if *ogly* guys like Harlan gonna take it. Just like on the plane to Puerto Rico. Hey, listen, they got new kids on that bus, right, Si? What kin' impression Harlan gonna make on them?" He pitched his voice into a higher squeak. "Hey, mister driver, lemme off, okay? I don' wanna go to camp no more. I couldn't stand to look at that guy's *ogly* face all summer."

"Yeah, yeah, sure, Heraldo," Harlan said. "We'll see.

Hey, look. I'll help you with your stuff, okay? You gotta meet the guys down at the cabin. . . ."

"I'll just check," I told them as they walked towards Buck, "and see if David's here."

The first time I saw David Taliaferro, he was standing next to Fisher Fleer and wishing that he wasn't. He told me that . . . oh, maybe two weeks after. Fisher had his clipboard in position and was leafing through the pages on it, looking out for David's name and cabin.

"You know what I thought, Randy? I thought I wasn't on the list." This is what he told me. "That maybe Mom forgot to send in all the forms or something. And then I thought that maybe that was good. Boy, was I *scared!* And then, when you came up and said . . . what *did* you say?"

"I said, 'David Tolliver, I presume,' " I said.

"Yeah," he said. "That really freaked me out. I was sure it wasn't me you meant."

The thing was that I'd guessed the kid I saw standing next to Fisher Fleer was David Taliaferro. Or maybe I'd just wanted him to be.

Hold on. I have to shift my gears a minute.

I have some real hip friends who seem to like to say they want to "share" a thought, or an experience, with me. I guess their thoughts, like mine, are shareable; thoughts consist of words, and all you have to do is get the words lined up and say them right, and then you've "shared" a thought. *Experience* is something else.

I am going to try to tell you an experience right now. Feeble attempt number 1,000. But "share" would be impossible. I'm sure you've never had an experience like mine. First of all, I don't believe it's what you'd call exactly commonplace.

*Exactly* commonplace?

To tell the truth, I've never heard of it before or since. And second, inasmuch as you're not me, you *couldn't* have ever had an experience like this. That's not conceit, that's simple logic. Think about it. We—each one of us—is like a super-sensitive machine, but sensitive in very different ways because we have such different parts. I can never feel like you because I'm strung with different wires: everything that's touched me all life long is part of my receiving system. And there is no other like it. Yours just has to be entirely different.

And you know one other thing? I'm glad that this is so. My moments are my own, one-time, unreproduceable, thank God. And they haven't got the slightest thing to do with language or intelligence.

So, with all that by way of explanation or excuse, I'll do my best to put this moment into words.

I looked at David Taliaferro and I loved him. Loved him not in any way that says "I want you" or "I need you," I don't think. I loved him in the way I love myself. As if he were a part of me. As if he were (let's say) my brother.

That is difficult to write, but it's not heavy. If you read it heavy, then you've got it wrong.

I didn't have some sort of psychic flash: Hey, that kid standing over there wearing a dungaree jacket and talking to the man called Fisher Fleer is son of both the people I am son of. It wasn't anything like that. But it wasn't entirely *not* like that, either. Of course there weren't any words.

What happened was this jump of recognition, way inside of me, and then this real smooth, happy kind of calm. And then I did think, silly as it sounds, I wonder if that kid could be my brother?

So I went and looked at him close up, and then said, "David Tolliver, I presume."

And he said, "No, I'm David Taliaferro," which made me burst out laughing.

"Well, then, you're who I'm looking for," I said. I'd blanked out Fisher altogether from this scene. "I'm Randy Duke, your counsellor, and I am *really* glad to see you!"

I'm perfectly convinced I could have spoken Swedish or Swahili, and he'd have heard the message, all of it. He smiled at me and shook his head, and said, "Whee-yoo. For a moment there, you had me really worried." And then we shook each other's hands, instead of hugging, and said, "Oh, boy, I'm glad to see you," two or three times more.

And here's the last weird thing I'm going to say, for now. I didn't know, till then, how much I'd missed him.

Okay. Now back to normal. David Taliaferro (tal-ya-fair-o, Harlan) does look a lot like me, in certain ways. In other words, his hair is real dark brown and slightly wavy, parted on the left, and thick; and his skin is soft and has a tan that never goes away entirely. We have big teeth and widish noses that just turn up a little at the end and seem to run a little, lots of times, which means that we are sniffers. Both of us have brown eyes and long lashes, and our eyebrows make us look surprised when we are not at all. My hair, though, is long enough to hit my collar, while his is only medium, and I am six foot three, one-ninety. He, I'd guess, is five foot four or five and maybe one-oh-eight. Looking at his legs, you'd guess he will be tall; right now, at twelve, he's pretty well-proportioned, just slightly on the slender side, and not the least bit awkward yet. Sometimes, kids can miss that stage—it must have much to do with genes. I did, in case you're wondering.

We got his things from deep inside the bus? a shiny foot locker that wasn't awfully heavy, and a flaking leather suitcase with a single strap, that was. Si came back and helped us—he was David's guide—and the three of us traipsed back to Bucks, me with the suitcase balanced on one hand, as if I were a busboy, and each of them on one end of the trunk.

Everyone assigned to Cabin 2 was there when we got back. Some had swum already, some were just about to go, so there was lots of tan and white bare skin and swirling towels and shrill excitement going back and forth, and covert looks, and thoughts of will-I-like-it-here?, I'm sure. I saw to it that everyone had said hello to everyone at least three times, and then I passed out name tags.

Mitchell Woodman groaned. "Oh, Randy, do we have to? These corny things! Don't anybody put them on a sweater. They take the fuzz right off with them, and then you have this big square patch that looks like you've got moths. Or leprosy!'' He looked around the cabin. ''Tiny! Where's that little thing? You need help with your name this year? If he'll just sound it out,'' he said to Rennie Watson, in a confidential teacher's tone, ''he'll get it right six times out of ten, at least.'' He wrote MR. MITCHELL WOODMAN on his tag in large capitals. ''This is for the other cabins,'' he announced. ''Cabin Two may call me 'Mitch.' ''

''Lemme see,'' said Gerry Ramos, and Mitch held up his tag. Everybody smiled or laughed, and Simon said, ''Oh, Mr. Woodman, *is* your son at camp this year? Michael, isn't that his name?'' He sounded like a very wealthy dowager, he thought. ''A *lovely* person, I don't think.''

At supper, I couldn't help but notice that Eddie Larrabee's name tag read, ''MR. EDWARD LARRABEE.''

According to the Raycroft way of doing things, after supper was the time for cabin activities. This could mean a slew of different things. Cabins often went on little hikes, and cookouts, not too far away; the Raycroft/Raylene property had webs of trails and bridlepaths and lean-tos and campfire circles, lots of them alongside brooks with little waterfalls. If a cabin stayed in camp, it'd be apt to challenge another cabin in softball or volleyball or capture-the-flag or something—stuff that didn't count in Red and Blue, and even counsellors could play. Of course there also were rehearsals, sometimes, or recitals, or a movie, or a show. And even nights with nothing planned at all. As dusk approached, activity would end, and everyone would head back to his cabin. Every night, in every one of them, was something known as ''Taps.'' At Rake-off, that was much, much more than just a bugle call. It was, in all its different forms, a cabin meeting.

Dunny'd told me there was such a thing as Taps; in fact, he'd said it was a favorite time of his, and he was serious. Every cabin's Taps was different, he explained, depending on the counsellor, but basically the time was there to use, in some way that would serve, and even please, the campers. Another facet of the Raycroft (or Raylene) experience. Some cabins' Taps were coolly Christian, Dunny said; others might do lots of story-reading-or-telling, or lean towards articles by athletes and other noted motivators. Some even read two burpless, pre-digested books a summer, passing them around from hand to hand. One dude taught his kids to meditate, and started up some chanting, till the cabins on each side of him complained.

When Dunny briefed me on this Taps routine, he was, as I have mentioned, serious. And, more than serious, he was, admittedly, a fan. I don't make fun of other people's pleasures, as a rule, especially my friends', and so I never said to Dunny what I thought of Taps. It sounded awful. Worse than that: impossible. Whenever I'd imagine me at Taps, icy beads of sweat the size of kernel corn would run on down my sides. Thank God that I had Harlan. Bases loaded? Extra innings? All the same to him.

"Got a great idea for Taps this summer, Randy," Harlan said the second day I knew him. He thought we ought to have a kind of seminar concerning, as he put it, "hard-core nitty-gritty." I asked him if he'd maybe get a hair specific, and he went on to say he meant that all of us in Cabin 2 could bring back things that we'd experienced, or seen, or felt, and tell them to the group. I swear that he did not say "share." "A nightly see-and-tell" is what he did say. "Bits of human drama: kindnesses and meannesses, good sportsmanship and bad. We can help the kids to get aware of stuff." I'm sure I nodded at that juncture. "I'd like to think our kids get more than tans and t-shirts out of camp," said Harlan, rather stuffily.

Getting serious might bring out the worst in him, I realized, but maybe it was my own self-consciousness that I was most afraid of. Frankly, I could not imagine me, at twelve or twenty-one, getting down to hard-core *popcorn* with a bunch of (other) kids, on schedule. Thank God for Randy Duke, the eager one, who said, "Sounds great. Suppose you more or less explain it to the kids tomorrow night, and kind of get us started—that make sense?"

"Sure," he said. "Be happy to."

So there we were, some friends of sorts, a few acquaintances, and a bunch of total strangers, getting ready for a night together. I guess it really struck me for the first time, then, that I'd be spending parts of most of fifty-six straight nights in this one room with these nine people. That David and I would be spending those nights with these eight people. Sharing a room with him seemed kind of nice . . . well, natural, if you want to know the truth.

I watched the kids as they undressed and put pajamas on. They looked so new and clean. Some were shy, and some were showing off; Si and Jimmy seemed completely neutral, un-self-conscious, I suppose. David shadowed Simon, half a beat behind: take pajamas out and put them on the bunk; take off shirt and put on pj top, put shirt on hook in locker; take off pants and underwear and put on pj bottoms, hang up pants and underwear on hooks; pick up towel and paste and toothbrush, head for washhouse, leaving socks and sneakers on. It was like he played a perfect game of "Simon Does." Just what I'd have done, I thought; how to get along in Rome, one easy lesson.

Eddie tried to penetrate the Mitch-and-Tiny Show, using lots of "Look at this, you guys," and making jokes that seemed a hair familiar, considering the source. Mitch and Tiny had their first-night manners on, but I could see—observant me!—opinions taking shape that I didn't really relish, but at the same time couldn't argue with. Gerry had begun a process that would last the full eight weeks: losing things of his and finding them again. "Eh, who's got my towel already?" moaned Heraldo. "What happened to my cap? Eh, Mitch, you seen my baseball cap? I put it on the table here, an' . . ." So on. Rennie was the cautious one, even more than David, listening and watching in that concentrated way he had but saying very little—just on the level of "Excuse me." But when Harlan came and lay down on his bunk and spoke to him directly, he smiled and answered and looked happy. Harlan seemed to know exactly what to do or say. I was the guy they'd send for the key to the batter's box.

When everyone had finished with the washhouse, we got the kids together on the window seat. I perched up on the table, facing them, and Harlan sat beside me, on a chair.

Sometime when I wasn't noticing, he'd made a little fire in the fireplace, so Si flicked off the cabin light.

"Anyone know any ghost stories?" Eddie Larrabee asked.

I guess I was the only one who laughed.

Then, seeing that I had the floor, I opened up our meeting with some necessary business: how the next day would consist of signups for activities and making out of schedules and (for the last time) swimming tests. ("Eh, Randy. I pass that stinkin' tes' las' year," said Gerry R. "Eh, man, I almos' drown. You mean I gotta do that thing again?") When I was done, I said perhaps I hadn't been entirely clear about the schedules and signups, but that everyone had told me it was easier to do than talk about.

"That's really true, Randy," Mitchell said. "No kidding. First year, it sounded worse than school to me. But it isn't all that bad. You sort of learn by doing it. And if anyone needs any help, in filling out their cards or anything, me and Tiny'd be Oonly Tooo Happy"—the wealthy old woman's voice seemed to be a standard—"to help them."

And Jimmy said, "Me, too," and Si turned to David and pointed to the two of them and raised his eyebrows, and David nodded back and also smiled.

"Now," I said, "I'd like to turn things over to Harlan for a bit, so he can tell you what we—"

I was interrupted by the sound of static and a scratchy, whirring sound that was coming from—my God!—more or less the place our chimney went up through the roof. Tiny flicked his flashlight on and aimed it so we all could see the small black plastic speaker nestled in the cobwebs by the ridgepole.

The message from on high was taps, the bugle call, a rather muffled version that could have been a little slow. Then there came a click, and the sound of heavy breathing. Of course! I had forgotten. Coming from above, the fond, paternal words:

"Good night, now, boys," gasped Martin Raycroft.

"We-all-say-good-night-Coach," Harlan whispered desperately, and just in time.

"GOOD *NIGHT*, COACH," we all chanted, hearing our own echo from the other Bucks, and Bears, and Bobcats.

A small bathrobed figure hustled in the door, trailing a dark-blue towel. "Oh, geezum," it said, "is *this* my cabin?" Everybody laughed, but Simon also asked him, "Who's your counsellor?" and when the boy said, "Barney," Tiny told him he was only off by one, and pointed to the left. "Hey, thanks a lot," the poor kid squealed, and hurried off, leaving Gerry doubled up and shaking still. "Eh, is *dees* my cabin?" he would rise to say, and then go back to knocking himself out.

"It wasn't that funny," Eddie Larrabee said.

Then Harlan took the floor and told about "our" plan for Taps in Cabin 2. The kids reminded me of freshman year in college: you hear a lot of junk you don't know whether to believe or not, so you try to look agreeable, and bright, but also cool and uncommitted.

"Tonight," said Harlan mildly, "tonight I thought maybe we'd talk about a feeling. A feeling that I bet we all have—uh—*felt.*"

"Love?" said Gerry Ramos, looking up with a wicked grin. Titters.

"Being homesick," Harlan said.

"Boo-hoo, I want my Mommie," Tiny wailed. And Mitchell turned around and punched him in the arm. I mean a good one.

"*Ow!*" screamed Tiny. "That *hurt,* Mitch."

"Shut up, you little baby," Mitchell said. He really sounded serious.

"Grow up," said Eddie Larrabee, and Tiny, Jimmy, and Gerry all turned to peer at him.

"All right," said Harlan, "hold it. Look, if we're going to joke around, this isn't going to be much of a Taps."

"Well, tell this megowumpus to stop hitting me," said Tiny.

"Mego-*wot?*" Gerry had to ask, rocking back and forth again.

"Mego*wumpus,*" Tiny said. "It's a mythological beast with huge, fat—"

"Tiny?" Harlan said, "Gerry? Mitchell? Look, suppose we *all* just cut it out, all right? If you guys don't want to have . . ."

I didn't know anything about Taps, but I do know what it feels like when an inning comes unstuck and every bouncing ball just seems to find a hole into the outfield. You just gotta rear back and fire.

"I was homesick the night before last," I said, and everyone shut up and stopped their wiggling and turned to look at me.

"No kidding?" Gerry Ramos asked.

"I think so," Randy Duke replied. "And I was scared, for sure."

"Scared? Of what?" said Mitchell.

"You, I guess," said Randy Duke. He smiled. "All this. Being ridiculous. Feeling strange." His eyes took up collection and got the nods he wanted.

"Homesick's more like missing something," Jimmy Gummage said. A mild correction. "Or someone. Like your folks."

Most of them were looking at the floor now, only picking up their heads to speak.

"Yeah. Take me, for instance," Mitchell Woodman said, looking straight at Randy, no one else. "I really like it here at camp. But, well, right now I miss my family a lot. I know that I'll get over it. I always have. But still, right now, I'm homesick, you could say."

So this was Taps.

"My mom says I'd better be a little homesick," Simon said.

"And are you?" Harlan asked him gently.

"Sure." He bobbed his head and made a crooked smile. "And not just, like, tonight. Later—whenever I mess up in something. You know, like play real awful in a tennis match, or strike out with the bases loaded."

"Any time you love somebody, you gonna have to miss 'em sometime," Gerry said, and nodded hard, agreeing with himself.

"You know it," Harlan said. "Right now I really miss my girl friend."

"*Har*-lan!" Simon said.

"And you can really miss people who died, like your grandparents. Or your dog, if it gets run over or something," Tiny added.

"You shouldn't say 'died,' " Eddie Larrabee said. "You should say 'passed away.' "

Mitchell groaned, but not too loud.

"So what can a person do about homesickness?" Harlan asked. "Should you try to stop missing the people that you—well—*miss*, or love, or whatever you want to say?"

"It kind of wears off, I think," Jimmy Gummage said.

"But mightn't that mean you don't love them anymore? The same?" said Tiny.

"No, of course not," Mitchell said. "It just means you don't think about them all the time. It'd be *sick*, if you did."

"Maybe what happens is you let yourself get into other stuff—like here at camp there's all this stuff to do—and then it's like what's happening is more important than what used to happen. You know what I mean?" said Harlan. "It isn't that you stop loving your home, or your mom, or your girl friend, or whatever. You just face the fact that you're not together anymore. But all I have to do is think of Mary Jean awhile and then—oh, jeez—I *really* miss her."

"Do you like that?" Rennie asked him suddenly.

"What?" said Harlan. "No, of course I don't." He shifted on his seat and chewed his lower lip. "Well, to be honest, maybe I do, too. That's weird." He said that almost to himself. "But anyway"—his voice changed—"I hope that none of you guys will feel ashamed of being homesick. Or feeling sad about . . . well, anything that makes you sad; or crying, as far as that goes. Any *honest* emotion is okay. And it's good to get it out where you can deal with it," he counselled us.

"I wonder if—like Randy said—we miss things more when we get scared," said David. He was sitting on the end of the window seat, nearest to my table.

"How do you mean?" said Harlan.

"I don't know." He shook his head. His voice was pure, so pure. "But if I'm scared of something new, it makes me think of something old a lot. And my gran, whenever something really awful happens—like when that girl got pushed under the subway train—well, then she thinks about the way it used to be and gets real sad. I think she misses being young then, too."

"Are you scared now?" I asked him. That may have been a damn fool thing to ask a kid in front of all his—whachacallit?—*peers*. I wasn't really thinking. Just about the question.

I could see him check that out inside himself. "Yeah." He said it right into my eyes. "I guess *so*. But I also think I'm awful lucky, too."

He said that softly, almost tenderly. No one spoke; I think, in some weird way, we all felt complimented. Then Harlan cleared his throat to close the meeting. Taps was over. He asked us if we'd circle up our hands a minute, stretching out a hand to either side of him, toward me and then toward Rennie Watson, nearest on his other side, on that end of the window seat.

I took his left hand in my right and held my left toward David. He smiled and took that funny hand in his as easily as if he were—oh, I don't know—a doctor, say.

"I hope that all of us will keep on being honest with each other . . ." Harlan started.

When the kids had gone to bed, I went around from bunk to bunk to say good night to everyone. It wasn't something that I'd planned to do, ahead of time; I didn't check it out with Harlan, even. He had had to go—"big JC meeting."

What I'd realized was this—that I was glad each one of them (yes, MR. EDWARD L.) was there. I had to tell them that, some way or other, no matter what they thought.

I started to the left of my own bed and worked my way around the cabin, counterclockwise. I didn't find it hard to do at all; the darkness helped. (Rennie said to me, "I don't miss anyone, is that okay?") It was a while before I ended up with David who, as last arrival, had had to take the bunk above my own.

I touched his shoulder. "You awake?" I whispered.

"Oh, yeah," he said. He picked his head up off the pillow, got an elbow under it. "I could hear you going round the cabin. I knew I'd get a turn."

"I think I feel a lot less scared," I told him.

"Me, too," he whispered back. "I'm so excited, Randy. This is like a whole new life for me."

"I guess you'll do a lot of music here," I said. "I've heard that you're fantastic as a singer."

"Well, actually," he said, "I'd sort of planned I wouldn't sing at all. You see"—he said this very slowly—"my voice is just about to go—to *change*, you know. And, most usually, that's it. As far as being any good's concerned. And so I more or less decided that, this summer, well, I'd just get into other stuff. And more or less forget about . . . you know."

I nodded in the flickered dark and squeezed his shoulder, said "Uh-huh," and wished him a good night. Then I just undressed and got into my bunk.

The day was buzzing in my brain. The Larrabees and big Bob Ingalls, David and the way he'd made me feel, and Taps. Could Kelly possibly have had a day as full as mine? What would she be doing now: checking in at Emil's for a ginger-flavored one or two, or lying in the darkness in her cabin? I'd better not imagine she is having thoughts like mine, I told myself. She isn't; she is not the same as me, as Randy Duke. Randy Duke is mostly her mistake, a small embarrassment.

Did I believe that, really?

Hmm. Yes, but maybe not so much as just this morning. Randy seemed a little different now. He felt a lot more workable, a good deal more *alive*.

I switched my mind to David and a different kind of wondering. What if the feeling that I'd had was right? Outrageous things did happen, didn't they? "Long-lost brothers meet on Staten Island Ferry," stuff like that. And it—whatever you might call it—it was something *he* felt, too.

So then I pooh-poohed *that* idea. First I make up Randy Duke, and start to like the guy a little bit, which makes me think he's gotta have a family, for God's sake. Ridiculous! I definitely was *not* about to check on David's parents' whereabouts when . . . blah-blah-blah, etcetera.

Which left me with a simple fact. I really loved this kid. The cabin was "terrific," just as Harlan had predicted, but David was, he was . . . I don't know . . . *forever*.

I lay awake for quite a while, counting kids and floating on their small night sounds.

# CHAPTER 5

Will you shout, "Shame on *you!*" if I say this? That there's a certain (not so tiny) part of me that *loves* routine—a schedule, the totally expected, planned-for happenings in life?

Some other friends of mine make gagging noises at the very thought of such a thing. They claim they have to be "spontaneous." "Don't you notice that the best times you have are all unplanned?" they ask, giving me a chance to reconsider. Surely, I am not *that* dull.

"No, not really," I reply, causing them to shake their heads and slip their eyes away; they've tried. The best time that I've ever had was standing on a pitcher's mound, my sophomore year. The place was Austin, Texas; the opposition, Arizona State. And the occasion was the NCAA baseball finals. Oh, yes, I got the *W*. I'd planned that day for half my life. The second through tenth best times I've had were probably doing basically the same thing I did then, to make it possible for me to do that thing, that day, at all.

Parties that just kind of happen may be fun; I'll go along with that. And inspirations, or ideas, may seem to come in blinding flashes. But parties, once you reach a certain age—or maybe it's awareness, Harlan—aren't quite the point of life. And inspiration's often just the dancing wave you see, on a huge Great Lake of sweat.

I look at it like this: a routine is a setting, or a backdrop. It puts me somewhere, at a certain sometime, doing something with a name—like driving, lunch, or baseball. But still, a lot of unexpected things can happen.

Here's the way my routine went at camp.

"TA-TA, TA-TA-TA; TA-TA, TA-TA-TA; TA-TA, TA-TA-TA, TA-TAAA-TA!" That—just slightly scratchy/slow/off-tune—came through the little plastic speaker by the ridgepole, just the way that taps did. But the next voice that we'd hear would not be that of Coach, but Harlan Klein.

"Tatatatata-TA-ta, tatatatata-TA-ta, tatatatata-TA-ta, tata-tatatata-TA," this jewel of all JCs would sing.

"Shot-op, Harlan. Shot-op, shot-op, shot-op," Gerry Ramos would reply.

"Why *Buena Mañana*, small banana," Harlan would carol cheerfully. "And good morning to *you*, the rest of Cabin Two. Who would care to join young James and me in Dipsville this fine day? Si-fi? Tin-Woodman? Ren-ten-ten?"

Harlan and Jimmy Gummage had vowed to try to take the morning dip in Beaver Lake on every day all summer. This would qualify them for membership in something called the Polar Bare Club, which had an ice cream social after Taps one night during the last week of camp. To celebrate survival, I suppose.

"And this year," Harlan bellowed, on the morning of day five, by which time no one but he and Jimmy were still in the running for membership, "the Polar Bares are going to have a final morning meeting of the summer over with their female counterparts—if you'll pardon the expression—at Camp Raylene. And everyone will wear official uniforms, Heraldo."

"Whaddaya mean, Harlan?" Gerry said. He never was to take a morning dip, all summer long. "I thought you didn' wear no bathing suits."

"We don't *hermano mio*," Harlan said. "And neither do they, in case you're wondering. The Polar Bares' official uniform is skin-tight birthday suits." With which he lapsed still further into song: "Farewell, Angelina, I'm glad to have seen ya, before I went back to New York . . ."

Once the morning-dip dynamic duo had gone on its warm-blooded way, the rest of us would ease into the light of day. I would rise and stretch and scratch my head and then look over at David, huddled in his khaki blankets, and feel great.

After breakfast, every day, was cabin cleanup, followed by inspection. The bunks got made, the floor was swept, the cabin clothesline put in order, the litter all around the place picked up.

After cleanup and inspection came activities: three periods, each an hour long, in which kids received instruction, practiced or whatever. I split the morning time between the basketball court and the baseball fields, with an occasional hour off. You can guess where I was happiest.

I think baseball's a beautiful game. Anyone who says it's slow or dull just isn't noticing. Baseball has a choreography (you hear me, Kel?) that other sports don't have; partly it's because the pitcher's always here and home plate's always there, and the bases are set so, and so, and so, and runners have to go around them counterclockwise.

To show you what I mean, let's say, for instance, that there's bases loaded, with one out. Places, everyone! Okay. The dance starts with the pitch; the batted ball becomes the choreographer. Ah-ha: a ground ball up the middle, close to second base. Thirteen men should move, as soon as they have seen it start; everybody has some steps to take, and, yes, there is a proper way to take them. Some move toward the ball, some head for a base; if the ball gets through the infield, other steps are called for. Runners alter course, just slightly, so that they run in arcs, and not straight lines; fielders change direction, retreat behind a man, or base, as backers-up, or take positions to cut off a throw. Everything the ball does changes things, but soon the fielders will control the ball, or hope to, and make it move the way they want it to. Here comes the throw, the slide, the tag, the gestured judgment: virtuosity!

Dancers all must *think*, as well; they're so much more than bodies. How many out? The score? The inning? Is the ball hit fast, or slowly? Did each passing runner touch my base? The answers to these questions call for certain changes in routine.

When baseball's played correctly it has pace and flow; the time between the pitches is when strategies are formed and tensions build. Baseball is a game of choices, thrust and parry.

Kids play baseball on another level, mostly. Oh, they pitch and catch and run and hit, all right. And yell, and throw their gloves or caps, and chase the ball on down a slope, and blame people. They do a minimum of planning or anticipating; everything seems unexpected, a surprise.

It seemed to me that Raycroft kids were old enough to start to do things right, in miniature. So Amos, Running Bear, and I began to try to teach them from day one. A learning experience that began guess where?

For all my life, I'd been part of the elite, as far as baseball was concerned. The kids I'd played with were the best, the ones who did things "naturally." I, for instance, fell right into pitching, without a lot of celebration, or the need to put the things I did in words, or think of all the steps involved. Just the way other people take one look at a problem having to do with rowing up, down, or across a stream, with or without some cannibals or missionaries for company, and—bingo!—there's your answer. They don't have to work it out. What I came to realize was that being a natural at something made it hard for a person to teach it, instead of easy. When something is real clear or simple to you, you have no sense whatever of the way another person feels who doesn't "get it." That is, unless you right away can force yourself to think of something *you* don't get, like playing bridge or billiards.

No wonder most teachers are only good at teaching people who are good at what they're teaching.

What I had to do was, first, find lots of different ways to say the things that I could do. And, two, to do things very slowly when I showed somebody how—like, break the action into pieces. Finally, number three, was then go back, repeat, and not look mad, or disappointed, just so long as people tried.

Of course we also had some naturals.

Gerry Ramos found he couldn't wear me out. As long as

he would pick 'em up, I'd hit 'em. He was one of them. Simon was another. He'd been coached a lot, and pretty well, but also he was natural. At home, he'd pitched and played first base, he told me; I had a hunch he might play center field, some day. A gawky kid named Harry Zacharias (of the Cabin 6 Zachariases) was number three. He played third and first and tangled up his feet a lot, but also he could throw and swing a bat so smoothly, with such leverage, I drooled. Wouldn't I have loved to have that swing? The fourth was David.

He was much the crudest, in the sense that he had hardly played. But he had the arm (not The Arm, mind you, but an arm), the feet, and oh, dear God, the *hands*. He could have made a living on the subway with those hands. I put him out at shortstop.

Every other day, at least, we'd have a little infield practice, those four kids and me, and anyone that we could find who was, or would be, catcher. These were the best of times, I promise you.

Gerry was the shortest and the lowest and the dirtiest. I swear he loved that infield dust. He wore gray sweat pants, grimy on the thighs from where he'd wiped his throwing hand on them, and slapped his glove. Balls did *not* go under him.

David had to learn to get his knees to bend the way he told them to; a person has a reflex fear of bouncing baseballs. At first, whenever he'd jerk up and pull his face away, he'd slap himself on one bare leg and kick the dirt impatiently.

But, soon enough, he got it going, and I'm not sure that made him happier than me. I'd send a grounder bouncing to his left, right over second base. Moving nice and low, he'd start for it, brown legs digging hard and body coming up a little at a time. In four steps he was striding, stretching out, and then he'd bend again; his yellow glove would chop the air in front of him, and he'd be leaned way forward at the waist. The ball would hit the glove, and stick, and he would straighten up and do a little twinkle with his feet to get them set and under him, and then throw on to first, still flowing.

" 'Way to go, babe, 'way to go," I'd chirp, and feel my

heart go boom-boom-boom. I had "taught" him the mechanics, but no one's ever "learned" that footwork or that balance or that quickness getting ball from glove and flicked away again. Gerry'd whistle through his teeth and shuffle up the dust in pleasure.

"Eh, Randy, sen' me to *my* lef'," he'd call.

When I was out there on that diamond with those kids, the ball and smooth bat handle in my hands, and smelling dust and grass, my own hot skin, and oily leather—well, I was no one then. Not Jonathan, not Randy, hardly even Kelly's "friend" (oh, sure) or David's brother. No past, no problems. Nothing in the future but another bounding ball.

"Hey, you guys, it's almost time for swim (for lunch, for something else, for supper) . . ." someone passing by would yell. And we'd pick up the balls and start on down the hill.

Before lunch every day, there was some free, unpromised time. A lot of people took a swim then, just for recreation and to halfway wash, cool off, and wear some different clothes. I liked doing that.

It's possible that one time, long ago, Beaver Lake was home for a family or two of "semi-aquatic rodents," as Mitch would say. I guess it must have been. But it was not at all like beaver ponds I've seen before: sort of swampy-looking with a lot of fishhook-snagging debris on the bottom. No, Beaver Lake, at least on both the waterfronts, got quickly deep, and it was very fresh and clear, its surface often rumpled by a breeze. When the wind blew down the lake, we'd hear the girls' camp's swimming squeals, as well as see the shapes and splashes in the distance. Then I'd think of Kelly, and wonder what her bathing suit was like.

That's the level I was working on those days. Pretty childish, wasn't it? Well, pretty human, too. Those early, early days of camp, I wasn't going out to Emil's. Why? Well, partly I was chicken, I confess. If I didn't *start* to hang with Kelly, everything was still in front of me. What doesn't start can't stop; I wouldn't be put down. Sooner or later, I told myself, I'd find out why she didn't want to date me, whether she was gay, or freaked, or what. Better not to rush it.

Then, too, as I have said, I liked the cabin, watching everything relax and gentle down. Hanging out with David was a simple, warming pleasure. We really got along. It was amazing the number of times I'd kind of catch his eye, and know that he was thinking just what I was. I'd get a little thrill from that: our special secret.

So, the place that Kelly fitted into my routine was when I'd go and watch her work—I'll get to that—and when I'd start the fantasy machine.

I thought she'd have a bathing suit that showed a lot of Kelly. That would be her style, and dancers, they were body people, anyway—like, pretty un-self-conscious. Sometimes I'd start to think about the way she'd look . . . and then just jump up off my towel, hot-quick, and dive on in the water. Maybe swim out to a raft and back, motoring real hard.

And there you have the sex life of the early Randy Duke.

Other people found a lot of different ways to handle their free time. I've noticed this before: the world divides between the ones who haven't got a thing to do when they don't have to, and those who easily could fill another lifetime with the stuff they haven't yet found time for. Then there are the sub-groups: for instance, those who feel a little insecure if they encounter chunks of time they don't have any plans for.

Amos S. and Bilgy, for example, always played croquet before their lunch. I don't think they ever finished a game. At more or less high noon, they'd stick their stakes and wickets in the ground in some new spots; size and symmetry of playing field would vary day to day. Sometimes, for example, their "lawn" would run from out in front of Bears over to the Fossel Fine Arts Building, snaking around the arts and crafts, and going right across the basketball courts.

"This is the way the American Indians used to play," Bilgy said. "Huge lawns, miles and miles in length, at times, and covered with trees. You've heard of 'Forest Lawn'? Well, that's a translation of an American Indian expression. *Squampatosquipee*: 'a place to play croquet,' or, 'a forest lawn.' It'd be tribe against tribe, of course. Hundreds of different colored balls. They used it as a substitute for war, I understand. Instead of putting warpaint on their faces, they'd paint their balls,'' said Bilgy.

It was during one of those games that canny Amos introduced the concept of the pinch hitter. Having just struck Bilgy's orange with his green—each of them would always play four colors—he enlisted passing Hillside Hildebrand to clamp his size fourteen on top of *his* ball and knock poor Bilgy's (nestled up against it on one side) as far as it was possible, for someone six foot six, two-sixty. Well, it so happened he had aimed Unc Bilgy's ball toward the lake, so when the mighty Hillside struck his blow, old orange just went shooting at the waterfront, aided slightly by the mildly downhill slope. Unerringly, it ran straight out one dock, and, dropping off the end, it fell in a canoe that Trace-the-Face had just begun to paddle.

Tracey had a routine of his own. Every Monday, Wednesday, and Friday of the week, he'd put a rod inside of a canoe and say that he was going fishing. Which is a sort of lie, in that he knew darned good and well (as Hillside put it) what he was going to catch. Which was, namely, ''that cute little catfish'' (more Hillside), Wendy R. Wendy's sport, according to the catalogue, was riding, so she hung out at the stables, which were over on the woods-side of the lake, and inland maybe half a mile or so. Usually people took the roads to get there, but Trace preferred an amphibious operation, feeling that'd mean he'd never have a witness who could truly say *she'd* seen him going to that place. ''She'' would be Raylene, of course. One moment he'd be ''fishing,'' right along the edge, and in an eye-blink's time, he'd run himself aground and have that red canoe dragged way up in the brush. The hike up through the woods was no big deal.

Gossip had it that he never even reached the stables. The big old comfy hay barn was nearer than the place the horses stayed, where Captain Larkspur had his office and the tack room. *That* wasn't gossip, that was fact; I wouldn't know about the goings-on, as Tiny's Mom might say.

What I did know was that Tracey dropped off Bilgy's orange ball, just beside the diving board, and nestled in a yellow towel, on the nearer of the two Camp Raycroft floats. Which left him a very difficult shot. Though by no means, impossible, as Amos said.

After lunch was always Rest Hour, a time that campers used for writing home, a rest, and "quiet games." So said the catalogue. And that was partly true, at least, especially in cabins where the counsellors took naps and made the kids be quiet, often with the help of bribes of candy, cake, and ice cream. It could be said that dentists either loved or hated camp, depending on your view of dentists. Kids were also known to read a comic or a magazine, especially ones containing photographs of people dressed for sports, or showers. Rennie Watson taught a lot of people cribbage, "but not well," Mitchell Woodman claimed. "If I'd had good teaching, I'd win a game sometimes," he told the cabin. "Well, wouldn't I?" he screamed, when no one said a word.

Harlan wrote a letter every day, right up until the Sunday after the Saturday night he took out Jennifer, the girl he'd met at the Dairy Queen in Wellington. "I'm not sure," Harlan told me, along with the news that Jennifer had returned to Bay Shore, with her parents, "but I think she was just out for a good time." It was hard to tell exactly where Harlan stood on "good times." Some place between wildly curious and scared-to-death, the same as most people, I guess. It wasn't long before he wrote it all out, with Mary Jean.

When Rest Hour was over, it was time for more activities. Again, three periods. Once a week, and always in the sixth (and last) were color baseball games: Bucks on Wednesday, Bears on Thursday, Bobcats on Friday. Red against the Blue, six innings worth or dinnertime, whichever came first. Basketball is played in neater time frames, and games would always finish in the hour.

And that was pretty much the way the routine days would pass, at good Camp Rake-off.

* * *

Monday, Tuesday, and Saturday, my last period of the day was fifth. Sometimes I'd have a little extra baseball practice sixth, and sometimes I wouldn't. But, no matter what (and other days, as well), I'd almost always wander over to the amphitheater, whenever I was finished, to have a peek at Kelly, hard at work.

At first—let's face it—you could say I kind of snuck my peeks (yes, sneaky-peeks), sitting in the top-most corner of what would have been the upper right field stands, if this were b'ball. I didn't know how she'd feel if she knew she was being scouted. Turned out she didn't mind at all, though I'm pretty sure that it was days before she noticed I was there. You know what it means, in baseball, when they say a player has "rabbit ears"? That means he's conscious of every little thing that the opponents or the fans might say—about his looks and lineage, for instance. Kelly wouldn't be the sort for "rabbit ears." My high school coach used to always holler at me, during a game: "Concentrate out there, Jon, concentrate!" I told him if I did I wouldn't be able to hear him giving me good coaching. He looked at me, and I could see him think: "Is this a wise guy, or what?" Kelly wouldn't have heard him in the first place.

I think I really got to know Kelly from watching her work with those kids. Hmmm. That sounds a little analytical, I guess—a little *medical*, in fact. "Why, yes, I've had the opportunity to observe the *subject*, a twenty-two-year-old Caucasian *female*, on eight *distinct* occasions . . ." Yas. Big deal. I don't mean stuff like that. As a matter of absolute fact, what I should have said, but somehow didn't want to, was: "I think I *really* fell in love with Kelly in the times I watched her work with kids."

I guess I didn't want anyone to say, "Oh, sure, right, *love*, you bet!" after I admit that one of the things I was doing on those big high concrete steps was, simply, grooving on her body.

Kelly seemed to have a lot of different clothes. Like scarfs in bright, outrageous colors which she'd loop around her waist or neck; shirts, both buttoned-up and slip-on, mostly blowing in the wind; baggy drawstring pants and those big, long, woolly footless stockings that dancers wear to keep from pulling muscles in their legs. Even, sometimes, a silvered, two-piece sweatsuit that looked like something Johnny Bench would use in Florida to try to cancel out a winter's worth of Heinekens. But often, almost always, she'd have stripped down to her working clothes sometime before I got there.

That meant a leotard, a sheer but sturdy second skin of, almost always, black, with silken cords of shoulder straps, cut V-necked in the front, and almost altogether backless. Frequently she'd wrap a colored skirt around her waist, a swingy little thing that covered up her muscled thighs and that most excellent, athletic ass.

No, Kel didn't have exactly what a lot of people think of as a dancer's body. For one, she didn't look as if she lived on carrot sticks and celery and Fresca. Her neck was long enough, but wasn't swanlike, and if you had a yen to count the bones between her throat and breasts, you couldn't do it just by standing there and looking. A lot of guys probably wouldn't look any higher than her breasts anyway, which were pretty classical: not huge, compactly beautiful, with nipples. All of her was rounded, you might say, but in a way that didn't seem about to overflow, or split the seams, or feel like this word: "squilch," if you grabbed her anywhere. What she looked was firm and ripe and juicy, which I finally got around to telling her, one time.

"You make me sound like a fucking fruitstand," she replied, "when all I am is fat." I've never met a girl who didn't say that; that part about being fat, that is.

The thing with Kelly was that just as she was frank about her body, and enjoyed it, so (it seemed to me) she didn't try to hide the fact that she was serious about her other parts.

What she was and what she taught (I thought) was graceful, energetic, sometimes sad and sometimes funny. Her classes copied her; there was a minimum of coyness or showing off, of bullying and balking, of bullshit or self-consciousness. She was the leader, model, coach, permitter, friend. She gave, and therefore got, respect. I called the stuff I saw amazing.

David called it lots of things. If the case of Kelly's excellence was ever brought to trial . . . well, there'd be other witnesses than me. David would be one of them. Can you believe he chose to take the class without the slightest push from me? And did the Easter Bunny visit your house, too? What happened was I'd told him that I thought he'd like it, ought to check it out. He didn't blush or squirm at all.

"Okay." He said this whole thing slowly, in that light and neutral way of his. "I've seen some dancing, and it looks like fun. The Cathedral has these programs. And if . . . Kelly, did you say? . . . if Kelly is a friend of yours . . ."

"Well, look," I said, and may have barely blushed myself, "I can't say we're close friends, exactly. I just met her, like, four days ago. I think I like her, though."

"Okay," he said again, "I'll try it." And he did. The very first day he came back smiling.

"I've gotta tell you, Randy. Dance is excellent. She had us do the *weirdest* things. You want to hear about it? Well, she starts the class with lots of exercises. Some of them are hard and maybe just a little boring, but she agrees with that and says . . ." He babbled on, with gestures. "Then she had us take each other's legs and . . . after that we . . . Kelly's really *funny* . . . think I did that pretty well . . . never really thought I could . . ." And, finally: "Boy, I'm glad you got me to try it, Randy. I've got so many favorite things! And, wow, I sure can see why you like Kelly."

He said that last part straight and looking right at me, with not the slightest bit of teasing in his voice. For one quite eerie instant, we were not a kid and counsellor, or even quasi-brothers, talking. We were two men friends who felt one way about a woman—who felt *attracted* by a woman. I'm embarrassed to admit it, but in that instant I felt a certain ugly and familiar twinge, not entirely different from the one I felt when I watched Lon Vicino warming up for Arizona State. But in the next breath I was smiling, touching David on the arm, saying I was glad he felt that way. I really was. I mean, what the hell.

My other witness and corroborator was even more authoritative. Or so the world would say. It came and plunked itself beside me on that Friday, which was, I think, the fourth day of my spy routine. It was the man who'd paid for what I sat on, Hyacinth Fossel himself.

"Ah, Randy," was his greeting. "I might have known you for a friend of Terpsichore." He offered me his hand and shook mine warmly; you would have thought this chance encounter was the high point of his day, so far. He was wearing a dashiki and his usual white ducks; his shades were pushed up on his head this time, perhaps because he lacked a proper pocket. The only times I ever saw him with them on, in fact, were when he was in swimming.

In time, I discovered that Hyacinth Fossel would usually shake hands, and that he really cared what people thought and said. Which really didn't surprise me, in light of the homework that I'd done.

Because after the conversation I'd had with Kelly in the parking lot outside of Emil's, in which she seemed to take for granted that I knew who Hyacinth Fossel was, I'd headed straight for Bilgy, my walking book of Rake-off knowledge, and exposed, to him, my ignorance.

Once he'd relieved himself of all the necessary jokes about the cultural deficiencies of my college and my sport (thank God I was the right color, anyway), he gave me the information that I wanted. And more, of course, much more.

"Hyacinth Fossel came to Raycroft at the age of ten, about the second year of camp," my mentor said, getting in the proper context right away. "He recalls those days quite frankly, and makes no bones about the fact he was an utter mess. Just bottomed-out. He told me once that if his scissors had had sharp ends he'd probably have tried to kill himself before he got here. I'll spare you all the details of his life at home, much as a _______________ man"—he named my college here—"might covet them. Suffice it to say that it was a blend of bedlam, brutality, and transvestism centered in a huge old brownstone off Fifth Avenue. I don't know why the family decided to send him to camp, or how they came to choose Rake-off, but they did, and that gave Martin Raycroft the opportunity to save his life, perhaps quite literally. Hy will tell you that, sometime; his gratitude is boundless and unending. Coach has always had connections, in civil *and* religious life, and once he had the story from the child—he's such a mild and gentle man, I'd guess young Hy was drawn to him at once—he got the screws put on the Fossels in a way that led to changes in custodial arrangements. Starting right away, at summer's end.

"Hy was moved out to the Island: an uncle who taught English Lit at Stony Brook or somewhere. He kept on coming back to camp for three, four years, and Coach and Uncle—that would be *his* uncle, not myself—both encouraged what they saw to be his talents. Soon he was enrolled in Yale, at some precocious age, and they put on a play of his called *Did You Burn the Toast or Is That Sherman Coming?*, freshman year. And Brustein, or whatever his name is, even let him direct and star. Walter Kerr came up and thanked him afterward. Two years later he was out of Yale and off Off-Broadway. And from there it's been one extra-base hit after another, you might say. On, Off, up, down—even out in Tinseltown. *Doomsday, Doo-Da*'s one of his, of course. And so was *Ego Sum*. He wrote the screenplay for *Fifty-Seven Chevy*, but under an alias. He was afraid it'd win an award, which it almost did. I guess he's some kind of a genius," Bilgy said.

"But he never forgot Raycroft, Coach *or* Camp, and maybe five or six years ago he went to Coach with a proposition, or a series of them, all connected. He'd put up the Fossel Fine Arts Building, and the amphitheater, with his own bucks, if Coach would let him work here for a while, for free. He said it'd be a wonderful change of pace for him, a terrific rest, a real favor, and so-on so-forth. Well, seeing as that was just about the same as having Koufax come and offer to teach baseball—no offense, Randy—better, even, seeing as he knew the guy, what is Coach to say but 'Fine and dandy' ? And Hy's been coming ever since. Coach's given him the right to stock his little pond with his own people—the Music, Dance, and Drama staff are all his hirees—and he and his wife and kids live in a house he built up along the road beside the Cottages. They love it here. As you've seen, he enters into everything, just like all the common wage slaves, and seems to have a grand old time. *I* like the guy, and you know how fussy I am," Bilgy said. "Why, even if he wasn't a Red, I'd probably still speak to him sometimes. Or wave ta-ta, at least."

So, in possession of that mine of background dirt, I wasn't too surprised that I was greeted (as "a friend of Terpsichore") by H. A. Fossel, Esq.

I grinned and said. "Well, not exactly that, I'm sad to say. More of an acquaintance—and the rankest tyro." I try to be a little stylish when I talk to guys like Fossel. "Use it or lose it," as the saying goes. "She makes it look like so much fun."

"Kelly?" I knew his eyes came back to look for mine, but I kept staring down the steps. "You bet she does. It was such a piece of luck that I could get her." He cleared his throat. "A piece of luck for *camp*, at least. I guess it takes some sort of special circumstance to get a person of her quality up here. Not that lots of others aren't *good*, of course." It almost seemed as if *he* was assuming that I knew some things I didn't, now.

"Is she that good?" I asked. Is it just me, or do most people want their friends to be good at things, but maybe not great?

"Oh, my, yes," he said, "oh, yes, indeed. She's perfectly outrageous, what she's done. And starting out so young." He gestured down the steps. "Her company just more or less grew up around her: people coming to her loft to talk or visit, starting in to work and trying things that she suggested. And coming back again. Not everyone could dig it, naturally. But I, for one, found it quite the freshest, most imaginative and human dance development in years."

"She had her own company?" I sounded like the yokel that I am, in certain realms. "What happened to it?"

Fossel was looking at me in a, well, *evaluating* sort of

way. "What happened to the people?" His tone was that's-what-you-must-mean-I-guess. "I suppose they're still around New York. Who knows?" And then, before some other nonsense could escape my lips, "But, Randy. The thing I wanted to ask you was . . . Cynt and I"—I'd heard that Mrs. Fossel's name was Cynthia—"are having some people over next Thursday night. No big occasion or anything. Just any time after Taps, until whenever. Perhaps you are not familiar with the term 'to fosselize'? Lucky you. It is the odious invention of my Uncle Bilgewater, who defines it as 'to meet socially at the Fossels' home.' He has also coined, I regret to say, 'fosselization': the consequences of such a meeting, and the 'fosselizer,' a concoction that contributes to this outcome. He, of course, is responsible for the mixture: a blend of grenadine and lemon juice and Demerara rum that tastes like a strong Life Saver but has the opposite effect. They are always served in paper cups so the children won't cut their feet in the morning."

I'd turned toward him as he spieled this invitation, not wanting to appear ungracious. Fossel was looking at me eagerly, like a dog at dinnertime. "Well, ah, gosh, sounds great," I said, figuring that's what Randy Duke would say. He'd probably love a fosselizer, too. "I don't think I know exactly where—"

"It's over there"—he gestured vaguely toward the fields behind him—"the big brown shingled one with all the porches? But Kelly knows; she's coming," Fossel said. It seemed as if he labored under what you'd call some false impressions, in terms of Kel and me. "Also Bilgy and R.B., and so-on, so-forth. I even think we'll have a Blue or two. They sometimes say the quaintest things—'collectibles,' I call them. Terrific smash in town. But basically we'll be a Red brigade, don't worry." He winked—our little joke, I guess—then rose and stretched, making such a grand thing of the movement that he made me think of Mayan priests and ziggurats. I think it was his great spread-eagled shape that first caught Kelly's eye. Her class was leaving; she looked up, and waved, and started up the steps.

"Well, time to bathe the surface of the man," said Fossel. "See you subsequently." And exited, throwing Kel a small salute in parting.

"What's this?" She'd stopped, oh, maybe halfway up the amphitheater. I was surprised to see her panting, and glad to see her smiling. "Checking out the competition, is it? The *non*-competitive competition, that is. You notice how *color*-less it is? I gave Hy the word on that, and you know what he said?"

"No," I said. "What?" She'd started climbing up again, taking huge, stretched steps, a couple at a time.

"He said he didn't give a shit. Whew, I'm really out of shape," she said. "But that the smartest thing to do would maybe be to give out points, but make the totals come out even. That'd keep the fanatics in their cages. So I'm going to have my kids draw slips of paper once a week. Every slip will have a number on it, and the number'll be how many points the kid gets for his or her team. And the Blue total and the Red total will always come out even. Won't that be amazing?"

She dropped herself down on the hot concrete beside me, with her legs spread and her toes up. She smelled of sun on skin and lightly scented sweat. *Lubricious* was the word that came to mind, given my kind of mind.

"You better not tell," she said.

"I won't," I promised. "Actually, I've got to tell *you* something. You're just fantastic. I've watched you every day this week. You are *fantastic*. Color points are just a silly game—how do you like that? But what you're doing is *important.*"

She looked at me. Her face had taken on that closed and wary look again. But when she saw I was serious, she smiled and nodded. "Thanks," she said. "I know that I'm enjoying it. And as far as I can tell, they seem to."

"They *are,*" I said. Mr. Certainty again. "There's a kid in my cabin: David Taliaferro? You know which one he is?"

"David?" She opened up her eyes real wide. "You kidding me? Of course I do. I'd heard him down in town, of course. Was I amazed to see him in my class up here! He may be the greatest treble who ever lived, do you realize that? And, oh, my God, he's so exceptional. And beautiful. And wise. You know what I mean? That kid could be a dancer, Randy. I'm sure of it. Wouldn't that be exciting—wonderful? What's he now—like, twelve, thirteen?" She yanked a leg up underneath her bottom; her face was all lit up with her remembering. David.

"Just twelve," I said. Apparently Fisher had gotten the straight scoop from Coach; the kid *was* great. But he was going to have to lose it—naturally, of course. I'd heard they used to fix (as vets prefer to say) young choirboys in Europe, in the old days. I'd wondered how much say they had in that. "And, you know," I said to Kelly, "the same thing's true in baseball. Not that I compare the two." I grinned and waggled my eyebrows at her. "He's hardly played at all—not ever, organized. But, God, he is amazing. I don't think I've ever seen anyone so well coordinated in my whole life. I mean, he's doing some things already that other kids—and not bad athletes—can drill and drill and drill on, and still not ever get down pat."

"That's right," she said. "He doesn't have to learn the movements; you know, one-two-three, like that. His body seems to solve the problem, where another person has to use his mind to send the message to his body. And then keep on correcting it. But the thing about David is—he's so much more than just another pretty body. . . ."

"Yeah," I said. "I know just what you mean. I see that in the cabin, in the way he treats the other kids. Knowing what to say and when to shut up—we've got one or two who need all the help they can get. He seems to understand so goddam much, for a kid. . . ."

"For *anyone,*" she said. "He's just so fucking full of grace I can't believe it." She shook her head. "How come some people know what's up like that, and all the rest of us get glimmerings? And then pretend we don't. Maybe he's a genius, for Christ's sake." She laughed.

"We-ell," I said. "I don't know about *that*. But he sure seems to think that you're one. Or anyway, the greatest."

She shook her head again. "That's nice," she said. "I really love him, Randy."

"Me, too," I said. And with that, I proceeded to tell her all about meeting him by the bus, and what I'd felt then, and the things I knew about him, just from what we'd talked about and what I'd seen. I'm sure I got a little carried away. At one point I felt my leg falling asleep, and I came back to the present so's to move it, and I realized I was talking more than I'd meant to. Again. That kind of scared me. But then I said to hell with it, and just kept going. I guess I was talking about love all that time, and it wasn't one of Jon's old speeches, something I pulled, canned or bottled, off the shelf of memory. This was Randy Duke, telling how he loved this boy—how much and why and how it made him feel.

When I stopped, Kelly was sitting with her head down and her hands folded in her lap. She looked up and nodded, when it seemed that I was done.

"Huh," she said. One of her dynamite reactions. "That's quite a story." She brushed some wispy strays from off her forehead. "And you know something? I envy you." She stood up then, and turned away from me, her face into the wind from off the lake. "I guess I envy David, too," she said.

I didn't know exactly what she meant by that. "Well, I know he thinks he's lucky to be here," I babbled. "And I know he loves your class, and he seems to think that mine's okay. And I know it really makes me happy to hear how much you like him, and how good he is." Now I was talking to the breezes, too, looking straight downhill. I was sort of heading for an exit line.

"You going to Fossel's Thursday night?" She didn't sound exactly like herself when she said that. I'm sure she hadn't already taken a breath to hold while waiting for my answer, but it sounded something like that—as if she'd sort of forced the question out, against resistance of some kind.

"Well, yeah, I thought I would," I said. "You going?"

I turned when I asked that. She was standing like a diver, with her toes hooked over the edge of the huge amphitheater row, and she had her lip in her teeth and was rocking back and forth.

"Huh," she said. A sort of small explosion. And with that sound she *did* let out a deep, held breath. Her lower lip was fat and wet and glistening. "Yeah," she said, and looked at me out of the tops of her eyes and skewed her mouth around the way people do when they're real dubious about something. "I guess I will," she said, and nodded. "So I guess I'll see you there."

"If not before," I said. I risked a smile. No question, I was feeling good. It wasn't quite as if we'd made a date, but it was something more than seeing her at Emil's, wasn't it? Well, wasn't it? "I really like to watch your class," I said, "if you don't mind, that is."

"I guess I don't," she said, and took a giant step forward, dropping down a row.

"You ought to come see David play sometime," I said. "Bucks always have a game the sixth on Wednesday. I bet he'd love it if you came."

She took another step. "Well, if *you* think *he* would, maybe *I* will," she said. "I haven't seen either of you at Emil's." She turned so I could see her grinning, too. And then kept dropping down the steps.

I didn't get around to asking her about the "special circumstance" that Fossel said had gotten her to come to camp, or why her company broke up. That could wait for Thursday night. Suddenly, there seemed to be a lot of time, and endless possibilities.

Dunny could be proud of Randy Duke's adjustment.

# CHAPTER 6

From time to time, I make remarks in total innocence that cause some other people to say this: "Get *him.*" My father, once, used different words to voice that sentiment. "Just who do you think you are?" he asked, in tones of some contempt. He didn't comprehend my snigger.

But, a little while back, I mentioned parties in a way that could have brought on that reaction. I said, if I remember right, that after you got to a certain age, parties aren't quite the point of life. My main defense, of course, will be that I didn't say what *is.* But anyway, parties . . .

First of all, you have to realize that people of my generation have, so far as I can see, a very different sort of party history than, say, my parents had. We began to party back in junior high, and "party" was an active verb, all right. That's one difference. My parents, at the same age, might *go* to a party; "party" was a noun, for them: a recreational gathering of friends, with dancing, and the bad boys drinking beer out on the lawn, someplace where the parents (always present) wouldn't see them.

But in *my* junior high, "to party" meant to listen to some music and to smoke some weed, in seventh grade; by ninth grade, it was listen to some music, smoke some weed, and maybe, if you could, (excuse my French) get fucked. And from what I understand, our neighborhood was fairly retarded, compared to, oh, the city, say.

Whether this is good for kids or not, I won't get into. Everyone will have his own ideas on that. But one thing I will say is: it's certainly ridiculous. Not at the time, of course, but once you reach a certain age, and start to retrospect a little.

Here we were, this bunch of little *nestlings*, almost altogether lacking in survival skills, spending countless hours of our time, and countless dollars of our parents' money. Doing what? Talking about, and buying, records and dope. And "turning one another on," as we were fond of saying. I hope my sister, Tish, doesn't have to pass through those basement-game-room-rites-of-passage, with the parents out of town, or at a party of their own. But I suppose she will. Even back in the Romans' time, people used to bitch about this sort of thing, you know. *O tempora, O mores*; that's the way they put it. Everybody, now: *"Get him!"*

In high school, I was hot and cold on parties. A lot of them seemed awfully *repetitious.* I had a spell where I was real, real serious—there was a girl involved with that, of course—and, too, I trained a lot, for basketball as well as baseball.

At first, in college, I went everywhere and anywhere and tried to feel at home by meeting lots of people. By baseball season, though, I'd settled down. Dunny and myself, we didn't party all that much, except with real small groups of friends. We kept on smoking, sometimes, or we'd have a bunch of drinks, like on a weekend; and, yes, we still had music on a lot. And, sure, our dates would spend some nights, and maybe we'd make love, depending. That's the way it was, for me, up to the accident, when I dropped out of social life.

Parties? Thanks but no thanks, fella. That became my attitude. (Won't someone please, please *get* him?)

Er, uh, unless, that is, it happens to be Thursday night, the second week of camp, and I am going to Fossels'.

"I always walk to Hiram's," Bilgy said to me that noon. "Everybody does, I guess, except for Coachie and Raylene. Why don't you come on by my cabin after Taps? Bring along your trusty Ray-O-Vac, and I shall lead you, as a horse to water."

"Sure," I said, "but I guess you know that you can't make one . . ."

"Nor would I *think* of trying," he proclaimed.

So Roger Redmond, Running Bear, and I convened outside our Uncle's cabin, our flashlights in our hands; from there, the four of us went strolling up the path to the athletic fields, which we would cross to get to Fossel's house. Only I, of course, was not entirely certain of our destination.

"Hey, Bilge," said Roger. "Is this a large affair tonight, or just the major talent?"

"On a scale of one to ten, I'd say a four," said Bilgy. "The Dance and Drama people, and the Music staff—as always. Plus certain wealthy patrons of the arts such as ourselves. But also many of the fresh new faces, I believe. Young Randall here. Mt. Hildebrand. Miss Helen Hastings of the Hawkeye State, the dead-eyed head of ladies' basketball. Maestra Kelly Carna - valli, of the Dance. I guess she gets invited twice, once for Dance and once for being new. And others of that virgin ilk, I think. Depends who shows. Coachie and Raylene will always go to Hy and Cynthia's. Fisher loves a free one; you figure he'll be there."

"And speaking of which," said Running Bear. "Free ones, not Fisher. It *is* true there'll be fosselizers served?"

"Oh, my, yes," Bilgy said. "I got a batch together during Rest Hour. Somewhere between a hogshead and a tun, I'd say. It's best to let it fume awhile, and give the flavors time to marry, if you get my point."

"Regretfully," said Running Bear, "I always get it. Every time, I swear I'm never going to touch those things, and then I take a little taste and . . . well, it seems so easygoing and down-home."

"Listen, Red-man," Roger said. "You know you people can't handle firewater. That's why we don't let you have it on the reservations. We know what's good for you boys—that's maize soup. Maize soup's *your* down-home drink."

R.B. laughed. "No worse than what I've seen some white folks go for. Ginger brandy and skim milk! Whoever heard of any drink like that? That Kelly's crazy, man."

* * *

That Kelly. Since meeting Fossel at the amphitheater, I'd seen her once or twice a day. I'd never thought that she was crazy. Beautiful? For sure. Mysterious? I guess so. Wonderful with kids? You bet.

It seemed that every day a few more people came to watch her class—not crowds, you understand, but twos and threes, more likely: people from the Cottages and other kids and staff. Christine (Tina) Garvey of the Dance department got to be a regular, I noticed. She was there on every one of my days, anyway, and sat down in a bottom row. After class, she'd always talk with Kel awhile. I liked to watch them.

Tina was a big tall blonde girl with a huge, expressive mouth, and gorgeous legs, and busy hands. She'd stand there looking down at Kel, her feet at angles, in the dancer's way, talking, laughing, touching Kelly here and there, and then herself, way high up on the breastbone. It looked as if she played a kind of stationary tag, for both of them. Kelly answered her in words and body movements: steps and bows and gestures; sometimes Tina shadowed them. Once, they had a movement conversation, back and forth, that made them shout for joy, and hug each other at the end of it. Some little dancers, who'd been hunkered down like setter dogs while waiting in the shade, rose high up on their knees and clapped.

I also went to Emil's every other night, a new routine for me.

JCs got two nights "off" a week, plus any other ones their counsellor stayed in. What those guys were, was eaters. They had a special refrigerator of their own up in the dining hall, which the kitchen staff kept stuffed with milk and remnants of cold quiche, roast duck, and so on. Right beside it was a shelf full of cold cereal, and all the necessary bowls and silverware and napkins. So, almost every night, some JCs got together for a "snack." Oh, a few Don Juans made contacts with their counterparts at Camp Raylene, and there were also (very rarely) little flings with tourist girls like Jennifer, but mostly, lacking cars, they stayed at home and played some pickup basketball, or cards, and ate. Freud could call it anything he wanted to; they believed—and firmly—they were having fun.

I still liked being in the cabin, lots—and so did Harlan, as it happened, which was good. But after I had talked to Kel, that day, and she had mentioned Emil's, at the end, I just—in spite of all I knew, and didn't know, and was afraid of—well . . . I went to Emil's every other night.

Kelly was there whenever I was, and I think the other nights, as well. Sometimes she came early, sometimes very late; the nights that she was "on," she must have hung around, stayed up, waiting until her JC got back in. If possible, she'd sit a long way from the door, with Tina and maybe Wendy, her back against the wall, tilted up against the knotty pine. When she was late, and guys and girls had mingled some, she'd sit off on the edge somewhere, and mostly by a girl. If someone had been watching her and trying to decide what her sexual preference was (as the saying goes), he probably would have said "neither."

The guys were equally predictable, on schedule. Running Bear and Amos tended to be there when I arrived, and still there when I left; Bilge and Barney seemed to manage to "look in," most nights. Hillside was an every-other-nighter, regular as a two-minute warning; Emil or his wife, Jackie, would have the tops off four tall frosty ones as soon as he walked in, so he could save himself some steps. Trace would stroll in late, always in a nice clean shirt and looking freshly bathed.

I noticed Kelly put away her share. As soon as Emil had seen she was serious, he'd made a Kelly's Corner in the bar. Above the cooler where he kept the orange juice and lemons and her skimmed milk, now, he'd stacked a half a dozen bottles of her ginger-flavored brandy, and Jackie'd cut a shamrock out of green crepe paper, which she'd tacked up over them. I think they thought her name was Something Kelly, instead of Kelly Something. Emil called her Sweet Mavourneen Kelly, in a fake-o Irish brogue, sometimes.

Kel did not correct him, she just laughed. She laughed a

lot at Emil's. It didn't take much provocation, as the night wore on.

"Oh, God," she'd say, "you people are too much." She made a joke of everything. That's the way she seemed to want it, jokes and nothing personal—you know.

I heard, oh, maybe half a dozen people offer her a drink—Tracey, Bear, and Barney to name three, but she would always laugh and say that she had money of her own. Sometimes, though, she'd buy for someone else, as long as she was sure he wouldn't take it personally.

"Here, Hubert," she'd say to Bilgy, setting down a Miller Light in front of him. "It's only that I had an empty hand."

"How can you drink this crap?" she said, another time, sipping at the scotch and water that she'd brought, before she set it down in front of me.

But when Running Bear got her a ginger brandy and skimmed milk, without permission, she let it sit there on the table all night long, untouched. "You're on the wrong track, Mark Trail," she told him, when she pushed the glass away.

One night I got a bag of peanuts and offered her a handful, just the way you do, more like a reflex than anything. "You sure know the way to an elephant's heart," she said, and took them. Our hands touched on the exchange, and she kept her eyes on mine as she put them in her mouth and chewed. I felt as if I were being weighed and measured and having my temperature taken. "Um, I could eat five bags of those," she said, and Bear leaped to his feet, as if to run and get them for her. "But if I get any fatter than I am, I'll be ready for the sideshow. So cool it, Keemo-sappy." He sat down.

"That there's the stuff that puts the weight on you," said Hillside, pointing to her glass.

"I know," she said, "I know." And for a second she forgot to laugh. "But everybody loves a jolly fat girl, right? And anyway, what else can a body do, of an evening, when she's all tied up in the boondocks? Or is it *to* the boondocks? What the hell is a boondock, anyway?" She grabbed Tina's shoulder and shook it for attention. "Dahling. We're discussing boondocks. Could you, perchance, enlighten us, as to the nature of a 'boondock,' singular?"

"Way-ull," said Tina, who sometimes liked to be southern, of an evening, "this one time, ol' Dan'l Boone was paddlin' down the Swannee or the Shenandoah, or one of them, and he sez to himself, he sez, 'I got the farthest-away cabin in the most remotest part of the entire Yewnited States, and every time I come on home by boat, I gotta step out of the gol-durn thing and get my rawhides soakin' to the knees. Mebbe what I ought do is build me, lak, some kinda . . ."

Mostly I just sat and sipped and went along with what was going on. I'd wait for Thursday night to ask her things. Closing time was one o'clock, a lot too late for me; the one night that I stayed to see how long she'd last, she left at quarter of, in halfway decent shape, enough to drive. I followed her, and she was slow and steady. I kind of think that was her quitting time; she'd said she couldn't get to sleep real early.

At least she always noticed I was there—a smile when I came in and left, which was that much more than other guys received. Or that's the way I chose to see it, anyway.

"You're looking awful droopy, Red," she said to me one time, and sort of underneath the noise that other folks were making.

"Well . . ." I started, then I shook my head. There's stuff that can't be mumbled, just the way there's stuff that can't be shouted. And particularly when you're not entirely positive of what it is you want to say. I went back to gnawing on my half a loaf. She shrugged and talked to someone else. I don't think other people knew I was so involved with Kelly. "Involved" in my imagination, anyway.

Running Bear, for instance, didn't seem to feel the need to sneak a look at me when he mentioned Kelly's drinking habits, as we walked across the ball field on the way to Fossel's. And neither did Rodge or Bilgy. I was thought to be a member of the all-we-are-is-good-friends group. Right.

And, as we angled off across the left-field foul line, with the small white weight house looming up in front of us, who should we encounter but the Kelly/Tina/Wendy show, arriving from the opposite direction.

"Hey, it's K.C. and the Sunshine Band," hailed Roger.

"Who's that?" said Kelly, peering. "Oh, might have known it." This to T. and W.: "Sly and the family Flintstone." Back to us: "Not that any of you heroes would have reason to know, but is the weight house open?"

"Yes-the-weight-house-is-open," said Roger-the-Robot, "and-no-you-may-not-go-in-it. That-is-an-order."

"We don't take orders," Tina told him. "Do I look like a waitress?" She had on skin-tight pants that flared at the bottom, in some huge flowered print; her legs looked six feet long.

"Raylene doesn't want her little ladies lifting weights," said Wendy, "but she must have given up on us. I'm sure she thinks the Dance and Drama weirds are safely gay. And *you* know how we cowgirls carry on." Hmm, I thought. Was Wendy joking, smoke-screening, or telling the plain unvarnished?

Bilgy had opened the door of the little house. "*I* don't see why you shouldn't go on in," he said, bowing toward the entrance. "Barbells for the bar-belles, didn't Shakespeare say?"

"Where the hell are the lights?" asked Kelly, going in.

"There aren't any." Roger slammed the door behind the three of them. "At last I have you in my power," he announced to it.

He put his face beside the door, and braced it with his foot and knee. "Do you swear," he whispered loud and savagely, "to fetch me all the treasures of Cathay, perform with me The Goat, The Rabbit, The Panther, and The Buffalo, cook me every kind of Rice-A-Roni, and give me backrubs Tuesdays during Lent?"

"Oh, sure. You bet. Why not?" said all three girls, and Roger opened up the door.

"Okay," he said. "I hope you didn't break anything."

"Shit, we didn't *see* anything," said Wendy.

"Are there really no lights?" asked Tina.

"Why should there be?" said Running Bear.

"Oh, *God,*" the girls all groaned.

"There really *is* nothing to do but drink around here," said Tina.

"Or try to learn The Buffalo . . ." said Roger.

"Speaking of drink . . ." suggested Bilgy, and so our group, now seven strong, wandered off around the farthest tennis courts and over the girls' lacrosse fields.

"I'm pissed that we can't use the weights." I'd put myself alongside Kelly; no question, she *was* angry.

"It's stupid. Maybe if I talked to Fisher, he could set aside some time for women, in the daylight . . ."

"I think I've decided to try to get back into shape," she said. I'd never heard her say anything so—what?—*portentously,* before.

I nodded, wondering how much she wanted me to ask.

"Shape? Shape?" said Running Bear, coming up on the other side of her. "Maybe I can help. I specialize in spot massage, you know. . . ."

I let out one of the loudest silent groans of my entire life. He seemed like such a kid—a cub?—sometimes. Not to mention, in-my-way.

"Hark, the sounds of revelry," said Tina. And very soon I saw the site of it, as well.

The summer house of Cynthia and Hyacinth Fossel, both fortyish, and their daughters, Hilary, twelve, and Kathryn, eight, was five years old and set in Wellington, Vermont. But it could have passed for sixty, and would have looked at home in Bay Head, on the Jersey shore.

It was, as Hyacinth himself had said to me, a "big brown shingled one with all the porches," and also something of a compromise. Cynthia preferred the seashore to the mountains, so at least she had a beach house. "Some time up the road," Hy told me later on that summer, "we'll build a mountain cabin on the Cape, as well. For now she's holding up quite nicely, though. We can get fresh lobster in Manchester, and I have sand I sometimes sprinkle on her towel."

When we climbed the front porch steps—that porch held huge and high-backed wooden rockers, with woven wicker seats—the door was standing open, letting music out, and party sounds, except for ice in glasses. Hy collected Ellington, and show tunes, Bilgy said, and Bix and Pops "Beshay," whoever they were. The music that was playing wasn't Ellington, I knew that much. It had a ricky-ticky sound, and pretty soon a guy began to sing who couldn't, really.

"Don't you think that Fred Astaire and I have the two most underrated voices of the century?" asked Hyacinth Fossel, advancing from the large, high-ceilinged living room directly to our right. He joined the record in a light, but also off-key, baritone: "Nothing now could take the wind out of my sails . . ." they sang. With which, he captured Tina in a ballroom grip and one-two-three-ed their way around the spacious entrance hall.

A wide wooden staircase, open in the middle, rose three storeys right in front of us; to the left was a formal dining room, with stacks of paper plates and napkins, plus food and snacks in quantity to warm a JC's heart. The floorboards and the staircase were a dark and lustrous brown, like buckwheat honey; the rugs were Navahos, I think, in cool, pale greens, and grays, and lighter browns. Inside the living room, the furniture was huge and deep, and there were cushions scattered on the floor.

Dancing with Tina, Fossel looked like a lion in resortwear and blue sneakers, his shirt as gaudy as her pants. They looked as if they'd done this all their lives. I felt like I used to feel in Latin class, when I hoped I wouldn't get called on.

Twice around the hall and then they stopped, and Hy shook hands with everyone before he turned toward the living room and made one big, delighted gesture.

"Randy!" he exclaimed, but not in my direction. "You haven't met my wife. This is Cynthia." No one's ever said my name like that, so far.

I didn't know that people ever really walked that way: the woman coming toward me could have been on wheels, instead of barefoot. Of course the long dress helped. It swept the floor, was white and silky, and had a wide gold belt around the waist. She was of a size you'd naturally put numbers on, like five-eleven, and perhaps one-sixty-five—but still you wouldn't call her fat. In my culture, goddesses are never fat. Her hair was thick and copper-colored, parted in the middle, and braided down her back. Her eyes were different colors—another first for me—one a deep, deep blue, the other kind of hazel; her lashes and her brows were copper, too. It was about the strongest face I'd ever seen, with broad, high cheek bones and a nose like Pocahontas might have had. She smiled at me and also shook my hand.

"Randy," she said. "Hy's told me about you. I'm very glad you came. Your secrets all are safe with me."

She didn't say the last of that out loud, of course. Jesus, I thought, you *are* in the Big Time. I'd never seen a Cynthia Fossel before, even at the NC double A's.

"We'd love it if you'd wander all around," she was saying to me now, "and get to feel at home. Kel will show you where the silver is, and towels. Everything is help-yourself, so help yourself. If you want to go upstairs and meet the children, go ahead. They're meant to be getting ready for bed. So they're probably watching TV, or listening over the bannisters."

"Thanks," I said, and looked up just in time to see two nightgown hems and four bare feet in quick retreat. "It's a great house. I can see that."

She nodded, lowering her eyes, and smiled, then wheeled back toward the living room. Coach was there I saw, being swallowed by a fat upholstered chair, with his little feet up on an ottoman. He was wearing his turned-down sailor hat and a "Remember Woodstock" t-shirt, and black high sneakers like the old-time Celtics used to wear. Raylene was sitting on the floor near his chair, on a big red tasseled cushion. She had on the sort of long, one-piece, baggy dress that I think my mother calls a moo-moo. Even if that's not the right word, it'll do. Hers had a design consisting of a lot of huge leaves in different colors. She looked as if someone had raked her up and piled her on that cushion.

Fisher was in there, too, and Rudy Red-nose, and Trace and Helen Hastings, who really *was* from Iowa and the head of girls' basketball and nice-looking, and some others. What struck me was how relaxed everybody seemed. Compared to guess-who. I mean, a lot of them were almost perfect strangers.

I decided on a drink-first strategy, and turned toward the dining room. Kel was watching me, and wearing half a smile, but not a mocking one, thank God.

"Yeah," she said. "I know. That's Cynthia. She *was* an actress, if you're guessing, but that's not an act. She's one of the few people in the world I actually believe. Come on. Let's start in this direction." She took my hand, as if she were my nanny.

"This is the dining room. See all the edibles? I've been told it's not the worst of all ideas to eat some greasy food before you sample Hagar's punch. Look at all this stuff. Isn't it marvelous?" She gestured up and down the table and the sideboard. "Cynt is something of a genius when it comes to making good food look like crap. You may think that what you're looking at is nothing more than American cocktail party belly-liner, but it isn't really. Everything here is good for you, can you believe it? Perhaps a little fattening in places . . ." She dug a cracker into something creamy looking. "But—I can always start to get in shape tomorrow."

I slathered homemade mayonnaise on two pieces of small dark bread and stuck a folded piece of healthy ham between them. "Here's looking at *you,* kid," I grunted, and popped it in my mouth. "Mmmm," I said, and made another one, to travel.

Kelly led me through a swinging door that put us in a pantry—sink and shelves, and glass-doored cupboards, plus a large refrigerator—and on through that into the kitchen. It was absolutely huge, stretching to the back wall of the house. Nearest to the pantry was where the food was cooked and stored, and cleaning up got done: stove, another icebox, table, counters, toaster, sink, and so forth. And farther down was like a little sitting-dining room, beside a large and brick-hearthed fireplace. There was a nice round wooden table, circled by some captain's chairs, and also a small couch and two upholstered chairs, and lamps, and paintings on the wall, along with antique things, some copper, some black iron. I had never seen a kitchen without any Formica, or linoleum, or lots of stainless steel. The big sink looked as if it was made of some kind of stone, and there was a bowl of eggs by the stove. I'd never seen eggs in a bowl like that before.

"Hy told me you had your own company," I said, as we stepped out the kitchen door and onto another, smaller, screened-in porch. If that doesn't seem too smooth to you—a little weak in the transition game—I'd have to say you're right. I was forcing it, all of a sudden, which doesn't work in basketball, or pitching, or relationships. I know that, and you know that, and Jon knew that. Randy Duke is not what you could really call left-*hand*ed nowadays, but if you want to see a guy with two left feet . . .

She kept on going, opening a door and walking down three steps to the back lawn. "Did he?" I heard, floating back in the dark.

"Yeah," I said, hurrying so as not to have to shout. "That's really something."

She seemed to have speeded up, too. "I was a big executive, all right," she said, and opened still another door, onto another porch, near the back far corner of the house.

"Well, how come you're not still doing that?" I trotted across *that* porch toward the lighted door that she was opening. "Hy said that it was the best thing that had happened in dance in a long time." I followed her in the door.

The room was part game room, part theater, part bar, and part dancehall, I guess you could say. To the far right, there was a bumper-pool table, and next to it was a Ping-Pong table. Hillside Hildebrand was looming over the former, lining up a shot. Watching him, and leaning on a cue stick that almost reached her chin, was a tiny girl named Bienvenida who wore her hair in a medium Afro and who'd been in the original cast of *Oh! Calcutta!*, I'd been told. Some wooden benches were stacked along the walls, around the tables.

At the other end of the room was a small stage that had a juke box on it—well, more of a platform, really, just a little off the floor, but with a curtain, now wide open, you could draw across the front of it. Just down from the stage there was a long table with stacks of large paper cups—the kind you get a milkshake in, some places—and a couple of white enamelware pitchers. Under the table and to both sides of it were washtubs holding ice, more pitchers, beer and other bottles, and a watermelon.

Kelly turned toward me. "The plumbing got fucked up," she said, "and I had to get it fixed. And now I think the wiring is shot. The place is a real mess."

"What?" I said. "Well, why didn't you just move, or something?"

"I couldn't," she said. "Don't I wish? It's hard to explain. The thing is, like . . . I couldn't break the lease. It'd make a lot more sense if you'd been there, you know? Like those jokes that people tell sometimes? You really had to be there."

At which point the door behind her opened and in trooped Bilgy, Tina, Running Bear, and Wendy, followed shortly by Roger and Rudy, all of whom maintained they might have known that certain couthless people would make a beeline for the . . . and etcetera. One trouble with parties is people. Everywhere. All over.

Kelly poured herself some punch and drifted to the right and asked for winners of the pool game. Hillside said that she'd be playing Bienvenida then.

"She's really waxed my water-skis," said the boys' camp's principal attraction.

"I'm stopping, also, Kel," said Bienvenida. "I got a little bet with this prime beef here. I said I'd slaughter him at pool, and then I'd drink him off his size sixteens. He's tryin' to wiggle out of it already."

"You come on now, Byenny," Hillside whined. "You know I don't drink stuff like Uncle's Kool-Aid, there. It's not in m' contract."

"Look," she said, "jus' try one little cup, okay?" She rolled her eyes at him and pouted. "It's full of vitamins, right, Oncle? I bet it makes you feel so healthy you won't know yourself. Before you say Yack Robinson." She laughed.

"That's what I'm afraid of," Hillside said, but let himself be led toward the bar.

Running Bear attached himself to Bienvenida's cue, and he and Kelly organized the table. I allowed a giant paper cup to get from Roger's hand to mine, and tasted from it. Whew. Not bad. My father would have set it down quietly and walked away; I at least had the smarts to drop in a handful of ice cubes. Kel and Running Bear had started playing; she laughed at something he said. I decided that I wasn't such a pool fan, and followed Bilgy out the door that he'd come in by. That put me in a hall that led back to the living room. And that's how come I landed on the floor at Coach's feet, and not too far from Raylene Raycroft.

No one seemed to notice me, and that was nice. I sipped my drink and listened to them talk about a Field Day and a Horse Show and the Camp Ondawa Day and someone named Carla Strasenburgh who had a timber wolf, it seemed, and how to make authentic black bean soup. Once or twice I thought of Kelly, too: what I'd say to her, the next time.

And then I heard the voice of Raylene Raycroft say: "You aren't Randy Duke." I turned and looked at her, with my heart guess-where. "Are you?" She was smiling, her eyes the merest slits.

"Yes, ma'am," I said, around a slow exhale. "I sure am." Feeling maybe ten years old.

"I thought you must be," she said. "You don't look like an All-American." She must have seen my hand. "Well, how are you getting along, Randy?"

"Just fine," I said. "I like it here a lot. It's everything that Dunny said it was. The kids are great. And of course the staff's the best." I raised my paper cup in her direction, sort of as a toast, and gave out with what was meant to be a youthful-yet-comradely, humble-but-confident, and somewhat-congratulatory laugh. She looked as if she might have missed my hyphenated modifiers but heard one of her own: feeble-minded.

"That's nice," she said. "My husband believes in hiring quality people. 'If you want the best, then get the best,' he always says. Actually," she went on, "he never said any such thing. He has his faults like all the rest of us, but an idiot he's not."

I couldn't tell if she was making a joke, or a comparison, or what, but she was looking at me very sharply now, with her head cocked to one side.

"That's obvious," I said, feeling that some halfway-Harlanistic honesty might work. "Everything I've seen and heard around here tells me he's a darn good man, with exceptional judgment. He should be plenty proud of this place. You both should be."

"He's more than proud of it, if you want to know," she said. "He *is* it. Literal-lee." She made the word two words. "Some people are gift shops, and some people are jails, or sweet sauterne, or games of chance, or circuses, or ciphers. Coach is a summer camp, that's what he is, all right. My father worked as a baker, so you might think he was a Toll House cookie or a Swedish rye. But what he was was numbers. Accounts, phone numbers, how many miles to Montreal, the speed of sound, extracting the square root, his nieces' and nephews' ages and their birthdays, the population of São Paulo, Brazil. That man was all numbers, I hope to tell you. Coach may have worked as a mortician all his life, but what he is is a summer camp. I never met a mortician who didn't think he was funny, except for Coach. A lot of them are glossy, big, resort hotels, it seems to me. My father could always relax with a road map or the World Almanac and just be himself. But Coach has this place."

"Dunny Dibble told me it was just like magic here," I found myself telling this woman. "I guess you know Dunny, all right—he's my roommate down at college." She nodded, narrowing her eyes again. I got a funny flash of feeling that she was trying to remember Dunny Dibble's roommate's name. I wondered what *she* really was: a lonely mountain top? a nurse novel? an all-purpose, antiseptic, contraceptive agent?

"Oh, I know Dunny well," she said. "He's a cunning little devil, yes indeed. Magic? Huh. His idea of magic is to change a girl into a rabbit. His father was much the same way in his own day. They're from Cincinnati, as you know," she said, as if that explained everything.

"Yes," I said, "but what he meant by magic hadn't anything to do with tricks. It's how he thought about the summer, here at camp, a kind of bonus in a person's life that doesn't *count* somehow. When people all are nice and mellow—just can be themselves, you know? And everything's in here-and-now, like they say in Gestalt psychology." Show-off. Liar. What a beauty I was! I finished off the liquid in my paper cup and felt an easy, confidential glow. That should have warned me, but it never does.

" 'A kind of bonus'? 'Real'?" she asked. "It could be just the opposite, you know. Totally irrelevant, unreal. Unlifelike. Useless. Who's kidding whom, young man? Answer me that one."

She put a hand down on the rug and leaned on it and turned, which got her to her knees. Then, helped by handholds on her husband's chair, she clambered to her feet. "Martin, we should go." She touched him on his sailor cap, and then looked down at me again.

"Or maybe summer camp is all the point there ever is. And all the rest of it is magic. Color: black. Either way, there's always some forbidden fruit, Sir Randy, and don't you forget it." Her paper cup was still on the floor, and it was empty. Martin Raycroft put his little sneakers down and rose.

"Cynthia and Hyacinth," he said. "This was wonderful."

My manners pulled me to my feet. I shook hands with Raylene; Coach punched me very lightly on the upper arm as he passed by, smiling very much the way a kid would. A mischievous, chance-taking little smile.

"Good night, Coach," I told him, as I always did.

* * *

With the Raycrofts gone, the party took a breath and started up again. I walked into the dining room with Bilge and stood and ate for half an hour solid, talking sports, Raylene and Coach, and sports again. It seemed to me that Dunny'd over-simplified a lot of things, maybe just to get a laugh, who knows?

By the time I'd circled back, to living room, to hall, to game room for my refill, Kel and Running Bear were playing Ping-Pong, hitting lots of smashes off the table, and Trace and Wendy, with the juke box on, were dancing on the little stage. Hillside H. and Bienvenida Something both were missing.

The food I'd eaten made me confident and thirsty, so I gave myself a nice-sized pour of Bilgy's brew, again with cubes, and headed through the door to the outside, thinking to reverse the route I'd gone with Kel. She seemed to be enjoying where she was. The food and drink were great, the evening a disaster, so far.

I went along the lawn toward the kitchen porch, hearing voices in the darkness not too far away, and thinking I smelled smoke; that made me think of junior high again. I opened up the kitchen door and stood there for a moment in the dimness. It was such a perfect room. I told myself I'd have a kitchen just like that some day.

"We got a range that size at home," Helen Hastings said. My feet probably didn't leave the floor, but various other sections of me jumped. She was sitting in the shadows to my left, on one of the upholstered chairs beside the fireplace.

"You must be from a big family," I said. The range in question was a big gas stove with eight burners and a griddle on the top of it. I guessed that it was new, but made to look like old, and quaint, with lots of metal scrollwork, and a warming oven.

"Uh-huh." She put her arms above her head and stretched, and I could see her small breasts rise, right underneath her shirt. She was tall, but not gangly, maybe five foot eight or nine, topped by light brown hair in a short Prince Valiant that'd keep it out of her face on a turn-around jumper. She had a clean-cut, open, Iowa look about her, I thought. An athlete. Strong but not sturdy. Definitely not trouble. "There're eight of us kids. And Mom's parents live with us, too."

"Jinkies," I said. "You must have come to camp to get some privacy."

She laughed. "Not really. I kinda like it when there's a lot of people around. Always something going on. The thing was, I wanted to see the East. I never had before. Particularly New England. Dad's got roots back here." She pronounced it so it rhymed with "puts."

"I guess it must be quite a change," I said. "I've never been to Iowa, but I think I saw it on a beer commercial once. This great big field, about a thousand miles in each direction? With a bunch of tractors going back and forth?"

"That's *it,*" she said, and laughed again. "One big old cornfield's all it is. Except part of it is soybeans, too. Corn and soybeans, beans and corn. It's gotten so we have to *import* all the hayseed that we use."

"What about the people, though?" I asked. "I'm really curious. Are the people all that different here?" I'd put a hip up on the table right in front of her, and set down my paper cup. I was suddenly having a pretty good time. It seemed very Randy Duke-ish to be sitting like that in a nice wood kitchen, talking to a pretty girl from Iowa, and kind of helping her to feel at home.

"Well," she said, "yes and no, I guess I'd have to say. A lot of people here in the East, they seem to act real smart—you know?—and I guess a lot of them *are.* And it seems like some of the kids back here are pretty used to having almost everything they can think of, about as soon as they can think of it. But once you get past stuff like that, they seem just like the ones at home." I wondered if she'd also just described yours truly. "Tell you one thing, though," she said. "People here—I mean at camp, now—they sure are *nice.* Don't *you* think so?"

"I surely do," I said, very much prepared to take that personally. I realized I was talking like her already. That was part of Randy Duke's desire to please, I guess. It seems to me, sometimes, that all he was was a reaction: like, with ice cream. Chocolate was that? Make that two. "My roommate at college was the one who got me this job, and he told me it'd be like this. I'm not sure I believed him, though." Dunny was getting a lot of air time tonight.

She nodded. "What gets me is how well different *sorts* of people get along up here," she said. "That's what I was thinking, sitting here. I mean, just look at me, as midwest as they make 'em and, I guess you'd have to say, a jock, hanging out with all these New York theater people. And I don't know about them, but I'm sure having fun. 'Course with actors and them, I guess you never know for sure just what they're feeling."

Well, we went back and forth like that, comparing first impressions of the camps and different people. I also asked about her sport, and what she felt about the future, having only one more year at school and all. She told me, pretty matter-of-factly I thought, that she'd be drafted by the WBL—that's the women's proleague, as hardly anyone knows—if it came back into existence, but wasn't sure she'd go for it. She shrugged. "I played in front of bigger crowds in high school than they used to get," she said. She thought she might like to play in an Olympics some time, she said, but she'd also have to face the fact that life was life and basketball was just a game she played for kicks. That, of course, was also true for Randy Duke, but he couldn't seem to get quite so matter-of-fact about it. "Life" seemed a bit more of a problem to the lad. Maybe having a choice made it easier for her. Something other than life. She *could* play if she wanted to—over in Europe, maybe, even.

"And speaking of kicks," she said, "I think I'm good for about one more cup of that punch. I mean, is that strong, or what?"

I laughed. "It's *sneaky*-strong," I said, and made my sneaky face.

We got up and walked on through the pantry, where Tina was sitting mostly in the sink with her legs wrapped around Rudy Red-nose's waist; they seemed to be having a face-making contest. In the dining room, I helped myself to four fast curried-tuna-salad-with-yogurt-on-whole-wheat-biscuits, while Helen went on down to the game room for her drink. Then, still chewing, I ambled to the living room again, where clearly it had gotten to be sprawl-time.

Parties often reach that stage, I'm sure you've noticed, when people start to look like puppets with their strings let go, or maybe after dinner at the Borgias'. Hy was sitting in the corner of the largest couch, with Cynthia's head in his lap and the rest of her laid out along the sofa's surface. Bilge and Roger both were on the floor, slouching back against the seats of matching lounge chairs, while Fisher, who'd been sitting up when Coach was there, was curled up on his side, his head upon a fat beige cushion. Amos was perched on the piano stool, but facing away from the instrument, with his elbows resting on the keyboard cover and his legs stretched out in front of him. Sprawl-time. Which is also a great time for the kind of argument they were having.

"Randy! My man!" Roger beamed delightedly to see me. That told me that he wanted something, probably an ally. "Just what we be needing here, a mind that's still elastic, open—that hasn't been *completely* fosselized. Randy. Listen. What I'm telling these dumb . . . *mastodons*—by which I mean my ancient relative, and Fish and Amos, the Fossels being neutral still—is this. That what they ought to think about up here"—he circled a long finger up above his head—"is having the camps stay open year-round. You hear what I'm saying? I mean, first of all, look at the facilities. Beautiful, 'm I right? A little insulation; you put some woodstoves here and there, a few storm windows and storm doors. No problem. Got wood for twenty thousand years at *least.* I mean, the *waste* to have a place like this just sit here empty, ten months out of twelve!"

I flopped down in an easy chair with canvas-covered down-filled cushions. I held my paper cup up on my chest and nodded, waiting for more instant replay. People having an argument love to repeat themselves, when a fresh set of ears comes in.

"There's no question about that," Fisher said to me. He remained lying on his right side, as if he were paralyzed, but his eyes moved and his speech was really quite clear. "It *is* a shame—a waste, as Roger says. And maybe sometime in the future, when Coachie and Raylene are gone, there may be other . . . *usages.*" He gave a sideways nod, as if approving of that word. "Some *work*shops in the arts, perhaps." He rolled his eyes way up in his head, in an effort to look at the Fossels. "Or perhaps a therapeutic *cen*ter of some sort. That type of thing." Fisher heaved a mournful sigh. "Of course there would be wear and *tear,*" he said. "And I can see a lot of *work* involved. But I suppose it could be *great.*" Another sigh. "For someone." He closed his eyes.

"Oh, Fisher, therapy your ear," said Roger. "I'm not talking workshops, man." He turned to me again. "What I'm saying, Randy, is: there should be *kids* here year around. Maybe you could have some kind of school, you know? So long as it was lots like camp—you get me?—with all the same good attitudes and that." He took a swallow from his cup. "I bet if Fisher here, and Bilge and Hy and some of them all got together and laid it on the Coach, he'd go for it."

"Rodge, you absolutely never listen," Bilgy said. He turned to me, the jury. "Here's what I've tried to tell this earless jackass, Randy. That he's got one of those great-sounding ideas that can't possibly ever work. Camp's camp. You can't have camp in wintertime. That's like a law of nature. Can't you see that, Red?" A chatter of voices came up the hall from the game room, and in came Kelly, Running Bear, and Helen. "You can't suspend reality indefinitely," Bilgy said. That captured my attention totally. Was that what I was trying to do up here? Was that what *he* was trying to do? And everybody else. And then we'd all go back somewhere and pick up, or maybe start on, life? I could feel a little worm of anger turn in me. You get a little worm in real tequila, don't you? Did this one come from rum, or what?

"Oh, yeah?" said Running Bear. "Listen, Bilge, when I have four or five of these"—he showed his paper cup—"reality becomes a mere expression. Seven letter word beginning with *r*. What *is* real, I ask you?" He sank down to the floor, his legs crossed, tailor-fashion. Kelly folded to her knees beside him; she looked significantly bombed.

"Shut up, Bear; we talkin'," Roger said. He widened his appeal. "How about it, Hyacinth? You been awful quiet over there. Don't you think I'm saying something right?"

"Whoosh. I don't know, Rodge, I really don't." Hy seemed to have been holding his breath. He threw out an arm, palm up. "I'm really not too into schools. On the one hand, what you say sounds wonderful. It really makes my heart start beating harder"—he shook his great black head and chuckled—"you know what I mean? And, of course, I think of my own case—suppose I hadn't had an uncle I could go to? Wouldn't I have loved to stay at camp?" He put his hand on Cynthia, and smoothed her copper hair. "But then I wonder. I think I see the point that Bilgy's making. To some extent, the strength of camp is *contrast*—the fact that it's so different from the other world. I have certain aches and pains—not all of them are physical—that stop when I come up here. That makes me grateful. And in my gratitude, I cease to deal out certain other aches and pains. My family's my witness. But what would happen if my memory grew dim, and camp was all the life I had? Much as I may love it here, this isn't Eden, is it? All the evil that I've ever known and been is still inside me somewhere—a cancer in its seasonal remission, you might say. So I think what I'm afraid of is that winter camp would soon recycle into, simply, *life*. And maybe in the process kill the summer."

"Jesus," Roger said. He took another swallow, eyes inside the cup, then shook his head. "I didn't mean that like it sounded, Hy." He crossed his legs the other way and stared at them. "Sure, I get the point you're making. Both of you. But I don't want to feel that's right. That if a bunch of people—let's say *us*—set up *something* here—a school, whatever—and ran it all year round, that we'd start treating one another different. Is that the kind of thing you guys are telling me?"

Running Bear said, "Hey, this sounds pretty serious to me." It's almost always an impossibility for one person at a party to yank the general mood in some other direction, but that doesn't mean that lots of folks don't try.

"That's an interesting question," Amos said to Roger, ignoring Running Bear. Amos was a world-class ignorer. "I suspect we *would*, you know. I think what we'd see would be that the past and the future would kind of make that happen. All of a sudden—or maybe gradually—we'd find ourselves getting concerned, involved, with stuff that went on in kids' lives—and ours—before we got here. And maybe especially with where they—or we—might be planning to go next. Unless, of course, we agreed to stay here forever." Amos smiled. My worm relaxed; hey, not a bad idea. "Which might not be the worst idea you ever had. Considering the food. But take, like, now. We never seem to bother with a person's other life. So what if some kid in my cabin can't spell 'immediately,' or multiply eight times seven? What's that got to do with camp? I couldn't care less. I don't have to. Randy there could be the Boston Strangler; don't tell me about it. We'll do business on the ball field in the morning, and he's great at that. If he goes back to work in Boston in the fall—well, that won't be my problem, either."

"Oh, come now, Amos," Fisher said. He sounded quite alarmed. "I grant you that the life at camp is very present-oriented, but if you knew that Randy was—"

"Okay. Okay. That was a little bit extreme," said Amos. "But still. You get the point I'm making. If we were here for any length of time, there would be certain . . . *alterations* in the way things are. Suppose, for instance, I—and Kelly—fell in love and decided to get married. That might not sit too well with . . . Running Bear, let's say. Major change in atmosphere, right there. And let's further say that Kelly thought she'd like to be a doctor. That'd mean we'd have to leave this place and make some money first, and then—"

"Or suppose we *didn't* fall in love and I just decided I wanted to be the Secretary of State?" asked Kelly. She was squashing her *s*'s a little, and cutting down on her *t*'s.

"Okay, fine," said Amos. "But the point's the same.

Life is much more complicated than camp. For eight weeks, it's great not to know a thing about these kids, or deal with the outside world, and plans, at all. But if it was a year . . . ? Pretty soon we'd be knee-deep in history, and also expectations. Past and future time, just like I said. I think I like it better this way."

Well, I thought, I'd been right. I *was* the only person around here who was bothering to think about the future, who worried about his plans, or lack of same. The veterans just went along on cruise-control, playing games of Red and Blue, and getting drunk, and getting laid where possible. And then rejoining planet Earth until it got to be July again, and time for camp. Well, this was a one-shot deal for me. I had to try to grab whatever goodies from this place I could, and take them home with me, and maybe try to make a life from scratch. So what the hell, why not? I think I thought.

"Say, listen," I said, "that reminds me. I've been meaning to ask someone. Is it possible to find out any stuff about the kids? I mean, like the ones in your own cabin? Are there any records somewhere?"

Fisher opened his eyes. "Like what?" he said.

"Oh," I said, "just simple stuff, mostly. I don't know. Parents' names and home addresses. Birthdates, schools—that stuff. You know, all the stuff that goes on a record." How casual could I be?

"Why? I mean, why would you want to know any of those kinds of things?" Fisher asked.

"I don't know," I said. "I'd just like to. Curiosity, I guess. Nosiness, you could say." I tossed a little laugh into the room. It seemed that everyone was looking at me with more interest than the situation called for.

Fisher sat up beside his cushion. "As a general rule, Randy," he said, "a camper's folder is considered confidential. Some of them have things in them that Coach and I have learned . . . in *confidence*. But I'd be happy to look things up for you." He pulled an ear and smiled. "If you'd tell me what you'd like to know, and why."

Amos laughed. Not pleasantly, it seemed to me. "See? As soon as you depart the good old present, or leave camp property, you right away get into problems. It's just like I was saying, Podge, you see?''

A lot of people then began to talk at once, and in from outer space came Hillside H. and Bienvenida, with Rudy C. and Tina G. in tow. They wanted to organize a carp and bullfrog spearing expedition. Hillside claimed that the shallow end of Beaver Lake—back near the parking lot—was thick with giants of both species, and that he, a hunter all his life, would be our guide.

I took the opportunity to rise and stretch; Kelly wandered to my side.

''I know you haven't asked for my advice,'' she said. Her eyes looked slightly glazed. ''But I know why you're asking Fisher that. You wanta find out about David, don't you? About whether you and him . . .'' She twitched a finger back and forth. ''Well, I think you'd be smart to jus' leave it alone. Go with the flow. Whacha don't know won't hurtcha. Let sleeping dogs lie. *Que sera, sera*. And all that crap.''

She was pretty drunk, but I wasn't focusing on that. I was too busy with myself, with my own great seething mass of needs, swimming around in alcohol themselves. It was up to everybody else to adjust to me.

''I'm not sure what I want to do,'' I said, as if that were the most important thing in the world. ''Look,'' I said to her, ''why don't we just take a walk, and maybe we can—''

Just then, Running Bear came romping onto the set, with a paper cup in either paw. I sensed that neither one was meant for me. Kelly took what she was offered and tipped it in her face, one time.

''Listen, Kel,'' I said. ''D'you mind? I want to go and talk somewhere, that's all.'' She was making some ridiculous face at Running Bear, so what do I add to that, but, ''And if you're at all serious about wanting to get back in shape, you really ought to . . .''

Wouldn't Hammarskjöld have thought that that was great? Can't you see old Waldheim cheering wildly? Shouldn't I be there at every summit conference, *especially* on nuclear affairs?

''Oh, stick it, Red, you poor self-centered bastard,''

Kelly said. And she was flaming hot. "You're not my nursey, mister, or my 'ought-to' man. So what *you* want is far from my command. I've been that route already, and it sucks."

Her anger came so fast and strong it took me by surprise. I guess I never think that *anyone* should be pissed off at me. Her voice was clear and straight, and then her eyes got wet; her cheeks were very pink. She turned and left the room, walking hard and steadily; in the hall, she took a left and went on out the big front door. Running Bear lived up to his name, in the same direction. Everyone else was sort of milling around in the entrance hall, considering the carp and bullfrog hunt. Except for Cynthia Fossel, who was lying on the sofa where she'd been before, but without Hyacinth's lap under her head.

She might have made some sound; I can't be sure. In any case, I turned and saw her, and my face was burning. *I'd* been pointed the other way, and hadn't been talking very loud, but she must have heard the stuff that Kelly'd just unloaded.

She sat up, and she smiled. A sympathetic one, it seemed to me.

"Let's see," she said, "*my* line might be something like . . ." She appeared to turn the pages of a nonexistent script. "Ah, yes, like, 'let her go, Randy. She'll be back.' " She did that in a stagey, over-acted voice. "But, hmm . . ." She wrinkled up her brow. "That really doesn't work, does it? I'd rather tell you something that's a little harder, but I think is so. I think that sometimes a person gets filled up with helpless, righteous rage that has to be used up. It won't evaporate or anything; it seems as if it has to be used up, which takes a little time. But when it's finally gone, it's gone forever. And when that happens, Randy, she'll be empty. She'll have to fill her tank with something else, or . . ." She shook her head and shrugged. "Or I don't know what," she said, "but nothing good."

"I'm afraid that it's too much for me," I said. Both what she'd said *and* what had happened. "And anyway, she's right. I am an asshole." I'd gotten to the point of being half-pissed and half-real-sorry-for-myself. And still a trifle bombed, of course. "Anyway, thanks for a mostly-nice party. The food was fantastic." I managed a rueful, grunty laugh. "I guess I'll move along to the bullfrog hunt."

She nodded as if she thought that sounded like a great idea. "Just do me a favor, all right?" she said. "Don't tell yourself it's just not worth it, or something really stupid and self-satisfied like that. Okay?" I couldn't tell if she was mad, or what. She walked on past me, heading for the hall, but stopped, and turned, and smiled, full brightness. "Not that you ever would," she said, and headed for the stairs.

I joined the forming frog hunt on the Fossels' steps: Hillside, Amos, Bilgy, Roger, Bienvenida, Rudy, Tina, Helen, Wendy, and myself. Trace was going to stay and listen to some jazz with Hy and Fisher; Cynthia had gone upstairs to bed. Running Bear and Kelly were wherever they were.

We moved across the fields, at times a bit uncertain of our footing, some of us, and took the path that went down to the boys' camp, doing lots of shhh-ing on the way.

"I b'lieve I saw a buncha old harpoons inside the boathouse," Hillside said. "I'll get 'em." We waited by the beached canoes. A minute later he was back, with four slim bamboo poles, with frog gigs on their ends. "There're only four of 'em," he said.

At that, both Bilge and Amos claimed fatigue and stumbled toward their cabins, which meant that we were now the perfect number: four canoes, harpoonists in the bows and paddlers in the sterns. Hillside and Roger both called dibbies on harpoons, and so did Tina—and Bienvenida, Wendy, and Rudy volunteered to paddle for them. That left Helen and me.

"Here you go, Queequeg," I said, handing her the one remaining gig, "and you can call me Ishy, if you like."

She didn't get it. "Okay, Fishy," she said. "You're on. Show me where the big 'uns are." I offered her my flashlight, too, and saw her settled in the bow, and pushed us off.

"They're all along in there," old Cap'n Hillside whispered, pointing to the shoreline to our left. "Good hunting, mates." We started out.

Running Bear would not have had too much respect for our flotilla, I don't think. Our paddles splashed, our wakes were crooked, and our craft all waddled slightly, I should say. I decided I could paddle rings around the other three (two girls and a Puerto Rican musical comedy star), and so I swung around outside and led the way along the shoreline opposite the camps, heading for the lily pads and reeds I knew were not so far away. There was a partial moon, not full but bright, and lots of stars, so navigation wasn't hard at all. My thought was we would work the farthest reaches of our range where, chances were, the game would not be sent to cover by our bibulous companions—or, in the words I *really* thought, "those noisy drunks"—behind us. And I would have to say my plan might well have been successful; we certainly got a good ways up the lake.

What we did there was tip over, in about four feet of water.

The thing was this: I didn't know that Helen planned to rise, just then, her harpoon cocked and ready in one hand, my flashlight in the other. If I had, perhaps I could have steadied the canoe, or anyway stopped paddling. But as it happened, I did neither. One moment I was feeling pretty good about my J-stroke—you should try it with two fingers on one hand—and the next one I was breathing Beaver Lake.

"Oh, *cripes*, I'm sorry, Randy," Helen said.

"Hey, buddy, you all right?" came Hillside's worried voice across the waters.

"Yeah, we're fine," I half called back to him. "Just leave us be. I think we'll maybe beach it and walk back to camp." My lust for frog blood had been cooled, I'd say. "Don't worry, Helly, it's okay," I also said, and waded up to her. A nice guy when disaster strikes, that Randy D.

Her short brown hair was plastered to her head; her face, all wet like that and lit by so much moon and stars, looked very white and perfect. She smiled and hung her head, a naughty little girl, but when I slid my arms around her waist, her head came up, and when my face got down to hers, her mouth was open.

This'll show you what a hick *I* am; I was surprised. Don't ask me how I thought they kissed in Iowa; don't also ask me what I—well—expected would/might happen next. I am not, in any way, experienced in frog hunts.

When we stopped kissing, she said, "Well . . ." and pulled in one big breath. Her shirt was stuck to her, of course. I'd probably expected she would have a bra on, too.

We pulled the red canoe up on the shore a ways—the bank was slippery and slightly steep—and then I tipped it over on its side to let the water out. The water made a little silver stream on down the bank. The woods along that shore were mostly pine and birches.

By the time I turned around to Helen, she had taken off her shirt and wrung it out, and thrown it on a little stunty pine. Oh, my, she had a body. Something like an eastern girl's, I'd say, but maybe better. She also had undone her belt, and while I watched, the button at the waistband of her jeans.

Of course there was that moment that you hear about, right then, when matters could have traveled either way. When she undid the button, she just stopped; she wasn't pushing it at all; it was more like she was saying, "It's okay, but up to you." She certainly had gotten my attention.

I *think* I may have had two thoughts, at that point—okay, well, really three. They didn't come in words, of course, but here's how you would read them, if they had. The first was that by talking in the Fossels' kitchen, we'd gotten to be friends; I knew I liked this girl, and she liked me.

The second was that she, a good farm-girl from Iowa, would know, by some uncomplicated miracle of middle-western insight, just what was right and best for us to do, and what the fallout wouldn't, needn't, be.

And third was what the hell did I owe Kelly, anyway?

Thinking those three thoughts, without the words, took maybe twice the time it takes to blink my eyes and smile, and half the time I need to pull a splashed-on sweatshirt over-head. It also took some tugs and hopping on one foot (and laughing all the while) to get our soaking blue jeans off, but seeing all of Helen in the halfway moonlight made me more than halfway glad we had.

Oh, well—I didn't think.

Oh, sick, I didn't think that, either.

Oh, Helen.

# CHAPTER 7

Long before there were any Bibles to swear on, or any words you spelled like this: "whereas," and "aforementioned," and "party-of-the-first-part," people were insisting that they *would* do this or that. No-fooling, cross-my-heart, I-promise-you, etcetera.

One of the things that people used to do in ancient Greece was walk out by themselves in the middle of a great big field, and say the things they really meant out there, where certain gods would almost surely notice them, and hear. That sort of solitary oath, those people felt, was many times more binding than the other kinds. Telling someone, or a bunch of someones, something—which is all a written contract really is—didn't mean as much. The Greeks knew (as I've already said about a thousand times) that words don't always tell the truth. A person who was shrewd and tricky, like Odysseus, was never called a liar or a crook back then, just smart. Which will give us an idea of how much civilization has progressed since Homer's day.

But anyway, I always kind of liked that open-field idea. If you walk out across a field, you'll have some time to think about the thing you're going to swear to, and maybe change your mind. And being all alone like that (except for the attentive god) almost deepens the commitment to yourself. If you can't trust yourself, who can you trust? There's no one's good opinion we need more than our own. Outdoors, in the middle of this empty space, there can be nothing shady going on; everything is open, seen—nothing up your sleeve, no fingers crossed. I promise *me:* the ultimate commitment.

Here's a funny question I just thought of: do people tend to tell the truth, or lie, when they are naked?

I, of course, have walked out to the middle of a lot of open fields and stood there by myself, in knickers. Nothing up my sleeve except, of course, The Arm. Sometimes I have sworn out there, as well. Those were commitments of another sort, to victory, and fame, and team and . . . oh, yes, excellence. Well, that part of my life was over. "Jet-fire Jon" was all flamed out, and Randy Duke was left behind to see what *he* could do.

Hit your kid some grounders at a summer camp, perhaps.

And fuck around with his commitments, maybe. My, but that was aptly put, good Randy.

But, on the other hand, I thought—all this on Thursday night—I'd been provoked. All I'd done was to retaliate, perhaps in kind. Quite likely, yes, in kind. Who wouldn't call my actions justified?

A few lines back, I used the word "commitments." Maybe you said "Huh?" or "What commitments?" Or maybe you've perceived the way I am, in spite of all the blabbing I do.

I am a certain kind of jerk, and that is nothing new. I was that way as Jon the boy and Jon the All-American, and now I'm still that way as Randy D. My mother has a quaint expression that she uses to describe this side of me. "He wears his heart on his shoulder," she's been known to say.

I do, and when I fell for Kelly, that was it. She didn't know it, but I did. I'd walked out on some open field, and promised.

So, knowing all that, I offer you the question once again: who *wouldn't* call my actions justified? Everyone who answered "Randy Duke" may paste a gold one on her forehead, hers or his.

That was Reason-for-Feeling-Like-Shit, Number One.

Number One. There's more? Oh, but of course.

Reason-for-Feeling-Like-Shit, Number Two was that not only had I absolutely overtly broken my word to myself, but also I'd involved someone else, and someone else's *feelings*, in my little Raycroft melodrama.

Reason Number Three was I'd enjoyed it.

So had she, apparently.

"I haven't felt this purely good in . . . seems like *months,*" she'd said when we were driving back to Camp Raylene. We'd put our clammy clothes back on—everything but jeans—and hiked back to the parking lot. Letting down the chain that was the Gate, I took her home by Squareback, driving up past all the Cottages (the Fossels' house was dark by then) and almost to her cabin in the Catamounts.

"Me, too," I'd answered. And months is what it was, try seven, since before the accident. Helen hadn't cared about the hand. She hadn't ever *known* about The Arm. And I, I hadn't really noticed any differences.

When I dropped Helen off, she just said, "Thanks a lot," and leaned, and gave me one quick, pecky sort of kiss. It sounded like "Nice game," if we'd been playing tennis, say. She smiled. As smooth and cool as Helen was, no wonder she was All-American. Never, in my hearing, will anyone from Iowa be called a hick again.

And I was left with Reasons One and Two and Three.

The next day, Friday morning, I got Reason Number Four.

My nine o'clock activity, on Fridays, was one that I looked forward to: Bucks baseball, one of three such periods we had with them each week. The one on Wednesday afternoon was when we had the Color game, but the other ones—the "clinics" as they called them—were for teaching.

In general, I got an early start up to the fields. Fields are lovely in the morning, empty. Put some people on them and whatever's going on becomes the feature: haying, baseball, shooting at the Redcoats, lying on the blanket, name it. But empty, early, they are simply beautiful, wet with spider webs that sparkle, tasting just like honeysuckle. At the edge of the fields at camp, the grass got longer for another thirty feet or so, and then gave way to brush and woods. So red-winged blackbirds buzzed, and flickers chattered, telling every other bird again-again-again that this part of the meadow had been spoken for.

Once, when I came off the path and walked out on those fields alone, I couldn't help myself. I just shot my arms straight up and screamed. For joy? In thanks to be alive? To promise I would try to try? Because I couldn't stand not knowing? I don't know.

This morning I was not the first. Running Bear was laid out on the bench behind the third-base line wearing, as he always did, white shorts and a copper tan. And when he heard my step and opened up his eyes, he also wore the face of one in pain.

"Henceforward," Running Bear intoned, raising his right hand in either oath or greeting, "henceforward and henceforth I shall drink only soup—maize soup, as Roger said. Oh, Great Spirit, guard me from all lower spirits, strike them from my hand. And notably the ones concocted by my cursed Uncle Bilgy, served in Fossel's shingled wooden lodge. Today, oh Chief of Baseball, I can only be a backstop, or third base, perhaps. Tell the campers they may step on me—I do deserve it, truly—but not the head or stomach, please."

He really looked in rotten shape. While I—I'm talking physically, of course—I hadn't felt better in . . . months.

"Hmmmm," I said, feeling about as sympathetic as a Pilgrim parson on a scarlet-letter day, "you sure don't seem too chipper, that's for sure. Where'd you go when you left Fossel's, anyway?" Subtle, aren't I? Delicate. "You ought to know you can't mix rum with *any*thing."

Running Bear let out a groan. "But that's the thing. I didn't," he maintained. "Kelly made a beeline for her cabin—wouldn't even talk to me." And there was Reason Number Four: Kelly hadn't done a thing but go on home, alone. You couldn't even claim "retaliation," Randy boy. "So I went back to Hy's and listened to the music with the Face and Fisher for a while—and Hy, of course. I might have had a little sip or two—that stuff's so mellow, man. Next thing I know, I'm waking up on Hiram's couch, it's six A.M." Running Bear groaned again. "But that's not even the worst part," he said.

He'd closed his eyes, which means he didn't see me lick

my lips. "God," I said. "What is?" My voice all treacled up with phony sympathy.

"I'm heading back across the fields, and figuring to get a shower, anyway, before the kids get up. And who comes strolling up the road, out walking with that poodle dog she's got but—yes, you guessed it, man—Raylene! So what am I to do? I know she knows I was at Hyacinth's, all right, but what I gotta make her think is anything but that I'm just now going home. I get a great idea, I think, and make like I don't even see her. Then I drop into a starting crouch and—zoom!—I sprint across the field. I stop and walk a little ways, and then I turn around and—whoosh!—I sprint on back. It looks as if I'm taking morning workout, doing wind sprints, right? Lucky thing I'm wearing running shoes and warmups when I go to Hiram's. Well, when I've finished with the second sprint, I make like I'm just seeing her.

" 'Good morning, there, Raylene,' I say. 'You *are* an early bird. Just getting in my workout here,' I say. Just about ready to puke, if you want to know the truth. An' you know what she says? She says, 'Bimbo and I are *always* early birds'—she's pointing at the dog—'an' you should see the worms we catch sometimes.' And then she laughs and laughs and heads on down the road, and I have to turn around and do another sprint before she's out of sight. I swear, I don't know why I didn't take a heart attack."

"*Rim*-baud," I said, "that's *Rim*baud, after the French poet, I'll bet." I *did* mention my Board scores and all, didn't I?

"What?" said Running Bear. "What did you say? I think I may be getting the DT's, no shit."

"Raylene's dog," I said unmercifully. "I don't think his name is *Bimbo,* Bear. I was saying that I bet she named him *Rim*baud, like the French poet. Though maybe you pronounce that, like, Ram-*bow*. I'm not completely positive."

"I'll tell you one thing." Running Bear let out a groan. "The *fleurs du mal* are growing in my stomach, I believe. Or was that Baudelaire? Of course it was, I'm sorry." He threw a hand onto the bench's backrest and hauled himself until he sat. I'm sure he missed my gape. "Oh, God," he said. "Hey, Randy. How about . . . do we get sick days on the baseball field? I'm serious. I don't think that I can . . ."

I gave him a comradely thump on his nearest shoulder. "Of course you do. Why don't you head on down and just rack out till lunch? I'll tell the kids you've got a virus. Amos and I can handle this okay."

He struggled to his feet and grabbed my hand and gave it one good pump. "You have done," he said, "more for the morale of my people than any white man since George Armstrong Custer. We won't forget this." And with surprising speed he headed for the path to camp. From which, almost at once, came Amos.

"Good Lord," he said, "I just passed Running Bear. He said you'd sent him down, that you'd explain. I'm guessing that you didn't want to look at him."

"Uh-huh," I said. "Dat boy, he done got fosselized last night. It's funny that he can't drink rum at all—he always seems to do all right with what he has at Emil's. Gin and something, isn't it?"

"I think so," Amos said. "But speaking of all right, what's this that Roger tells me of your frog-hunt escapade? A small capsizement, followed by a disappearance from the group—you and Helen H.?"

I looked at Amos and disliked his small, expectant smile. Last night he hadn't joined us when we went to spear the carps and frogs, but this morning, on the ball field, he was fishing.

"Well," I said. "I guess the things you heard are true. We *did* fly up to Sainte Agathe—her plane—and yes, I did tie into one, a sixty-three-pound cow-frog. It's being stuffed, and later on we'll mount it. You can be the fourth, right after me, the Podge, and Bilgy. . . . No? Well, try on this one, then. That little dip in Beaver Lake turned out to be a trifle sobering. All we wanted after that was getting dry, and so we walked back to the parking lot, from whence I drove her home. My teeth were chattering like cariocas or whatever they're called."

Amos looked let down. "How boring." And he shook his head. "I'd hoped for something more eventful, along the lines of this: Can Red-the-Fed's Assistant, Randy Duke, go one-on-one with women's All-American? The details of that match would be the biggest thing since Riggs met Billy Jean. Were there any fouls or violations? Stuffs? Rejections? Cries of 'In your face!'? That kind of thing. The language of basketball is so wonderfully . . . *adaptable*, n'est-ce pas?''

''Sorry, Amos,'' I replied. ''I hate to disappoint the fans, but . . .'' I shrugged. ''And speaking of that kind of thing, I have to tell you I've been worrying. It's about our cabins' hiking trip next week—I just hope I won't be too much of a burden. Did you know I'm used to sleeping with a night light? And where will we 'go potty,' anyway? Is Jean-François going to come with us to cook, because I'm sure that I don't have the slightest . . .''

Amos laughed, and we were off the subject of my so-called escapade. I'd never been the sort who likes to tell those stories anyway, or even hear them, come to think of it. Noses don't belong in certain parts of other people's lives. If it's fiction, that's another matter; nothing's private in a story, and the characters don't really hurt. With all the books there are these days, the guys don't need my action to get off on.

The sort of hiking trip I'd planned to take with Amos and his kids—and ours, of course—was something standard on the schedule at camp, for girls as well as boys. Two cabins would pair off and plan their own excursion, according to the tastes of those involved. Some were very hard and physical and known as ''expeditions''; their goal would be to climb a lot of ''major'' mountains in the Adirondacks, say. They'd be taken to their base by bus, and picked up three days later, totally exhausted and bragging of the ''records'' that they'd set. Other trips were more relaxed, and nowhere near as tiring. These were known as ''scenic strolls,'' and popular with members of the Music, Art, and Drama staffs—as well as a lot of fat kids in both camps. Luckily for them, a kid could swap a trip with someone from another cabin. So if your cabin planned to do something you really didn't want to do, you could look around and find a substitute. Sort of the same thing that rich people used to be able to do in wars. Counsellors, however, couldn't do that, and so they tried to always double up with guys who shared their tastes in roughing it. Then the two of them could shove their joint opinion down the campers' throats.

I am not what you would call an Eagle Scout. It's not that I am anti-roughing-it; it's just that I had never done it much. That's apt to happen if you're really into baseball, and stick to that all spring and summer, from the age of six or seven.

In the section of New Jersey I grew up in, everyone had hiking boots and sleeping bags and knapsacks, though. You got them during junior high, and what they were was, like a pre-car car. With that equipment, you were mobile, sort of. Independent, in a way. Those boots were made for walkin'; you could put them on, and gather up your sleeping bag and knapsack and take off. You'd have a place to spend the night (that sleepin' bag), and all the stuff you needed packed inside your Kelty.

What you did in fact was this: you'd walk as far as some main street and hitchhike to your friend's house, where you'd put the sleeping bag on the other bed in his room. They you'd look at his TV or listen to his stereo, and eat the things in his refrigerator. When his parents left the house, you'd dig your stash out of your knapsack, and you'd both get high.

By the time I got to high school, I actually did take "camping trips" to Stokes State Forest and places like that. Then we'd always wish they'd invented an "instant" wine or beer, some powder you could mix with water, which didn't weigh a ton to carry in a pack. Those trips were always co-ed in my group, and girls all knew what "getting back to nature" meant.

If you want to know how many camping trips I really took, the answer is just two. Which made me pleased that I could double with a woodsman who had skills like Amos S.

Not that he was Dan'l B., or Running Bear, but in his years at camp he'd learned some tricks, he told me.

"*If* you're lucky with the weather," Amos said, and "*if*

you can describe the trip in such a way that all your best kids want to take it, and all your whiners don't . . . and *if* you sweet-talk Jean-François and get the perfect meals for the conditions, *then* you have a trip that isn't really dreadful. Not at all. Why, I've been on a few I'd have to say were even mildly pleasant.''

Here's what we decided on. We'd start on Monday morning, hiking out of camp on something called the Old Coyote Trail (every group since 1955 had claimed to see this beast on it, said Amos). Eight miles out of camp, this trail would hit Clinch Hollow Road, and there, in Amos' master plan, we'd rendezvous with our supplies, which would have come by truck. In that way, we'd be guaranteed an excellent cold lunch with which to celebrate our pleasant hike (no really major ups or downs, a lot of shade but not too buggy, Amos said). And furthermore, it meant that we had only half a mile or so to carry the supplies and sleeping bags and packs: our campsite was that distance from the road. It was, he said, a favorite of the Art and Music staffs: two Adirondack lean-tos just in case of rain, beside a clear, cold pool, below a lovely little waterfall. We'd spend that afternoon on such important tasks as ''bringing in supplies'' and ''organizing camp'' and ''checking out the area''—English translation: lolling around and swimming and getting in the wood on which to cook a sumptuous dinner. After dinner and cleanup, we could make final plans for the next day's expeditions (harumph), and get a good night's sleep.

Tuesday we'd probably get up early (''What's a camping trip without a sunrise?'' Amos asked), take our light-pack trips all day, and have another banquet in the evening. We'd mellow out on Wednesday morning, take our gear down to the road at noon, and load it onto the waiting truck. Another easy stroll on Old Coyote Trail, and we'd be back in camp in time for swim and supper.

''I don't see any reason why we shouldn't have a ball,'' said Amos.

Well, I could have given him Four—and wished I was able to. Give them all to someone else, that is.

* * *

From Friday morning, when I talked with Running Bear, to Monday morning when we started down the Old Coyote Trail (Cabins 2 and 5, in Bucks, some twenty strong) I tried, and also didn't try, to get in touch with Kelly.

Until I'd talked to Bear, I'd had one slim line of defense: that even though I'd been a jerk to talk to her that way, her going off with him and doing who-knows-what (I did!) meant I could not be blamed *too* much for doing what I did with Helen.

But when I learned that she had gone straight home and hadn't even passed the time of night with him, that single, puny stone fell from the casting-hand of Randy Douche-Bag Duke, which was his right one, and not much good to start with.

All day Friday, I just moped around. One time, back at school—one midterm—I got into a mess made up of equal parts of mono and a girl who'd missed a period and a religion course I couldn't do the reading in, and what happened was I all-of-a-sudden (so it seemed)found myself facing two exams and two papers and not the slightest hope of doing anything decent on any of them, and not even knowing where to begin. Friday I had that same feeling. I couldn't think. My head was full of huge black rumbles when I tried. I'd ruined myself with Kelly. I'd used Helen, who was innocent and likeable and good. I had no fucking idea in the world what I was going to do with the rest of my life, or what exactly I was doing at this strange summer camp with all these integrated, easygoing guys that nothing ever seemed to bother.

With rotten thoughts like those carousing in my mind, I got through Taps on Friday night and crawled into bed right afterward. I told myself I was over-tired, and I wasn't thinking straight. I also doubted thoughts or words were going to save me now.

Sometime later—had I been asleep?—I heard a whisper, Simon's: "Well, is he awake?"

My eyelids glowed. I opened them, and there was Rennie Watson, with a flashlight, bending over me. When he saw I was awake, he answered "yeah," and then he took his empty hand and tugged a little on my blanket, just the way I sometimes did for him. "Good night, Randy," he said to me, and went back to his bunk. Jimmy G. was next—then Mitchell, Tiny, Eddie, Gerry, Simon, David. It was just like every other night, except that I was them and they were me. But none of them made out like it was anything special. David kissed me, just as if he always had before, instead of saying anything.

Saturday I felt a little better. Who wouldn't, given that good night? I lingered over coffee in the dining hall, and Bilgy came and sat with me and chatted.

"I didn't see you at ye Rustic Inn last night," he said. "In fact, I didn't see a single one of all my fellow tosspots of the night before. I wonder why? Did everyone—save present company, of course—come down with thimble-belly ache?"

"Come on," I said, "you mean to tell me Kelly wasn't there? Or Tina, Wendy, Amos, Hillside?" I added hastily.

"None of the above," he said, "and more. Emil seemed a bit concerned. He asked me if there was something special up at camp. I improvised: a mammoth two-day, all-night jacks game down at Larkspurs'. Seven dollar minimum, nothing less than fivesies. I'm not sure that he believed me, though."

"Hmmm," I said, and shortly afterward I left.

Later on that morning, during second, I snuck up to the amphitheater, peeked around a column at the very back, up top. Kel was there, all right, and looking great and hard at work, as usual. *Of course* I knew she hadn't taken off, but still. . . .

After lunch I wrote a letter during Rest Hour, just like Harlan almost always did. I tried to keep it very simple, very truthful (just like Harlan almost always did—my God!), and I didn't try to explain or justify anything. I just told her what I thought of her and how much I liked being around her, and that even though I'd almost surely always be an asshole, I'd never stop trying to change—or feeling sorry when I hurt someone, or made them angry. I also told her that ever since

Thursday night I'd been feeling pretty Blue, which, mixing with my basic Redness, left me looking kind of *mauve.* I'd gotten funny glances at the waterfront, I said, and anything she could do to help, I'd sure appreciate. I didn't dare ask to see her, but maybe I could make her smile, and let her know I wanted to.

I gave the letter to David, to deliver it before his class with her that afternoon. He took it without question or remark.

I had Bobcat basketball while he had dance with Kelly, and when my game was over, there he was. He must have run right down, and he was looking serious. Kids are so beautiful the way they are, but very early on they start to practice grownup faces.

"She opened it and read it right away," he said.

"How'd she look?" I asked him, trying to seem a bit offhand.

"Oh, fine," he said, with triple my amount of cool. Then the kid in him (which is the truth) took over, and he had to grin and say, "Real happy, if you must know. She said to tell you she would be in touch."

I must have looked relieved, delighted—maybe just a hair self-satisfied. Because he added, in a whisper: "Romeo."

So of course I had to grab him, throw him on the grass beside the courts, and poke him in the ribs until he took it back.

"I didn't mean it, Randy," he shrieked out, between the squeals of laughter. So I let him up. He started toward our cabin, turned, and mouthed a silent "Ro - Me - O," then sprinted off in full, high cackle. Out loud, I swore I'd get him later, but wordlessly I loved him more than ever.

That night I went to Emil's, just in case she planned to get in touch that way, but Kelly wasn't there, and Tina didn't seem to have a message. Helen wasn't one for Emil's much, so her non-presence didn't mean a thing.

When I got back to Cabin 2, still early, my flashlight showed a letter on my bunk. The envelope said "Randy," and I took it to the washhouse and some light—and flying bugs and smells of Irish Spring, and Crest, and piss.

"Dear Randy," said the letter. "There's something that I have to tell you, and it seems to me a letter is the way to do it." Her handwriting was neat and clear, no frills. No shit. "I've decided not to see you anymore—not because I don't like you, but because I think I like you a lot. I guess I know you're wonderful, in fact. . . ."

I wrinkled my nose and ran my right little finger around the edge of the sink I stood before. I looked in the mirror and saw myself in full, wide stare, expressionless, not good for much, and then I dropped my eyes into the sink and saw a little pale-green blob of toothpaste halfway up the side of it. I turned the water on and pushed the toothpaste down the drain.

"The thing is," said the letter, "I'm engaged, and I want to stay that way. It happened just before I left, a kind of sudden thing; I never should have come, I guess, but I had promised. And I didn't think I'd feel as lonely as I've been. Not for what you'd call *acquaintances*, and all. I wasn't lying when I told you everyone has been real nice . . ."

I had to see my face again. This time it looked stupid, with its eyebrows lifted high. I turned the letter over, saw the "Always, Helen" at the end.

"Dear God," I said aloud, and turned to put my back toward the mirror. I leaned against the sink and felt the edge of it, all wet against my pants. I read the letter twice, and closed my eyes and tried to do what people claim to do at times like this—to think.

It didn't work out right. A great deal later on, I could maintain that I was sad *and* happy, proud *and* humble, grateful *and* deprived, etcetera. But at no time did I ever think, "How could she?" I don't think.

Monday morning we were on the trail by nine o'clock. Amos, looking very much at home in hiking boots and khaki shorts and a kind of floppy bush hat, took the point. He'd set a pace, he said, that'd get us to our rendezvous with the camp truck (and jellied *madrilène*, he thought) in perfect time for lunch. He suggested that I put myself, say, halfway down the line of march, leaving Harlan and Bobby Brownlow, his JC, to bring up the rear and keep all stragglers ahead of them. Barney Rothman, our beloved Unit Head, was there to see us starting down the trail, his clipboard in hand. "I'll make sure they bring your comic books with lunch," he promised Amos as they parted.

Old Coyote Trail was probably a logging road in other days, or maybe it was parts of more than one. In any case, its ups and downs were not too steep (as Amos had promised), and its footing was quite comfortable. Some time in the 1800s Clinch Hollow had been cleared for sheep—the valley and the lower slopes, at least. It blew my mind to think that this was done by hand, and then that it was all let go to woods again, those fields and pastures taken over by the birch and beech and ash and maple trees. Twice the trail passed near old cellar holes, and not too far from them were apple trees, all overgrown and wild. Every little while there was an old stone wall, lying low and stumbly these days, sometimes hiding in the sprouted ferns. Evergreens mixed in among the leafy trees, and little brooks ran sweet and silver down the hillsides.

At first the kids all walked in bunches, chattering like chickadees and stepping on each other's heels and swearing that they'd seen the "Old Ki-yody" lurking in the underbrush. But in a little while a lot of them got out of breath and started to drop back and stay in line, while others forged ahead to be with Amos and be first to see whatever could be seen. Some of them found walking sticks along the trail, and everyone who'd started with a sweater on soon had it tied around his waist.

I thoroughly enjoyed the hike. David, Si, and Rennie kept me company; we didn't talk a lot, just "yeah," or "Wow," or "Nice," to things that one of us had pointed to. We drank from almost every brook we crossed, getting on all fours and dipping down our heads, like deer and old coyotes.

From time to time, along the trail, I thought of Kelly. I hadn't seen her Sunday, either (she was not at Emil's, once again), but she'd said she'd be in touch, and so she would

said that smaller groups would make for better expeditions, by doubling our chance to make some rare discovery, or do something outrageous we could brag about. I *was* a little sad when David's name got picked by Harlan, though.

After much negotiation, we agreed on plans for both the groups. Our ten would go in search of . . . Lost Local Legend; they would merely undertake an . . . Impossible Journey.

We would try to find a something called The Bear's Den, a mammoth cave that certain local people in their nineties said they'd visited when they were under ten but no one else had seen in more than eighty years. The story was that it was huge—at least fifty feet deep by thirty feet wide and twenty feet high—but kids were pretty small back then, and maybe they exaggerated some. The postmaster in Sandgrove had given Amos clues on where it used to be, as best he could remember hearing, though he thought that there'd been rock slides since that could have covered up the entrance. Finding The Bear's Den would make us as famous in Bennington County as whoever it was in whatever county that happened to be in Central America somewhere, when he discovered Chichén Itzá.

The other team would set out to circumnavigate Clinch Hollow. Jimmy Gummage loved the sound of that. Leaving at first light, they'd climb directly up the hill called Haystack, and then just circle clockwise all the way around, on the lip of this huge cereal bowl of land, coming down Bear Mountain at the end, a short way up Clinch Hollow Road from our base camp.

"All we have to do is keep our right foots lower than our lefts, and we will have it made," said Bobby Brownlow to his forces.

"How far would you say that is, around the rim?" I asked him.

"Oh, maybe fifteen miles," he said.

"A piece of cake," said Harlan.

"With not a single trail on it," said Amos, *sotto voce*.

"Great!" said Jimmy Gummage.

"I t'ink I glad I go with my boy Randy," Gerry Ramos said, and twirled a Frisbee on his middle finger.

The modern-day Magellans left as we were getting up, just shortly after dawn. David looked excited—also nervous, full of energy; I told myself it was perfectly okay that he was going with the other group. As they moved out, I realized this would be our longest separation since we met, four weeks and a little bit ago. That stunned me. First, that it was so, and second, that I'd think of it just then.

"Good luck." "So long." "Be careful of skunks and lions." "Have a hobby." "Don't forget to fenestrate." We told their parting backs all that.

David turned and waved. "I hope you find the cave." His call came pure and clear and easy, like any morning bird's.

"Ran-*dee,*" Simon scolded from beside the fire. "For the last time—fried or scrambled?"

Our day-hike was a quite successful failure. It took us to a far part of the Hollow, along another logging road a ways, then following a stream up to its source, below some mossy, huge, and tumbled boulders, at the bottom of a really steep incline.

"Looks as if there *could* have been a rock slide, sure enough," said Amos, pulling on his stubbled chin.

"Oh, wow," I breathed adoringly. "Just listen to that mountain lore."

From that point we were on our own, direction-wise; the postmaster had merely said it was "above" the place the stream began. What we did was crisscross up the slope until we reached the ridge, and then come down again, a little farther east than where we'd started. We saw two porcupines, both up in trees ("Watch out, he shoot his sticker at you," Gerry Ramos said), and possibly a bobcat, jumping off a sunny ledge of rock a ways above us ("Catamount!" yelled Tiny).

"Are there really any bears up here?" asked Rennie at one rest stop.

Amos answered: " 'Deed there be, young polecat, 'deed

there be,'' and I slapped pockets, looking for a pen and paper.

But Gerry told him, ''Don' believe it. He jus' try to scare you.''

Later Amos showed us what he said were claw marks, old ones, on a tree where ''Bruin stopped and scratched, just like a tomcat,'' Amos said.

''Ahhh,'' said Gerry, ''who you try to kid? Some dude, he did that with a knife, I bet. Right, Randy? Looks to me like knife cuts, right? Don' you try to kid *me*, Amos.''

After lunch we took two other trips up to the ridge and back, in different places east and west of where we started. We never found *the* Bear's Den, but we did discover one substantial cave. Its entrance was too small for Amos or myself to squeeze through, but we could shine our flashlights in and look. There was a chamber, maybe six feet square and four feet high, with a hole in the right-hand wall that seemed to lead into another. Maybe that one was The Bear's Den! Simon volunteered to wiggle in, far enough so he could look and see; we agreed to let him do it, though I kept my right hand on his ankle all the way.

''Can you see anything?'' Amos whispered after him.

When asked that exact same question by Lord Carnarvon, as he peered into Tutankhamen's tomb, the archeologist Howard Carter supposedly said, ''Yes. Wonderful things.''

Simon simply said, ''Yes. Bats.'' And put his wriggle in reverse, his eyes as big as doughnuts. ''I'll bet there are a hundred of the things, hanging from the roof,'' he said.

''Ugh! Yikes! Gross! Disgusting!'' everybody said.

''And on the floor—you'd never guess,'' said Simon.

''Bat shit!'' answered Hughie, making it come out a sneeze.

''No,'' said Simon solemnly, ''something much more . . . marvelous than that.''

We guessed: ''A bearskin rug.'' ''A golden idol.'' ''Harlan and his girl friend.'' ''Rip Van Winkle.'' ''A Ford Fairlane.'' ''Nothing.''

''Wrong. You're all wrong,'' Simon said. ''On the floor are piles of . . . *bases! chest protectors! catcher's masks!*

*batting helmets! gloves and gloves and gloves!* You should have seen it, Gerry. And the bats, they all were Louisvilles and Adirondacks, the best bats in the world."

"Simon, you *stink,*" yelled Gerry, and we all piled on and mugged him—and The Bat Cave got its name in Raycroft legend. The second "room" was just a shelf, no more than three feet deep, and empty. We headed back to camp, arriving slightly after four, quite proud of our discovery. So what if it wasn't The Bear's Den, we asked each other—The Bat Cave was original. Gerry couldn't wait to "get to" Mitch with Simon's story.

By five we'd had a swim and, roaming through the woods in pairs, collected all the fuel we'd need for dinner and the evening. Then we talked it over and decided to get breakfast wood as well. Those other guys could clean up after supper. By six o'clock the cooking fire looked real close to being perfect, and that *other* group was still not back. Amos put some fresh wood on and stalled around; there were mutters from the mountain men: "Where are those idiots, anyway?" "Don't tell me we're just going to sit around and wait for them." "It could be *hours.*" And etcetera.

Amos strolled up to his lean-to, and I followed.

"I think we might as well just eat," he said. "I'm guessing that they've found it's longer than they figured. Harder, too. Like, over there"—he pointed—"that's all beechwood, and beech are tough to walk through when they're small. From here it *looks* as if the Hollow's just a bowl, but actually the ridge has lots of ups and downs. Two brooks cut into it right there and there"—he pointed at two other places—"and what they have to do is go right down to cross them and climb up again. It's over twenty miles, I guarantee you."

I could feel the pump start going. "Why didn't you tell them, if you knew all that? What if it gets dark, and they're still out there?"

"I don't think that'll happen," Amos said. "And if it does, it'll be okay. Part of the adventure. Both of our JCs are good, and they've got some kids who know their stuff. What Bob and Harlan have to learn is how to plan a little better and to ask for information they don't have. This'll help to teach them, that's for sure."

"May-*be,*" I said, "but I kind of doubt the parents of those kids would like to think we make them stumble down a mountain in the dark so we can train the junior staff a little. Jesus Christ, Amos. They could break a leg out there."

"Randy, listen," Amos said. Already he could fit behind a gleaming walnut desktop, hands folded, with a most disarming smile. "Believe me, if I thought it was all that dangerous, I never would have let them go. I think it's good for kids to deal with minor fuckups. And part of growing up is having your ass scared off sometimes. Anyway, I bet most of them feel safer on that mountain than when they have to bat against that wild man Zacharias. And they're no more apt to get hurt than they are sliding home, I bet you. It all depends on what you're used to, doesn't it?"

I knew he was right, but that didn't make me used to mountains in the dark—and David wasn't, either. If only I had drawn his name instead of Harlan, then I could have pulled my nose and solemnly agreed with Amos that the best times up at camp were unexpected. Sure.

"Hey, Amos," Hughie yelled from near the fireplace. "Are we gonna eat tonight, or what? This fire looks just perfect, and we're *starving.*"

"Coming, little Pew-Bear," Amos called. "I guess it's time we made the *chateaubriands* walk on burning embers. Whose turn is it to pour the wine, I want to know. . . ."

We cooked and ate, grouching at the other group but stuffing down the meal as if we weren't even slightly scared. I'm not sure the kids *were,* come to think of it. In general, most kids make rotten worriers. It's something that takes time to learn, worrying about people other than yourself. The judgment was that the other group was "feeble," "slow-pokes," "spazzes," "stupid," and "the pits." *Hubris* didn't get a mention.

Clouds had gathered as the sun got close to setting; dark would come a little earlier, and maybe rain. Through dinner I just sat there, eating but not talking much, doing a classic Parent: waiting for the kid to call or come on home. My

God, I thought, is this the Great Divide I've crossed, and now I'm one of Them? He who used to do it now gets done to? I'd learned in college that the human body starts its slow de-gen-er-a-tion at about the age of twenty-five. Could that be the story of one's life in general? I'd always been precocious. Had the good times rolled on down the tubes? Must the woman that I marry call me "Dad"?

I helped with washing-up. It got to be what I call dusk; I swear my ears hurt: nothing.

"Well," I said, "I guess I'll stroll on up the road a little ways and see if I can hear them." Amos nodded; he was playing with his jackknife by the fire. Si and Rennie asked if they could come, and I said "yes," and the three of us got flashlights and went down the path. When we reached Clinch Hollow Road, we took a left and walked up toward Bear Mountain. Si and Rennie didn't talk to me; it got to be what I call dark.

I knew I would find David, if not that night, the next morning. The knowledge didn't make me much less worried; it was just a feeling that I had in addition to being worried: I would find him, get him out of there, and then take care of him. I knew that I could do it; I'd never felt so strong in my entire life. Don't get me wrong—I was worried about all of them. And I assumed that when I found David, I'd find the rest of them, too, and get them out of there, as well. But David was the one I knew I'd find.

It suddenly came over me I'd felt this way before, or *he* had, anyway. Standing on the mound with, say, the tying run on second base, and someone pretty awesome coming up. And knowing I would do it, end the inning, get the out. Hey, Randy—Randy baby!

We heard them on the road before we reached Bear Mountain. At least we heard some *people* up ahead. My heart gave one big hopeful bound, and then I bit my feelings back till I was sure. Si and Rennie weren't so inhibited.

"Hey, you Bucks! Is that you, Harlan? Where the heck have you guys *been?*"

"Sounds like Simple and The Wrap," came Harlan's voice. "You having such a lousy time you ran away?"

"Hey, Simon, Rennie—hey, guess what? We did it! All the way around! Can you believe it? Who's that with you? Randy? Randy, hey, we did it! Have you eaten yet? You what? I don't believe it!" On and on, etcetera. Everybody talked at once, and flashlight beams went whipping back and forth.

I shook with Harlan. "Well, nice going, Har," I said, old Señor *Frío*-face, "and yay for you, you little circumnavigators." I touched a lot of heads and shoulders.

"But couldn't you have called?" I put my voice into an ancient quiver. "Your mother, there, and I were worried half to death. You know it's way past eight already." We headed down the road in one rambunctious group, everybody trying to tell the story of the day at once.

David wasn't fooled by all my easy-riding, I don't think. He got right next to me and stayed there, saying little things like, "It was fun, all right, but boy, I'm glad we're back." I'm sure he understood that I was, too.

I couldn't see the sense of putting all my worries on him then—or ever, come to think of it. What would be the good of that? Soon enough (I didn't know if I should laugh or puke) he'd know, himself, from over on the other side.

That night, before we went to sleep, we had a weary Cabin Taps inside our lean-to, telling one another one last time that it had been A Day.

"I wish that all of us had been on *both* trips," Mitchell said. "I'm sorry that I missed the Bat Cave, and that you guys didn't suffer all the hardships we did. Cabin Five's okay, but they're nothing like the good old Fam-a-lee."

"Boy, man," Gerry Ramos said, "I'd have been some scare' to be up on Bear Mountain when it's starting to get dark. You know, they's *bears* up there, man. Amos show us where they scratch a tree today, an' man, they got some *claws*, I tell you! Dint you guys get scared?"

"*I* did," Eddie said, and there was silence for a moment.

"*Everybody* did," said Mitch. "I guarantee you. Though

maybe some of them in Cabin Five are still too baby to admit it."

"It's smart to be scared, sometimes," said Harlan. Harlan had a sermon-sonar that would flip on during Taps. If there's a lesson to be spun off anybody's smallest statement, Harlan's sure to notice it and teach it. "We *should* be scared of coming down a mountain in the dark; that'll help you to be careful." He always had good things to say; it was just the tone that got me sometimes. "And if you're scared of . . . well, nuclear power, let's say, that maybe means you'll work to make darned sure no more plants get built, and the ones we've got up now will slowly be—"

"Oh, *Harlan,*" said Simon, whose father worked for some huge company that made reactor parts or something. It looked as if the time had come to get some sleep.

David made a little sound. "I just wanted to say," he said, "when we were going up, this morning, in the light, some of us were in a rush. You know the way it is, sometimes when you've got lots to do, you really want to do it fast, at first, and kinda get as much out of the way as you can, right off the bat." He was talking softly, in a slightly husky voice, not to anyone, exactly, just the night.

"And those people kept griping at the rest to hurry up, and let's get going, and all that. And the people who were going slower had to gripe right back, and ask them who put *them* in charge, and tell them they were on a hike not a race, and stuff like that. And Harlan finally said *he'd* set the pace and everyone would have to keep up close enough to see the guy in front of them. Well, that worked out, 'cause he walked kind of *medium.*

"But what I noticed was, when we were coming down, and it was getting dark, everyone just bunched together all the time. No one griped that we should speed it up or slow it down. And all of us kept checking one another out, to see that everyone was there—*you* know—and making it okay. That was, like, the best part of the day, when we were coming down the mountain. I was scared then, too, but in a funny way that made me feel . . . well, almost *happy.* I thought that that was really *neat.*"

He stopped, and it was quiet in the lean-to.

Before I fell asleep, I got another weirdo question in my head.

"Can there be life after camp?" I wondered.

# CHAPTER 8

Off and on, the past five years or so, people have been saying this to me: "I've got to get my head together."

But wait, that's not completely right.

Let's see, there's something missing. . . . Ah, I've got it. What those people *really* say—and, no, they're not all Humpty-Dumpties—is: ". . . *but first* I've got to get my head together."

It figures, given certain tendencies of mine, I've had to mess with those nine words a lot, and try to figure out just what the hell they mean, exactly. Here are some conclusions I've arrived at.

Sometimes, apparently, they mean a person must "collect his thoughts," "make up her mind," "set some priorities." Other times, it seems they mean that what the people want to do is iron out the differences between their thoughts and feelings: get their heads "together" with their hearts, or glands, or something. Then, too, they *can* mean that the person's saying he or she must sober up, get straight, retool, calm down, come-off-it, or etcetera.

But also they mean none of these occasionally. "First . . . together" is a kind of code; those words, the eight of them, still mean some things, all right, but not at all like what they're saying. *Example:* A father is bugging his son, who's taken off a couple of semesters to check out Alaska, and learn how to work a sound board, and see if the Navahos are really being screwed. And the son says: "Look, I'm planning to go back to college, but first I've got to get my head together." All he means by "First . . . together" is "*Not now.*"

And also: "Please stop bugging me."

And even, maybe: "If I don't come up with a better idea."

A very useful, and elastic, row of words.

When I got back to camp, on Wednesday afternoon, just in time for swim (as planned), I took a speedy survey of the message situation. There was no letter in my mailbox, no memo from the office saying I had had a call. There was no letter lying on my bunk, or propped up in my locker. Or even underneath my pillow.

It seemed I had not yet been got in touch with. My stomach did a sort of queasy number; not butterflies—more like an eel or two.

I found I didn't want to go to Emil's. If Kelly wasn't there again . . . well, probably I'd sit around and brood. And if she was—what then? The last time I'd seen her was at Fossel's, still. What if David had been wrong, or hadn't understood just right—or she had changed her mind? Without some sort of cue, or signal from her, I didn't even know my lines. My mother would've said I was "two jumps ahead of a fit"; I'd say about a jump and a half.

So, after Taps, I exited Cabin 2 and headed for the ball field by myself.

I planned on seeing Kelly *sometime* (yes, for sure), but first I had to get my head together.

Four weeks and more before, I'd walked out to the pitcher's mound and sat down on the rubber; this time, without a thought, I headed for the left end of the bench, the one that paralleled the first-base line. A weather front had stalled somewhere, and so the air was still, and warm, and humid; I thought I heard some thunder in the distant west. It was a lazy, hazy night in summertime, all right.

And summer (all my life: vacation/holiday) was more than halfway gone. We were slipping down the other side of equinoctial time, and soon, for almost everyone at camp, it would be almost-fall, and back to school, and stacks of empty notebooks. Exit, magic; enter, everyday. Oh, yeah.

Dunny'd told me that the weeks at Raycroft wouldn't

count: "No carry-overs, no one keeping score," he'd said. That seemed attractive, then. I'd wanted out of what I'd had to deal with, and who I'd been but couldn't be again. I hadn't wanted in to anything, particularly—or, put it this way: I didn't know, could not imagine, what I might get in-to. The safest thing, and what I wanted then, was nothingness. The future was literally unimaginable.

But no more. Meeting Kelly and David had managed to change . . . well, only everything, is all. I wasn't even close to having things worked out, or even *working* in the case of Kelly, but at least I seemed to see a way, a possibility. No carry-overs, Dunny? Fuck that. There had to be. I saw a whole new ball game, one that kept going after camp: a real perfecto, the ultimate *W*. And pitched by plain old, good old, Randy Duke, the guy who just threw straight ones down the middle.

I shook my head, and twitched, and even tried to give the semi-dark a smile. I wiggled on the bench; it was a sticky night, indeed. I stood and started pacing back and forth, up and down beside the first-base line.

But what if Dunny was completely right? Suppose—by some great cosmic weirdness—there really were no carry-overs? Suppose this was—not actually, but *like*—an extra gift of time? Suppose this wasn't . . . well, the *world*—as Dunny had said? It isn't meant to be, he'd told me. And that, of course, would mean that everything that happened here at camp would be completed here at camp: beginning, middle, end. The whole package, Aristotle. And what did that imply? Would everyone either win or lose, or could a game be "no decision"? Called on account of . . . darkness? This was going much too far, I mentioned to myself. This Randy's getting just a hair peculiar. I wondered if I could be cracking up, having some kind of delayed reaction to everything that had gone on in the last two hundred and twenty-some days. It was all so odd, so impossible, beginning with what had actually, provably, happened. Maybe, starting with this whole Randy Duke business, I'd just been imagining things.

I'd walked down to home plate and then turned right and

walked on up the third-base line. I was slightly past the infield before I saw the funny light.

That's what I said inside my head, sort of: "Hey, that's a funny light. . . ." In the next moment, my head was working semi-normally again, and the message that it offered was: "There's a light inside the weight house; that's peculiar." The light *and* the fact, that is. Both of them were funny.

Of course I kept on going. Thc weight house door was closed, as usual; the light was showing through the windows. Inside this little blocky building (as I've said) the walls on either side were mirrored; the back wall was all racks for different kinds of weights, plus one or two contraptions you could pull on, hang from, or whatever. That meant the windows were up high, above the mirrors and the racks, and over six feet off the ground. They opened from inside by cranks—the whole rectangular face of them would lift up from the bottom, as wide as anybody wanted. With the heat we had that night, they all were saying "Aaah."

But because of the height of the windows, all I could see from outside was the ceiling of the weight house, a kind of mottled white, and shadows. The "funny" light was very dim and flickery. I then remembered that there weren't any lights in there. Someone had brought candles, or a lantern of some sort. I could hear the metal "clink" of weights in motion and, so it seemed at least, the sound of someone breathing.

I turned and tiptoed off a ways. Of course I tried to figure who was in there. *Of course* I recollected who said what to whom, right here, the week before. It *could* be Kel (thump-thump), or Tina, Wendy, Roger, or Joe Blow. Or all of them at once. I licked my lips, then chewed the lower one in lieu of cud. Idea. I padded to the baseball shed and opened it. By feel I found the bases: one, two, three. The stack of them would make me close to seven feet, a perfect height for peering into high-set windows.

It was easy being quiet on the grass. I piled them by a side wall and stepped up.

The "it" was Kelly, by herself, alone (oh, super-thump).

She was lying on her back atop a weight bench, which is a narrow, padded, plastic-covered thing with black steel legs, and maybe eighteen inches high. She was also doing presses: an exercise in which you slowly push a barbell off your chest until your arms are straight, and then you lower it again, and also slowly. Up-and-down is one. I'd messed around with weights when I was back in high school. One up-and-down, with weights, is called a "repetition." The eight, or ten, or twelve you do at once are called a "set." All the sets you do make up a "program." Isn't that exciting?

Even if it isn't, Kelly was. I plan to know her for a hundred years or so, but I doubt I'll ever see her more . . . well, *edible*, than then. She'd laugh to hear me say that, but she'd also understand. And probably agree. I like that.

She was pretty close to naked, and of course that didn't hurt at all. I don't know how styles and sizes go in women's two-piece bathing suits, but whatever she had on was only for the righteous and the confident. Her hair was coiled behind her head, and her face was pink and sweaty. All of her was wet, as far as that goes; her skin looked honeyed in the candlelight.

Lying on her back like that had flattened out her breasts to nippled mounds, with bands of working muscles at the tops of them. Below her rib cage was another stretch of muscles, clearly sectioned off, the way it's meant to be, on well conditioned bellies. Her bare feet were braced flat on the floor, and her legs were spread to let the bench between them; her thighs were smooth and round as any statue's, and looked about as hard. And low down on her belly, just above the fringe of curly hair that showed above that small bikini bottom, there was a thin pink scar, perhaps five inches long, or six, running side-to-side.

She pushed the weight up two more times; then, straining, slowly, three and four. With her arms fully extended, she placed the barbell on the rack above, and just behind, her head.

Panting, she stood up and walked down toward the door and back again. She gave both arms a shake and hunched her shoulders up and down. Her breasts, no more than half inside her bright-red little bra, bobbed up and down as well. Then, bending at the waist, she wrapped her arms around her thighs; she could have kissed her knees.

Straightened up, she went and got another barbell. With her hands set wide apart, she lifted it over her head and let it down behind her neck, so that it was supported on her shoulders. Then she faced the mirrors on the wall directly opposite, which meant she'd turned her back to me. I'd thought she had a fantastic ass when she had blue jeans on it. Without blue jeans, and scarcely—barely—anything else, just a sort of silken triangle of brilliant red material, it could be certified as . . . *perfect*, if I do say so. I do.

The exercise she started on is called a "lunge." What you do is step way forward, with your right foot first, let's say, and bend that knee, and dip. That means your left leg has to bend as well; it almost kneels, and that heel comes way up off the ground. Then you bring the right leg back and make the same step once again, but this time with the left leg. And so on, alternating. If you choose to work with weights, you have to like and-so-on's. ("And be a counter," Kelly told me later. "I've always *loved* to count things out," she said.)

Well, on about her ninth or tenth step forward (I am not a counter), Kelly's mirrored eyes came up and saw me, looking through that open window. She didn't start, nor did she stop. But on the next pause, when she stood there straight, she said, "Why don't you come on in; I'm almost done."

That's the way she got in touch. She didn't sound the least bit angry, anyway.

I got down off my bases, walked around the house, opened the door, and stepped inside. I quickly closed it after me. Kelly kept on with her set of lunges. There were eight candles stuck in stubby candlesticks and sitting on the floor. The mirrors multiplied them lots of times, and Kelly, too. She drove her oily looking, nearly-naked body back and forth; I watched her muscles stretch and bunch, and listened to her breathe. The air was hot and thick with sweaty incense smell. Patchouli. I must admit that I was gulping slightly. My sister, Tish, keeps guppies in a tank; my guess is I resembled them somewhat.

When she was done, she put the barbell on the rack and turned around and faced me. She was really panting now, and sweat was pouring through her plastered bangs, on down her face, and off her chin. Her hands were on her flanks, below the waist, resting on the stretchy, bright-red band of stuff that kept her skimpy bottoms somewhat up; her sloping shoulders were a little rounded, deepening the soaking space between her breasts. *My* chest felt full of something: passion, wonder, tears—you name it. Never, never in my life . . . was how I felt, if that's a feeling.

She did a number with her mouth that ended in a sort of smile.

"Well, now you know," she said. "My guilty secret."

"You sure have got in some terrific shape," I delicately said, following an old rule of my father's: "When in doubt, punt."

She swatted that one down with her right hand. "Not *this* secret, Red, the other one—down here." She ran a fingertip along the pinkish scar. "Say 'hi' to zipper-belly Kelly," she ran on. "You know what one of these is from, Red Ryder?"

I must admit I blushed. But not because of looking at her body, or the scar; her cool made that unnecessary. I blushed because I hated to be ignorant.

"I guess I don't, for sure," I said. "Could it be you had a baby?"

"It *could* be, yes, I *think,*" she said. "But no, I didn't, and now . . . well, now the train's out of the station, as they say. Lady's had a *hys*-terectomy, my boy." She distinctly made the first part sound like "his," not "hiss." And stared at me. "Above her mount of Venus, there lies a barren plain."

Absurdly, I felt guilty, skewered by her eyes like that.

"Wow," I said. "I'm sorry." I gave my head a few quick shakes and breathed in through my nose. "That seems like such a two-bit-nothing thing to say. Jesus." I looked up again. "I'm assuming you had to—like, didn't have a choice. Me, I'm not real sure I'd ever want to have a kid, myself. But for a woman . . . I don't know. I'm very, very sorry, Kel."

She turned and bent, and picked up a flowered towel from off a pile of mats, and put her face in it for quite a while. And then she rubbed her arms, her dancer's shaven underarms, and down her sides. Next she dried her legs, the whole way down, and didn't have to bend her knees at all to do it. The mopping didn't do a lot of good: by the time she straightened up again, she was just about as wet as when she started.

"I guess I want to tell you. Assuming that you want to hear it. And if it isn't here and now, it might be never, so . . . why don't you have a seat?" She walked down to the racks, and took a folded terry robe from off the top of them, and shook it out, and put it on. I flopped down on the mats; she kept on standing.

"Your guess was on the money—yes, I had to," she began. "There'd been this pain, for months and months and months, that came and went. No one seemed to know exactly what it was. One Rex Morgan guessed appendicitis, even; he should have lost his place in the strips. But, generally, they called it 'an infection,' type unknown, a stubborn little case of P.I.D., you know?" I shook my head; she stretched her face and gave it to me syllable by syllable. "A pel-vic in-flam-a-to-ry dis-*ease*. That kept on coming back and back. After a while, I'd just sort of ride out the attacks, and they would go away. I was awfully, awfully busy, then, and I'm not into doctors much. But finally there was so much pain, this one time, that I couldn't stand it. I ended up in the hospital, and they decided that they'd better knock me out and take a look in there. 'Exploratory surgery,' that's called. I signed a form so they could do repairs in case they found a leaky valve or something. Well, when I woke back up again, I got the word from Columbus and the gang. A gonorrheal infection. So advanced they had no other choice. They had to do—*had done*—a 'total' hysterectomy, which at least, thank God, it isn't. They leave a girl her ovaries, unless they absolutely can't, so you can keep on making hormones, anyway. My ovaries were not 'affected,' I was told.

How fortunate I was, they told me. No reason that I shouldn't have a 'normal' sex life, they went on. Unless, of course, you call conception part of 'normal' sex. As fast as you could say 'Shazzam,' they'd made me Sally Spayed, Sam's semi-sister.

"I don't think any man can understand how stunned I was. What do they call it in boxing? The old one-two? Well, I'd been given the old one-two, all right. First that I could never, ever make a child with anyone—no matter how much love and wanting and all that jazz, forget it. And second, that some other person *did* this thing to me. I'm not referring to the doctors, now. No matter what your mother told you, Red, you don't get gonorrhea off a toilet seat. A guy *gave* this to me. The story is, it doesn't always show in tests, on girls, especially in what they call the 'early stages.' So when I had *my* test, and they told me that I didn't have it—way back when—I scratched it off my list of worries. Whatever was wrong with me was 'something else.' It couldn't be that serious, I told myself. Ho, ho.

"Now that guy had to know he had it, didn't he? I mean, a guy will *always* know. Right, Randy? Isn't it a fact a guy will *always* know?" It almost was as if she'd gotten out of breath again.

"God, I don't know," I said. The word "hysterics" came to mind, but I wasn't sure what it was, exactly. The thought of slapping Kelly in the face was more or less . . . what is it they say in Washington? *Inoperable?* "I guess so." I nodded to agree some more. "That's what I've heard. I've never had it myself." I shifted around on the mats. "I mean, it just so happens that I haven't. Absolute pure luck, I guess. What I've heard is that it's reached the epidemic stage, and anyone is apt to have it. At school, there was a story that the student health facility had treated . . ."

I was being serious. Mildly panic-stricken, babbling, but serious. But Kelly laughed, and not hysterically, thank God.

"All *right,*" she said. "all right, already. I think I get the point. You really are nice, Randy." She put her hands into the pockets of her robe and shook her head. "You'd think by now I wouldn't get so wild about it. The simple fact is:

guys do know. But some guys haven't got the kindness, guts—you name it—*decency* to tell a girl. All he had to do was tell me. Three little words: 'I got it.' Even afterward, for Christ's sake. And all this could have been avoided. *That's* what makes me so damn mad I want to scream—the goddam *unnecessariness* of all this." She turned and took a few steps toward the door, her shoulders hunched, her hands now fists inside her pockets.

"Actually, I did try screaming for a while. A friend said that might be a way to get the anger out." She turned and walked back to the edge of the mats. "Mostly, what I'd get would be a sore throat. And, as you found out at Fossel's, I keep on doing numbers. I don't seem to blow up at women like that, just guys. If Tina'd said what you did, I would have shrugged it off, or maybe even thanked her. But let a man give me anything but strokes, and I go crazy: a man is *doing* it to me again! How dare he? The slightest little thing will set me off."

She took her hands out of her pockets and undid the coil of hair on the back of her head. When it was loose, she spread her fingers wide and ran them through it.

"You'd think that if I can see that, and if I know it's crazy, I could stop. But I can't quite seem to. That's pretty alarming. Have you ever *not* been able to do something that you want to do? It's some awful feeling. Maybe I don't really want to—that's occurred to me a few times. I think I still like men as much as ever, but maybe I'm just kidding myself. In any case, the whole thing's pretty crazy."

"It doesn't sound so crazy to me," I said. "It doesn't sound crazy at all. I'm sure I haven't gotten over this." I waved *that* hand at her. "But in my case, I didn't have anyone to get mad at, except myself. And that makes everything different. When you talk about self-pity, though—I'm a specialist in that. A real major leaguer. That's been *my* biggest problem."

"Do you mind talking about it?" she asked. "Whatever happened to your hand, I mean?"

"Oh, no," I said. "Not really. It's pretty gross. I did it with a log-splitter, up at my parents' place in Brandon, just before last Christmas. Not a very merry one, I must admit. Even after it healed and all, I was still pretty sensitive about being . . . deformed. *You* know.'' The old self-conscious chuckle. ''I mean, as you found out.''

Earlier, I said that I can tell about The Accident in lots of different lengths. At camp, I seemed to be going for the shorter ones. It crossed my mind to tell her all my story—all about The Arm and Jonathan etcetera. But, right away, I thought that would be stupid and insensitive, kind of like playing a game of surgical/psychological Can-You-Top-This. Wait until you hear *my* story, if you think you got it bad. I really didn't want her feeling sorry for me, and it surely wasn't Jon I wanted her to love. And anyway, we were talking about *her*, and if we kept on talking about her, and about her feelings about stuff—about *men*—we could conceivably get to what she thought of *me*. There'd be plenty of time for my little soap opera later. Later, much later, I thought.

''God,'' she said. ''And so I did. Find out, I mean. I blush to think of it. Actually, I'm still surprised your lovely introduction to The Fat Broad didn't turn you off completely.''

An opening: I pounced. ''Well, obviously it didn't,'' I said, ''as you read in my letter.''

''Yeah,'' she said. It was as if she'd suddenly let go the strings that were holding her up: she sank down on her knees and then sat back, with her fanny on her heels and her hands flat on her thighs. She looked at me, then looked away. ''That was the sweetest letter I ever got. Which is surely one reason I kept putting off getting in touch with you. What I've been doing for the last five or six days—other than the job, of course—is dieting and working out. I wanted to show you that I wasn't *total* bullshit. That I *had* meant what I told you, even if I didn't act like it on Thursday night.''

''The other part''—she pushed some hair back off her forehead—''of my not getting in touch, that is, was that I knew I had to tell you''—she shrugged and pointed to her middle—''*this,* somehow. You remember I told you I wasn't dating? Well, aside from all the other stuff, there's

. . . well, there's the simple fact that—this sounds like such a melodrama—that I'm not a whole woman anymore. Literally. And unless a guy just *happens* to see me naked, or the next thing to it"—she couldn't help but steal a glance at me, and make a little grin—"the only way he'll know is if I tell him. Which never having done, I wasn't sure if I could or not—if that makes any sense. It isn't exactly one of those 'Guess what . . . ?' deals, is it? And it didn't—doesn't—seem right to let anyone think he has some feelings about me when he doesn't even know what he's getting into." The grin again, without the glance. "As the saying goes."

"Listen, Kel," I said, "all I can tell you is that I don't think I could care less. About your having had the operation, I mean. I just told you: I've never been sure I wanted a kid. For a lot of guys, I'm sure it's a really big deal, or, like, some kind of an assumption. But not with me. I don't know why. Maybe it has something to do with—*you* know—being a foundling and all. And anyway—I know that this is just a hair ahead of where we are right now, but anyway—if it ever did turn out that we got married or something, and we decided we wanted a kid, we could do what my parents did—the ones I grew up with, that is." It was my turn to grin now. I put a hand on my breast. "Adopt a little boy as wonderful as me. Or David. Maybe his mother would let us adopt *him* for a while. . . ." I laughed. "So we could practice up."

She smiled and dropped her eyes. "David. He's amazing. You should have seen him when he brought your letter. Solemn as a bishop: 'Randy's written you a letter, Kelly. Could you possibly—please—read it now? I think it's important.' He may have held his breath until I'd finished it."

She shook her head and sighed. "He's just so beautiful, so talented. I wish I could get him to sing for me, just once. I keep asking him. But he just laughs and tells me he's retired. I guess it doesn't matter." She smiled and turned to me. "Any more than being blood-related does. I guess it's good I feel that way, just in case I ever do want a kid of my own. And *that's* what I was trying to tell you at Hy's. The feeling you and David have got, between the two of you . . . well, that's the thing that counts. Lots of brothers hate each other's guts. Suppose David's mother put you in that basket. Would you want to find that out? I mean, wouldn't that make you hate *her*, maybe? And wouldn't that be *really* awful?''

''Oh, I don't know,'' I said. ''She could have had her reasons.'' I'd turned this over in my mind before, and being Mr. Fair himself, I'd come up with a few. ''And seeing things worked out okay for me . . . It's just that now, because of meeting *him*, I think it might be neat to know I'm not a total single.'' I threw a rootless laugh in there. ''And if I knew we were brothers, then I wouldn't have to worry about after camp, and all. I mean, staying close to him. Am I meant to go back to college, and he goes back to the city, and that's that? I mean, what's his mother going to think about his visiting me, or my coming to New York all the time and taking him to, like, ball games and stuff?''

''Yes,'' she said, ''or, like, dance recitals and *stuff.*'' She was grinning again.

''Yeah,'' I said. ''Actually, the *three* of us could go to lots of things like that.'' No carry-overs, Dunny, did you say? Just listen to this. ''Well, couldn't we? You're going to be in New York, aren't you? And if you're working out again, doesn't that mean you'll have a company again, and all that kind of stuff?''

She was shaking her head, not ''no,'' but more like ''hopeless.'' ''Randy, listen, you keep on going much too fast. Nothing's as simple as you make it. Never mind my work and the company for the moment—though, let me tell you, that's going to take a lot of time, too. But as far as you and me . . . you *think* you don't care about this . . . thing of mine. The hysterectomy.'' She pronounced it right this time. ''But, I promise you—you don't really know yet. You think you do, but you can't. Even if it turns out that you don't care about having kids, there's still a lot more involved than what you're thinking of right now.''

''Well,'' I said, ''I don't know exactly what you mean by that, but . . . so . . . .'' I'm not absolutely sure I had an ending for that sentence, but she interrupted anyway.

"For instance, I can still fuck," she said. That grin again—perhaps at my expression—then a grimace and a shrug. "I told you they said that. And I'm meant to feel stuff just the same as before. But I'm not sure. I haven't tried. I haven't wanted to." Was that a past tense that I heard? "*I* don't know why. Maybe I'm just nervous. And that's just another example of what I'm talking about. What we were talking about before. This leftover craziness. *You* know what I mean—all you have to do is look at the way I've been with you. The way I hot-and-cold around—I *hate* to be like that. I've never been a tease, for Christ's sake." She shook her head again and looked down at her hands, still stretched out on her thighs. I got the feeling she was all stretched out again, inside, just the way her hands were.

"Well, I don't *know,*" I said again. The problem was I didn't know in any way that I could demonstrate, like with knowing the infield-fly rule, or the sum of two and two. Can anyone prove he knows anything that matters? "All I know is that whenever I'm with you, or watching you, it's just as if a theme starts playing in my head. But it isn't music, this theme. And it isn't words, either. But if it were words, you know what they'd be?" I laughed. "I feel so ridiculous even trying to tell you this. It sounds so *weird.* They'd be: 'Of course.' Isn't that romantic? But that's as close as I can come, in words, to what the feeling is. 'Of course.' That sounds like such bullshit. Do you have any idea what I'm talking about?"

Now she really looked at me and didn't stop, and her voice had lost its tightness. "Of course," she said. "And Jesus Christ, I'm grateful. And I'll tell you the truth, too, Randy, though not as beautifully as that. I really do like you. I mean, I really, *really* do. Not just the edges, or the frosting. Right down to the layers, I think. It got so—down at Emil's?—that I'd catch myself just waiting, hoping that you'd come. Can you believe it? Whenever you were there, I'd feel myself relax; I felt all right. Just sort of safe and happy. When you followed me home that time . . ." Her smile was so completely sweet. "And now I'd like to spend more time with you. Have a little summer romance, you know? The kind that doesn't have a lot of expectation in it. Look at it this way, if you like: I'm just protecting myself. Because of what I think about you not having really taken in my . . . status yet. I believe the other things you say—what you wrote me and all—but this is something new, less than an hour old. . . . You have to give it time. And give *me* time. To work out all that other stuff I talked about: the way I act toward you, and men, in general, and sex.

"So who knows what will happen?" She held out a plausible palm. "And, as you said, we have to go back in . . . what? Three weeks. Maybe, in a different setting, things won't be the same at all. Here, there're all these kids, and summer in Vermont, and hardly any pressure, and a kind of neat community. . . . You must have heard that old story. About the girl who fell in love with the pilot during World War Two, and they got engaged and everything? And then, when the war was over, and she saw the guy in his regular clothes, and he showed her this restaurant he planned to buy, she knew that she could never marry him? Well, my mother claims she knew a girl like that. And you may be that girl yourself. Or I could be. You really don't know."

I didn't know if I did or not, and I probably didn't care, at that point. Kel was being super-cautious. But, somewhat typically, my mind was still mostly back at the point where she said she really, *really* did like me. Imagine a big, fat, jolly mind with a napkin tied around its neck and knife and fork in hand: just feasting, feasting, feasting.

And hadn't she just said she'd like to have a little summer romance? With none other than his highness, Randy Duke?

# CHAPTER 9

Like almost everyone else my age in the entire country, I have a number of friends who are vegetarians. Most of them turned veggie sometime during high school, at least partly (it seems to me) so as to put some philosophical and domestic distance between themselves and their parents. The philosophical distance could be measured vertically, and the domestic distance horizontally, and both could be summed up in the fragment, ". . . so I just stopped eating with those creeps."

But, regardless of their motives, all my vegetarian friends proclaim their diet's benefits to health, two of which are "feeling light" and "plenty energetic and alert."

If they are telling us the truth, then love, so often spoken of as carnal, may be mostly beans and rice and buttercrunch. Not to mention yogurt, ginseng root, and sprouts.

At least that's my experience. For quite a run of days, starting with that evening in the weight house, I was almost light enough to float. Nothing was an effort; I was never bored. Gravity *existed*, same as always, but nothing (neither "I," nor "it," nor "he or she") was heavy. People seemed a little nicer than before; whatever faults they had would surely be outgrown. Sleep, though there was less of it, was better: sweeter, smoother, easily-awakened-from, refreshing. Time flew by, and work was easy, playful, nourishing. "Oh, yum," as Martin Raycroft might have said.

On Cloud Nine, there is a very small Office of Problems, but a huge Department of Solutions.

Take, for example, how I finally filled one nagging little

pothole in my conscience: this matter of my name, my True Identity, and telling "All" to Kel and David.

From the moment(s) that I knew I loved them, I knew I'd have to tell, before the season ended. That was obvious. I wasn't going to wait until one of them came down to school, or over to my parents' house, and just happened to notice that everyone was calling me Jon. But for a while I didn't want to go into all that with Kelly, for reasons I've already mentioned, and there didn't seem to be any big, pressing reasons for letting David know, while keeping it a secret from Harlan and the rest of the cabin, not to mention all the other Reds and Amos and etcetera. Explaining something to one person, or even two, one time, is a hell of a lot different than explaining it over and over, or on national TV.

Anyway, what I decided to do—my brilliant stroke—was tell them both together! And make a kind of ceremony out of it. What I'd do would be to take them out to dinner at that place the Woodmans talked about and feed the story to them there, the Saturday before the end of camp. And furthermore, to mark the day indelibly, I'd give them both a present, a memento. How's that for perfect planning? *Letter*-perfect, as you'll shortly see.

What I did was hie me to the All-Camps Store and buy, right there, two running-*R* lapel pins. You can get them in Red or Blue, and you can guess which kind I chose, if you are really sharp today. Then I took the pins to Wellington and got a jeweler to engrave them on their little gold-filled backs.

I know you're thinking "corny," right? But wait, you haven't even heard the best part. Imagine the back of a capital *R*, okay? Which is like an *R* turned around, right? On both the pins, I had the guy put R-A-N-D-Y, but going *down* the big long right-hand side of the letter. Then I had him put J-O-N going down the upper left-hand part. On the top bar of Kelly's pin were her initials, going across: K.C., and on the middle bar were David's: D.T. On his pin the initials were reversed, his on top and hers in the middle. And on the slanty leg of the *R*, I had the guy put 3 - 4 - 1, but going down, from upper right to lower left. Isn't that about the corniest thing you ever heard of in your whole life?

Well, here's what I think. "Corny" is for other people's rings and rituals. When I got the pins back from the jeweler, they looked *great*. I stuck them in my wallet, where I wouldn't lose them.

But hold on, back up. I'm getting way ahead of myself. You surely want to hear about our "little summer romance." It made for certain changes in routine, and mostly in the hours of the evening.

I've always liked my sleep. I prefer to have it once a day, when it is dark outside, and have it last a good nine hours. Dunny used to tell me this was not "collegiate." He said if God intended we should sleep that long, He never would have made the University, or given Dexedrine to man. I informed him that I needed sleep, and that if Thomas A. Edison had gotten a little more of the stuff, he might also have invented *important* things, like the blow-drier. If I didn't get my sleep, I told him, I'd be grouchy and catch lots of colds, and how would he like that?

It was hard to win an argument with Dunny; he came from legal stock—I think I mentioned that—and always had a brilliant closing statement up his sleeve. "Baby! Baby! Baby!" is what he said that time.

But anyway, for two whole weeks and more, I cut my hours-slept-per-night from nine to five or six, and never blew my nose or spoke a word that could be called "discouraging." It's true that during Rest Hour the sound of Harlan's Bic on Raycroft stationery did have a rather sedative effect on me, but a nap in the middle of the day is by no means fatal, as anyone would know who's checked the population of Mexico City lately.

What Kel and I would do, most nights, was meet down at the parking lot and then take off together. We went to different spots, depending, but always to a place we figured we could be alone, or not with anyone from camp, in any case. The first night of our romance—that was Thursday—we drove way down to Valley Falls, New York, and sat around a bar for . . . I don't know, it must have been two hours. Then, more or less at once, we took a look at one another, laughed, and said, "Let's go." With which we sprinted out of there and jumped into the car. And there we stayed, just holding/touching/hugging/kissing/breathing hard for three or four hours, I don't know. We sat right in the parking lot, I know that much, outside a bar named Shady Rest, in Valley Falls, New York, swept from time to time by old Impala headlights, with pickups crunching in and out across the gravel. We didn't think of moving; we weren't moved to do much thinking, either. It's funny: people's bodies know the way to get acquainted, step by step; it's only in our minds we're shy.

From that night on, we stayed away from bars and other public hangouts—except to get provisions—and went to places like the campsite off Clinch Hollow Road, and others that the camp maintained. If cabin overnights were using them, or someone else was parked before us, we'd go to places by the Battenkill, where fishermen could nose one car just off the road in daylight, and folks like us would do the same at night.

I don't remember details of those first few dates; they blend together in a long, sweet, easy process. Getting to know someone has to do with learning how she smells and feels and tastes, and learning where she's come from, step by step. You pay attention, and you love it; it's exciting time. She talked a lot: when and where and what, and how she felt while doing all those things. I was candid, too, but more selective, hiding Jonathan the Great. "All in good time," my mother used to say—instead of "No," in her case.

One Sunday night, as we were driving back to camp, Kelly pointed, smiled, and said, "Hey, why not there tomorrow night?"

"There" was called the Copper Kettle: sixteen units, off the road, AAA and big-screen color.

"Sure," I said, above the drumroll in my chest. The subject of her hysterectomy had not come up since we'd first talked about it. And no, indeed, we "hadn't." "I heard that they're predicting rain," I said.

So, in we checked, at nine-fifteen P.M., tired from the drive up from New Jersey—as we told Ma Kettle at the check-in desk. "Mr. and Mrs. Jonathan ____________," I wrote down on the card, just in case she asked to see my driver's license for some reason. I hadn't gone the motel route before. Kelly never looked to see who she was with; I guess she thought she knew. At any rate, her "husband" wore a coat and tie, while she had on a dress but not (she told me in the car) the smallest stitch of underwear.

That night was everything you might imagine—and also just the opposite of that, which really covers everything. Later on, it all made perfect sense, but then we were surprised. What idiots.

The thing is this: we tried to act as if we hadn't any company.

When I unlatched the door of Unit 8 (forty bucks a night, TV, with bath and shower), it could have been a subway car at five P.M. on weekdays. Kel and I got in, all right, but with us came a crowd with names like Fear and Tension (a.k.a. Anxiety and Hope and Expectation), plus a gang of relatives and friends of theirs. Sweating, elbowing, and carrying lots of smelly, greasy packages, they sat on both the beds, and all three chairs, and perched atop the dressers. And also lined the walls and stood there, swaying, staring straight ahead at us, pretending they were not the least bit interested. *We* behaved as if we were alone, or as if we'd worked this kind of crowd a hundred times before.

Our bodies weren't fooled at all.

Bodies can't stand static. Call it mental interference. What they'd like to do, a lot of times, is give those bratty minds that sit up on their necks a five or ten and send them to the movies. But no, the little dears prefer to stay and make suggestions: "How about a sip of this, a sniff of that, a pop or puff of something? It's just for *your* sake, body," says the mind.

That's one kind of static that is pretty common nowadays.

Ours—or, face it, *mine*—was different.

I've never wanted any body, anytime, as much as I craved Kelly's, I am sure. Nor have I wanted anything for anyone as much as I wanted the manifestation of my wanting Kelly to go right for her, in just the way she wanted it.

Say, *what?*

Hum/buzz/crackle/garble/pleasestandby.

My body fiddled with the tuning knob a bit and then, with one rude gesture, went on strike. Too much. My mind refused to understand that. It got confused, and then annoyed, and then (let's face it) frightened. *I* wasn't the one who was meant to have these problems; what *I* couldn't do was *throw* hard. Gulp.

Poor Kelly. Exactly what she needed—right? A little extra load of Gosh-how-am-I's? How about a side of Guilts? What we got was one Depression, two scoops, sugar cone.

Things got pretty sticky before we finished that. What saved us was a miracle, no less. You may not call it that, but I do. I think it's a miracle whenever people are allowed to scrape life really clean and see what's going on, instead of just what seems to be. Truth's good body is the thing they see, without a layer of ego fat.

It started when we laughed. We'd been lying stiffly, side by side, siamesed together by self-pity—and suddenly we got from there to laughing, I can't tell you how. Maybe we were tickled by an angel. And when we laughed, we stretched and rolled and let the tension go; we looked at one another, and we saw how beautiful we were, as well as how ridiculous. That made us shake our heads and laugh some more, and pretty soon we simply laughed for joy, knowing it was great to be the way we were: beautiful, ridiculous, and all.

I wouldn't try to kid you. There was a moment when our minds—I may mean *mine*—came rushing back on duty, shouting things like "Oh-oh, careful now!" and "This is it!" and "Howzit going so far, do you think?" But what our bodies seemed to do was not pay real attention. I took a job once, back in high school, hauling groceries out of trucks and stacking them in storerooms, and stocking supermarket shelves. The manager, a man named Mr. Moncrief, always buzzed around and hollered things like, "Watch it!", "Easy . . . ," "Hurry up!", and "Over there!" He made me pretty nervous till I saw that all the older clerks ignored him altogether and just went on about their business at the same calm pace as always. That's what our bodies did in Unit 8, I guess, subtracting "calm," you might say. And just like at the grocery store, the work was nicely, neatly done.

By then it was gray dawn, and both of us were almost of a mind to throw the windows wide and tell the peasants. Never mind how "good" it was—as if there was some Celsius of sexual satisfaction. In terms of learning and accomplishment, it was—in Rennie's kind of language—"merely awesome." Kelly chortled her delight, put my head between her breasts, and told me that she felt "much woman." I moved my face from side to side and mumbled my agreement. Then we both fell fast asleep, which almost made us late for reveille.

And so began our time of being lovers. Not just making love but being it; a not-so-technical distinction. I lacked three fingers on the hand that once could throw a baseball at astounding speeds. Kelly lacked a womb that might have harbored geniuses. Too bad for me, too bad for her. Too bad for all the ways that people aren't perfect, aren't God. But yay for that one way they are. We are completely lovable. Believe it. Every one of us. I didn't say *deserving*.

I loved the way I felt and looked and was, perhaps because I loved so much the way she felt and looked and was. Or maybe it's the other way: that I loved *her* so much because I loved myself. Or maybe—this is what I *really* think I think—there was no first-then-second, chicken-egg or cause-effect. Maybe love just *is*. Sort of like a hundred-mile-an-hour fastball: you can't say where it comes from, it just *is*. You either got it or you ain't. And if you can, you do.

Ready for another set of questions? (1) Do more people love their own minds than love their own bodies? (2) Should they? (3) What part of them decides the answers to the first two questions?

Anyway, Kelly Carnevale and I were lovers, starting with that Monday night, I guess. And oooh, we wallowed in the fact. In soft, warm, honey-colored moonlight, we two rolled—yes, barely rolled—around and across each other's bodies, feeling every part of her or him with every part of him or her you could imagine. Everywhere and every way felt wonderful.

"Oh, my goodness!" I'd exclaim. And she'd say, "Yes, indeed. And more so."

"Why is everything completely new?" she asked another time, not meaning one specific act, but everything. I didn't answer then, but one or two nights later on, I said, "It's more or less as if whoever I am now has never been before, you know?"

To which she answered, "All ways and forever, Randy."

On nights when one or both of our JCs were "off," we also got together, but not till later in the evening. We'd rendezvous at Emil's, at no specific time, each leaving camp whenever his or her JC got in. That way we'd keep our membership, we figured, and give the group a chance to mock us to our faces.

"My gosh," said Bilgy, grabbing Roger's arm as I walked in one night. "Don't tell me . . . *Bucky Dent!*"

"No, no," said Roger, "*that* is Burt Reynolds, I think. Bucky Dent looks younger, doesn't he?"

"In any case, how fortunate we are," breathed Amos, "that he should come to this poor Rustic Inn, rub elbows with the riff, and also raff, and dance the hoipolloi." He spoke to me directly then. "No consort, then, tonight, Great Pasha? The Pasharess is locked in the seraglio, perhaps?"

"What?" I said. "You see through my disguise so quickly? Rats. I'd planned to mingle with you people, find out your needs and hopes and fears, and then, when I returned to Camelot . . ."

"Camelot or Id, Sir Rodney?" Running Bear threw in.

He smiled, but half his lip appeared to be a trifle curled. Since when did R.B. quote the comics?

"My gosh," I said, "could that be Bung? Still safely on his stool, and close to midnight?"

"Uh-uh," said Running Bear, "me Little Beaver, Red." No one called me that but Kelly. "Don't tell me you forget so soon. Me know that Little Beaver, he not much compared to . . ."

"In point of fact," said Amos, interrupting, "we are mighty glad you came. We think they're watering the gruel in here, and also, with inflation what it is, a piece of eight won't buy a piece of . . ."

"Rhubarb pie," yelled Wendy from the table next to ours. "You watch your mouth now, Amos; there is some ladies in the joint."

"What I would like to know," said Roger, wiggling his eyebrows and fondling a large, invisible cigar, "is whether there are joints on any ladies . . ."

With which the conversation got to be what passed for normal, of an evening, out at Emil's, during camp. There wasn't any doubt that everyone was curious and interested: why and how do two such social tortoises sprout wings? But by and large the mood was tolerant amusement, I should say. Let the children play; they'll learn. The season's almost over anyway.

Kelly said she got the same impression, there and at Raylene, though Tina'd given her a squeeze, and Cynthia Fossel'd sent her one huge yellow rose bud, wrapped up in the Rutland Herald sports page.

But, tortoises or lovebirds, we'd always stay at Emil's till the crowd began to thin, goofing back and forth and showing that we hadn't really changed at all. After we drove back to camp, I'd walk her home across the fields, making maybe one sweet stop along the way. There was a poncho and a blanket in the Squareback nowadays.

You'd maybe think—considering the time I spent with Kel in those two weeks, and all the sleep I didn't get that I was used to—you'd maybe think that other aspects of my life at camp would have to, sort of, suffer. Or, to make what I am saying crystal-clear: that I would start to do a crappy job.

Well, I don't think that was so at all. Really. There seemed no limit to my energy, no bottom to my well of caring (kaff). *Amor* not only *vincit*s *omnia*, it also seems to make the time for it.

Exhibit A: the cabin. I think I've said already that the cabin was evolving, week by week—getting more involved with one another (or should that read "itself"?). Seldom did a guy from Cabin 2 spin rough-or-smooth, or shoot for some award in Rifle, or leave the starting line in a canoe, without a small group watching him and rooting. Silently and diplomatically, perhaps, but they showed up. Their loyalty to one another dripped across the color lines, as well, and when they had to play against each other, man to man or team on team, the sportsmanship they showed would make a Billy Martin puke.

One incident, from fairly early on, is maybe worth retelling, just in case (by any chance) I haven't made completely clear the kind of kid that David was.

David didn't just pick people up when they were down, he *put* them up, as well, in what you might call little ways. For instance, he'd spot Rennie heading for the movie by himself. "Hey, Ren," he'd call to him. "Save me a seat, okay?" Or there'd be Jimmy, walking to the dining hall, and he would holler, "Jamesie Gee! Wait up!" and run and catch him. Other kids had laughed at Tiny's vitamins, till David bummed a couple from him. And when Mitch came back to camp from a three-day canoe trip, guess who was there to help him with his pack?

I don't think he did things like this by plan; it was more as if he felt like it, you know? Even with Eddie Larrabee.

Eddie was a loudmouth, just the way his father brought him up to be, and pretty much the ayatollah of the tactless squad. Mitchell upper-lipped it for a week or so, and then began to cut him down, using only blunt ones. "Tell us all about it, Larra-baby," Mitch would say, as Eddie started in on yet another story of his feats "back home," or told us once again that something that he owned (dirt bike, fishing cruiser, English saddle) really was the best, far and away.

Others took the cue from Mitch, and in a little while Vast Eddie (still another Woodmanism) had himself more limelight than he wanted. At first he answered back defensively: "You're all just jealous . . . ," and then geared down to insults: "Well, at least I'm not so fat/small/stupid/ugly that I can't . . . ," whatever. He started to get that look about him that a picked-on kid will always seem to have: a kind of sulky, fugitive expression that makes him even less attractive than he is, which isn't very anyway.

What David mostly did for him was do things *with* him: tennis, shooting baskets, going fishing. Anything that would remove him from the cabin scene between-times—the hours of the day that weren't scheduled. The less the other kids saw Eddie, the less he could annoy them, and the more he hung around David, the less obnoxious he became. Not quite so loud, not quite so big a show-off. And, then, one day, with help, he even got to be a hero.

The setting was a baseball game, Red-Blue: Red is leading 6 to 5, in the top of the sixth, and last, inning. Two out, with Blue at bat, and Eddie Larrabee the batter. We are—remember, I coach Red—one out away from victory, and not a hard out, either. Amos, mentor of the Blue, does not look hopeful; his bench is wrapped in heavy gloom. A kid with glasses starts to pick up bats and slide them in the bat bag. Amos yells at him, then hollers toward the plate: "Come Eddie, come babe! You can do it, kid!" But he doesn't sound all that convincing.

Well, wonder of wonders, on the first pitch Eddie swings the old aluminum in the place the ball is thrown and shoots a ground ball into right, a foot past Gerry's desperate dive. He's on: base hit; Eddie Larrabee has singled, and the Blue is still alive!! And Mitchell Woodman up!

Ed is so relieved he's hardly even happy yet. Amos shouts to him: "Way to go, you Eddie-babe. Two out now, kid. You're running on anything, okay?"

Eddie nodded, and the pitcher pitched again, and Mitchell, who is first-ball swinging, too, connected. But this was no ground ball with eyes. Mitch doesn't hit one often, maybe, but when he does, it goes. This one plain took off, both hard and high, a little to the right of center field; for distance, say, three dollars in a cab. As soon as he connected, I said, "Gone"; there wasn't any way it would be caught, or Mitchell either. That could be the ball game—damn!

But still, I did what I'd been trained to do: I watched the bases. Those runners have to touch the bases, and sometimes, all excited, and going superfast, they don't. And when a runner misses any base, he can be out, provided the defense notices and tags that base, while in possession of the ball, and appeals to the umpire for a judgment. Umpires, of course, are also trained to watch the bases, but it isn't up to them to call the runner out, unless appeal is made.

You've surely guessed what happened. Eddie Larrabee, the potential tying run, running on "anything" with two men out, missed touching second base by maybe half a foot. He touched third and home all right, and Mitchell, thundering around behind him, touched them all—a task made a little easier by our right fielder, who first kicked the ball into the goldenrod and then threw it ten feet over Gerry, who'd run way out to be the relay man.

The ignorant Blue bench went absolutely bananas. They'd taken the lead 7 to 6, and "good old Eddie" and "good old Mitch" were hugging, dancing happily around. Their only problem was that neither run would count when we appealed the play and Eddie was called out for missing second base. Third out, the ball game's over.

I'd gotten to my feet and was pointing down toward second base. My mind had put together the sentences I'd yell: "The first runner missed second. Get the ball and touch the base."

And then I looked at David, who was looking straight at me, and very serious. He shook his head, just twice, but unmistakably.

In the three and a half weeks of baseball clinics—and our little extra practices—I'm sure I'd mentioned to the infielders that they should watch the bases when they could, but I hadn't made a great big point of it, or drilled them on the play. There are a lot of high school and college infielders who never think to look. Yet, at this crucial moment, he'd remembered and he'd seen. And now he didn't want to call it. No one else, of course, had noticed but the ump—assuming that *he* had.

I dropped my arm and closed my mouth and sat down on the bench. The next Blue batter hit a grounder down to Si, and so the inning ended. Red came in and took its last at-bat. We got a runner on, but didn't score, and so the game was down the tubes.

We gave them a cheer, which was the thing to do at Raycroft and Raylene, and I shook hands with Amos, like the good sport I'd learned to seem to be. I also yelled, "Good game, you little rats," to Mitch and Eddie as they walked on by, surrounded by a knot of happy Blues. The Reds had trooped away by then, mostly each one by himself, and looking at the ground. Winners stand around and talk; losers get real scarce real fast. You can see that on TV.

When I started to collect the bats and stuff, I noticed David sitting on the bench, his elbows on his knees, bent over. He wore an Expos cap, and he had pulled the peak way down around his eyes. Every little while, he'd pop his fist into the pocket of his glove. I wandered over, touched him on the cap.

"Look," I said, "you shouldn't feel so bad. That was one of the finest, most important things I've ever seen a person do. You saw how great old Eddie felt. He needed that." I sounded strained and foolish.

He didn't raise his head. "How about all the guys on *my* team, though? Did you see how great *they* felt?"

"Well," I said. "Think of it like this. In a way, the Blues deserved to win; they got the hits and all. And besides, it's just one game. And it seems to me that winning or losing one game is a lot less important than—"

He'd gotten up. He turned and lifted up his head so I could see the tears still running down his face. "Oh, shut up, Randy," he said. "Will you just shut up? You could have called it anyway, you know." And then he turned away and trotted toward the path to camp.

When I had put the stuff away and headed down the path, I found him waiting there beside it, sitting on a stump this time.

"I stink," he said. "It wasn't your fault, Randy. I'm a baby."

"The hell you are," I said. "Sometimes, well, there isn't any way to make it right for everyone. I still think you made a good choice." We walked on down together, shaking our heads at the way life was.

That was how the cabin—David—was.

I hope it wasn't overdone. I can't be sure; do people ever tell you what they really think your baby looks like? No question, I promoted it. The latest was I'd started making stops when Kel and I were heading home, and picking up some treats—well, mostly ice cream—for the cabin. That started from the fact that we (that's she and I) got hungry almost every night, and needed . . . well, if not another meal, at least a snack. Right away, I thought: why not the cabin, too? I always got enough for everyone (except Harlan, who's sworn off it for the sake of Mary Jean's new diet), and some nights we'd have a party: everybody sitting up and dripping on their flannel sheets and ssshhing one another. There were also nights when only one or two would rouse themselves to eat: an awful waste of ice cream.

David woke up like an Indian, and usually was last to go on back to sleep. One night—I'd fed the dying fire in the fireplace—he slipped on out of bed and sat beside me on the window seat, his feet up on a chair, and split a final pint of chocky-marsh. And as we ate, he asked me what was going on, that I was getting in so late so often. It made me happy that he asked. I told him I was seeing Kelly.

He smiled. "I thought so. I thought it must be that. I hoped so." He nodded to himself emphatically. He had just pajama bottoms on, and in the firelight his skin was perfect satin, deeply tanned; his eyes were big and round, with lashes Kelly would have swapped for. David wasn't perfect, any more than you are; I'd seen him angry, thoughtless, selfish, sulky, miserable. But never in a way that stuck or marked him. It's funny that we use the word "unspoiled" to talk about a kid or piece of country that is clean and pure and natural, more or less as if we thought that state was only temporary. Why don't we call a shirt "undirty," or a piece of food "unrotten"?

"That must be great," he said to me.

"It is," I said. "Sometimes I have to pinch myself."

"I bet," he said. "A girl like Kelly—wow." He shook his head, and bent, and rolled up one pajama leg a little. "Sometimes I worry that I'll never even meet a girl—*you* know—I really like. I mean, really, *really* like, like Kelly. There can't be all that many, I don't think, and me . . . well, I don't go to lots of places all that much. And, like, in New York, the perfect girl could be living right in the next building, and there's still no telling you'd ever meet her. It seems like there's a lot of luck in finding girls." He sighed. "And even if I do meet one, what are the chances she'll be available? I mean, the perfect boy for *her* may be living way over on the East Side someplace." He shook his head again. "But I guess the thing I worry about the most is: what's a girl going to see in a little dip like me anyway?"

It struck me then that what he didn't mention—maybe didn't even *think*—was how, when he went home from camp (or shortly after, anyway) he wouldn't be the famous boy soprano anymore. He hadn't mentioned that at all, all summer, except on that first night. But he had to care, didn't he? It had to be eating at him *some*. Kel had said he wouldn't even sing for her.

"I know," I said. "I know exactly what you mean. It's scary. You know what I used to do? I used to make lists of interesting things to say, and memorize them, so in case I met a girl I really liked, I wouldn't have to stand there like a moron. I could talk to most girls all right, but as soon as I met one I really thought was neat, Tap-City. But, you know, my lists didn't work, either. I'd say one of my interesting things, like, 'I heard that if you live-trap a mouse and take it a mile away from your house and let it go, it'll find its way back in no time.' And the girl would just look at me for a second, and if she was really polite, she'd say either, 'Oh, gross,' or 'That's interesting,' and then remember she'd promised her mother she'd help her with the baby or whatever. So, after a while, I started memorizing lists of interesting *questions*, like 'Do you think it's fair to put kids on detention for chewing gum in class?' But that wasn't any better. Mostly, I got, '*I* don't know,' or 'Sure, why not?' and then they'd say 'Wow, I'm meant to meet Miss Dorplething to see about a radfateetle, 'bye.' ''

David turned his head to look at me. He had a small smile on his face, and a slightly cut-the-kidding look.

''And then,'' I said, ''when I finally had my first real girl friend—and she *was* one of the ones I thought would never in a million years go out with me—well, then I got afraid that maybe she was *it.* My 'one and only,' as my mother used to say. What I thought was, if I didn't drop out of school and get a job or something so's I could support her, I'd blow the only chance I'd ever get. So I went from worrying I'd never find a girl to being pissed I'd found her much too early.''

''I guess my mom did that,'' he said. ''Sort of.'' The fire snapped; the dark outside the cabin was completely quiet.

''What?'' I said. ''Drop out of school . . . ?'' I didn't want him to hear my heart beating, so I cleared my throat a little.

''Yeah,'' he said. ''Except that it was college. She dropped out and got married and had me, and then, two years later, I guess, they got divorced, and my father went to live in Oregon.'' He stopped talking, but not as if he'd *finished* talking.

''It's sort of weird,'' he started up again; his voice had gotten softer, ''to think that you're, like, part of a *mistake.*'' Of course I had thought that no one else had ever had that thought before. ''My parents getting married. My mother dropping out, and stuff like that. I know it isn't my fault, but still . . .''

''I know,'' I said again. ''It's funny how that happens. I've had the same kind of thoughts.'' And I told him, in a very easy, offhand way, about my being a foundling. I'd been wanting to, and that seemed like a good time; it got him caught up to Kelly on his Randy-facts. When I was finished, I said, "But in your case, I'm completely sure your mom would do the same things over, if she had the chance." I had my arm around him; he was warm against my side.

"I know," he said. "She's told me that, and I believe her. I guess what I'd like is for her to get married again, and have a really nice marriage." He turned, looked up at me. "Too bad that she's too old for you." He smiled to let me know that he was kidding.

Well, there it was, my chance, the perfect opening. How could I resist? "So how old is she, anyway?" I asked, "like, thirty-five?"

"No," he said. "She was just nineteen when I was born. She's thirty-one. I know that isn't old or anything. And, jokes aside, she's been seeing this guy. . . ." He told me about a man named Rick, in his early forties, nice, and kind of rich.

I sat there holding him and listening. Well, that was that. I wasn't David's brother after all. But still, I felt okay, not any more alone than usual. Having him beside me helped, of course.

"The big thing is"—he'd simply gone on talking softly, huskily—"that she gets married for herself. Not just so I can have a father. I never could get up the nerve to tell her that. But what I did—oh, weeks ago—was write her. And I told her . . . well, I told her *that,* and then I told her all about you, so she'd know I had an older man-friend of my own—and wouldn't need for her to get me one. Not that you're so old." He gave a little laugh and straightened up. "I told her you were lots different than any teacher, or my choirmaster, or anybody. The thing I told her was you just seemed like the way I always thought an older brother would be. Should be. Right from the first. Remember? By the bus? I wanted her to see that this was different than with other men I'd liked. I wanted her to understand I *love* you."

He said that in his soft, rough voice as easily as if he'd

said he loved vanilla fudge. I guess he knew he didn't have to be afraid of saying it.

"Boy, I'm glad you told her that," I said. "And I hope she knows I feel the same as you do. What I'm planning, after camp, is that we'll keep on seeing one another, lots. Kelly'll be in New York, too, and I can come up, and we can go to a ball game, or a dance thing with her. And you can come down to school—it isn't very far—and visit, meet my roommate, Dunny, and all. I'm hoping, once your mother meets me, she won't mind."

"I'm sure she won't," he said. "She wrote me that you sounded great. She said she'll really like to meet you. Kelly, too. I told her how amazing it was that my two favorite counsellors were good friends with each other, too. She said that wasn't so surprising, when you think about it." He paused. It was one of those moments that you'd like to bronze and put up in the trophy case. "Are you and Kelly going to get married, Randy?" David asked.

I wasn't really set for that one: knuckle ball. But there are times you'll swing at anything. "I hope we are," I said. "It's sort of up to her, I guess." I think, as I said that, I really understood the things she'd told me in the weight house. Sitting in the darkness, snuggled up against this child I loved, I understood we'd never have a child. I pulled him even closer.

"We haven't talked about it yet," I said. "But, yes, I know I want to." And I did. I knew. It really *didn't* matter. "I've got another year of college still." I laughed. "It's really weird to hear myself talking about getting *married.* I mean, six weeks ago, if anyone had said . . ." I shook my head. *That* thought almost cracked me up. "How's a married person meant to act?" I made my voice much deeper. "Now, David . . .," I began.

He laughed and punched me on the arm.

"Time for bed?" I said. He nodded and I picked him up and carried him. I set him on his upper.

"Thanks a lot. Good night. Sleep well." We whispered back and forth and kissed each other on the cheek. I crawled into my lower bunk.

I think, right then, I put my past to bed as well.

Other guys my age had both their parents dead, and never had a brother or a sister, and didn't have a lover yet, or maybe ever. David's parents weren't mine, any more than Kelly's were; the bond between us didn't start with stuff that guys in labs could count, and name, and split, and analyze. I thought I liked that even better, somehow. It seemed to make our brotherness more . . . (maybe you will think I'm mental) . . . *thrilling*. I'm sure I smiled my way to sleep.

On the Sunday before the second to last week of camp, Reynolds Ormsby Watson, Senior ("Buzz" to his old roommate, Rennie's dad to me) finally made the scene. His Jersey license number was ROW 1.

I, as luck would have it, was standing in the gatehouse by the parking lot, the Gateman (then) On Duty—playing, as we called it, GOD. For weather, I had made an undecided day of showers off and on. I stood inside My little house, with the cottage door half-opened, leaning on the sill it made and reading. Some other GOD had left a paperback behind, and I had gotten lost in it. The book was *Billy Budd*; I'd read the thing before. Or written it, perhaps.

The small gray Porsche snuck up so quietly I almost didn't see it coming. I looked up just in time to read the license plate and bumper sticker: "U.S. Open—Baltusrol." My father's club. I had the chain in place across the road, and so he had to stop.

"Oh, hi!" The driver's face lit up, much as if it were a good old friend of mine. I didn't think I'd seen it anywhere before. It was a lean face, tan and deeply lined at each end of the mouth, but young, and very closely shaved; the tan was drawn so tight across the cheekbones it looked as if the guy had got a suit of skin a size too small. He wore a white and floppy tennis hat, and a white knit shirt with some peculiar emblem on the breast, and vivid madras pants. A newly lighted cigarette was deep between his fingers, near the palm.

"It's nice to see you," he went on, and took his right hand off the steering wheel and stuck it through the window.

I closed my book and held it in my left, while giving him my right. He saw the hand that held the book; his eyes went quickly up and checked my face again.

"Hi," I said. I could be as nice as anyone. "I'm Randy Duke. I'm a counsellor on the Raycroft staff here. And currently the Gateman." I gestured toward the sign above the Gatehouse door. It was the same one that was posted on the far end of the parking lot: all those things you couldn't do, and I can't make exceptions so don't ask.

"Oh, yes," he said. "Of course. I'm Reynolds Watson, and my son's a camper here."

"I know," I said. "I'm Rennie's cabin counsellor, in good old Cabin Two, in Bucks." I also said this to myself: Oh, shit.

"Of course, of course," he said. "I thought I recognized the name. I'm really dreadful when it comes to names." He took a hit of soothing nicotine and another close gander at my face. "*Randy,* isn't it, you said?"

"Uh-huh," I said, not being very helpful. I tried to put the film on rewind, find the place in it where I had talked with Mr. Ingalls (good old "Bob") about this very moment. A good fat forty days ago, or so. And I remembered everything verbatim, or anyway the next thing to it. Rennie's mother was our client, but I could still be fair.

Reynolds Watson, Senior's eyes flicked upward to the sign; I was sure he'd seen it once already, coming in. "I thought I'd pick up some of Rennie's gear," he said, or quoted, "as long as I was driving through these parts." He sucked his cigarette again and waited for some gate activity from me—a little game of drop-the-chain, perhaps.

"Well," I said, "I'm sorry, but . . . there's still two weeks of camp." I mumbled, pointing upward toward the sign, as if it were its fault.

"Hmmm." He read the sign another time. "I guess you have your orders. And clearly no . . ." It could have been "discretion," but he mumbled, too. "So . . ." He snatched the gearshift knob and backed the Porsche up faster than my Squareback goes in third. He braked, then shot it forward and around into a parking space. I heard the car door slam, and there he was again, now walking toward the Gate.

I left my little house and met him, as they say, halfway.

He smiled; the lines cut deeper in his face. "Guess I'll wander in and locate Ren. Maybe take him out for lunch," he said. He pointed at the road beyond the Gatehouse. "I gather that's the route?"

"It is," I said. And then I shook my head. He wasn't going to make it easy, was he? "But I'm sorry, Mr. Watson, you can't do that. Take him out for lunch, I mean."

He stopped. "Why not?" He took a box of Benson & Hedges out of his pants pocket. "Why can't I take him out? I've never heard of such a thing. You mean that children can't have luncheon with their parents on a Sunday? Is Rennie being punished? Or is this some other idiotic rule that you are not allowed to make exceptions to?"

"No, not exactly, Mr. Watson," I replied. "And Rennie isn't being punished, either. He's a wonderful kid." I dropped my eyes to the asphalt and saw he wore white leather shoes, those rough-out bucks that have red rubber soles. "I'm really sorry, but . . ." I had to look at him, in fairness. He had a cigarette in the very middle of his mouth, and a gold lighter in his hand. ". . . but *you* can't take him out, I'm afraid. The person who enrolls the camper has the right to . . ."

He'd lighted the cigarette, and now he snatched it from his mouth; his words came out in little puffs of smoke.

"Why that's absurd!" he said. "Ridiculous! If Mrs. Watson made some list and didn't put my name on it . . . why you can be assured that's just an oversight. You see? A pure and simple oversight. She probably assumed she didn't have to put the boy's own father's name down on a list of visitors, for heaven's sake." He shook his head and even sort of pawed the pavement with one foot. That was a first, for me.

"Now, look here . . . Randy," he went on. "I don't blame you at all. I'm sure you're doing just as you've been told, and I know you've done a *super* job with Rennie"—was that a snowflake on my cheek?—"so I *know* you won't be angry or . . . *offended*, if I take this matter up with the

Director. Right?'' He smiled a large one; he was such a gentleman. His teeth were somewhat stained. ''I mean, that's what a director's for, I guess—to handle irate parents and misunderstandings. Right?'' He chuckled, touched me on the shoulder; there's a good lad. ''Now if you could tell me where . . .'

I smiled right back at him: a *very* good lad. ''I can do better than that,'' I said. ''I'll take you to his office. *He's* where Rennie is, right now, at our Sunday chapel service, but we can go and wait for him. My relief will be here any minute. We can head right up there now.'' This lad was not real easy to dispose of.

We hadn't even gotten to the Gatehouse before Rudy Caceres, the next GOD, appeared from the direction of camp. I saluted him as we passed, but didn't introduce my companion, who had his head down and was walking fast, not waiting for me.

''The thing is,'' I told the side of his head softly, when I caught up, ''that we were told not to let you take Rennie out. It wasn't just that your name was left off a list or something. We don't have any lists like that.'' I could have waited for Fisher to tell him, just let Fisher handle the whole thing. But I didn't want to do that. Sometimes there's a hitter that you want real bad. In painful bits and pieces, since the start of camp, the story of this guy, this Buzz, had come squeezing out of Rennie, some to Harlan, some to me. I'd rather be abandoned than be hurt like that.

The words I'd chosen stopped him. We'd just about come out of the pine grove and reached the place where you first see the lake. He took a puff on his cigarette and turned around to face me.

''What-do-you-mean?'' His almost-whisper sounded almost-British. ''Do you mean to tell me *she* did that? She told this camp I couldn't see my son?''

''Not *see,*'' I said. The guy was looking pretty wild. ''Just not take out—like, off the grounds. Except for regular activities, campers aren't meant to leave the grounds too often, anyway. We like to keep them—''

''That goddam-tricky-little-*cunt.*'' So said the gentleman. He *interrupted* me. Tut-tut. And then he did a weird one. He took his lighted cigarette between two fingers and a thumb and jabbed the ember end into the other palm. Not once, but twice, and three, and four, until it turned to blackened, flattened, frayed tobacco.

I took a step away from him and folded my arms across my chest. I hadn't been given a clue as to what was wrong with this dude. Just that he wasn't "stable," or some such word. So what was he, then? "Un-stable"? "Anti-stable"? Bullpen, pigsty, horse-shit, maybe? The last thing I needed was to get blown away by a raving lunatic in madras pants. My father'd say the trousers should have warned me.

There was a big flat boulder there, right beside the road. He turned and sat on it, with his elbows on his thighs and his hands tightly clenched. He looked like a person sitting on the toilet.

"I admit"—he said this quietly and clearly, talking to the ground that was between us—"I admit that she had reason, once upon a time, to feel the way she did, and does. I'm not denying anything that *was*, you understand. And it's true I signed those papers giving her . . . control. My God"—his head snapped up, his eyes blinked very fast—"d'you know what she'd have done if I'd resisted? She and my boy Bob-o? Of course you don't. How could you? College snotnose. Why should you? It's none of your damn business, is it?"

"You're right, it isn't . . .," I began, not gently. It was a funny situation. He was treating me like a kid, but I was feeling like an equal. I actually felt completely equal to a grown man. He might not have been able to see that, but I wasn't going to have him mistaking me for the rug that runs into the men's locker room at Baltusrol, the one you can even wear your golf shoes on.

"But that was then and now is now," he said, ignoring me again. He'd unclenched his hands. "I'm different now," he said. "I've changed, and so the circumstance has changed. You must see that."

I suppose he was talking to me, but he wasn't looking at me, except maybe my feet or knees. And he was speaking softly now, in a sort of gentle, conversational tone, more as if he were talking to an old friend, or to himself.

"Of course I signed the papers. I hadn't any choice. And in all fairness to Laney, she was right. I shouldn't blame her. I was just in rotten shape back then. But now"—he gestured with one hand—"I'm not. I've changed. I'm getting things together. I want to have a son again. I need him. It's really very simple. Every person needs a motive force, a *raîson d'ètre*, you might say. Rennie fills that need for me. I *know* he loves me; soon, he will be proud of me, as well." He stretched his hands in front of him, palms down. They shook, but only just a little. I got the feeling that he gave himself that test a lot, and that he believed the scores he gave himself on it were all that mattered.

He looked up at me. "You may not understand the things I'm saying. *I* couldn't have, at your age. The world is rather simple when you're twenty-one or two. I *knew* I had it made in those days. Nobody pushed the Buzzer. All you have to do is eat and drink and fuck and study just enough to keep your parents off your back. Right? You don't need anything you haven't got, and getting things is easy. You need a car? A lay? A drink? A wife? A kid? You got it. How about a kick in the ass?" He smiled a phony, tight-lipped smile. "You don't have the slightest idea of what I'm talking about, do you, Buster Brown? Well, the only thing you have to understand is this. . . ." He bent his head and rubbed both palms against his cheeks.

"I *need* my son," he said, and stared at me through slitted eyes.

I just looked back at him, sort of holding on to my chest with my folded arms and trying to figure out what to say. Nothing I could think of seemed to fill my present needs. I hated this guy, really hated him. It occurred to me that my mother would say I should feel sorry for him, and inside my head I said to myself, or to my mother, in a really pissed-off tone of voice, "Of course I feel sorry for him." And then had to add "too," in all honesty. I really hated this guy.

"I guess you're right," I finally said to him. "I guess I don't understand. I don't understand where someone like you gets the right to have a kid at all. And then fuck him over like you have. And *then* try to tell me you need him. Bullshit, Mr. Watson, it's too late. Rennie's turning out okay, but it isn't up to him to solve your problems. Even if he wanted to or could, both of which I kind of doubt." I think I wanted the guy to come after me, right then. I think I really wanted to hurt him.

He'd shut his eyes while I was speaking, and I could see him take some quick, deep breaths, the way a hitter does, sometimes, when the ball game's on the line. But after a bit he relaxed, stood up, and smiled again, not showing any teeth at all.

"The kindest assumption I can make," he said, in an easy, educated drawl, now, "is that having your hand . . . *deformed* like that"—he pointed to the place my left was parked, under my right bicep—"has made you bitter at the world. And so you try to take revenge wherever you can get it. *I* seem a vulnerable target. Well, that's for sure." He turned and started to stroll toward camp. "Rennie *hasn't* written me this summer—he hasn't my address—and so I *didn't* recognize your name at all. I was just being diplomatic when I said I did. But I suspect that Rennie, being bright and sensitive, will be glad to see the last of you, just as I will be. Now take me to the Director's office."

I stalked along a half a step ahead of him, on up to the main lodge porch. By the time we got there, chapel was just letting out, and kids came streaming back, some sauntering sedately, others at a gallop, loosening their clothes. I was afraid we'd see Rennie before I saw Fisher, but, thank God, that didn't happen. He ambled up; I made the introductions and was blunt about the rest. "Mr. Watson has a question that I think I should hear your answer to." Not eloquent, but straight. We went into his office.

Fisher did it nicely. Guys like him can do it all from memory: "We're sorry, but . . ."; ". . . a nice clean fracture, said the doctors . . ."; "his grandfather? How sad . . ." This time he smiled and said he understood. He went to Rennie's folder, and he opened it and read. He said he didn't really have a choice; surely Mr. Watson could see that? Of course, there wasn't any reason that he couldn't *see* the boy. Would "Randy round him up, please?"

I did as I was asked. Rennie's eyes just flickered sideways when I told him, as if some portion of his feelings shied away. Then he nodded, licked his lips, and made a little sigh. I told him that he couldn't leave the campus with his dad; he said he understood and didn't want to. He went up to Fisher's office.

I shadowed them. Maybe I should be embarrassed to admit it, but I'm not. I wasn't going to let this guy try anything.

He didn't. Not in any way I was afraid of, that's for sure. Rennie took him on a tour of everything there was to see, except the playing fields. And then they went and found a bench that looked out on the waterfront and sat on it awhile. Mr. Watson smoked and talked a lot; Rennie mostly gave short answers, looking at the ground between his feet, though two or three times he looked up and seemed to tell a story or whatever. Those few times, he smiled a bit, and gestured with his hands.

When the bell began to ring for lunch, he jumped right up and started for the dining hall. I paralleled their route; Rennie saw me then, and waved. His father looked in my direction and made a funny motion with his hand. Then he started talking rapidly. When they reached the main lodge steps again, they stopped. Rennie now looked up at him; his lips moved very fast. His father answered. Rennie shook his head a lot of times and shrugged. His father spoke again, lifting up his hands, palms up, in front of him. This time Rennie shook his head hard, twice, and turned and sprinted up the steps and into the building. His father pivoted on one white shoe and paced off toward the parking lot, striding long and quickly, his shoulders round, one hand in one side pocket, digging for his cigarettes.

I hurried to the dining hall. Rennie'd put himself way down our table, next to Harlan's seat. He ate a little, but he didn't say too much. He seemed to look away from me. ROW 1's revenge, I thought. He couldn't let the kid just go on being happy.

* * *

Kelly shook her head and said that Mr. Watson sounded like a hundred percent polyester asshole, coming-ready-or-not. That was Monday, during Rest Hour, the first chance I'd had to tell her all about it. Sunday night the JCs had stuffed their yearly JC Banquet down, so both of us had had to stay on cabin duty all night long. To compensate for that, we'd met on Monday at the parking lot, right after lunch, and motored to the campsite off Clinch Hollow Road. Later on we finished off by jumping in the pool. And then we lolled around and talked while getting sun-dried.

Kel was a world-class loller. I know that dancers, speaking of each other, talk about a person's "line." I'm not exactly sure of what that means, in terms of posture or technique, but in general I think it means the shapes that dancers get in—how they look when they are doing different things. A cat, by and large, has a terrific "line." And so did Kelly, lying bare-assed naked on a big striped towel, turning this-and-that way in the sun, catching rays and glances everywhere. She liked for me to look at her, I knew. She'd said to me, some days before, "I don't want any secrets—ever, ever, ever. I want to give you everything, to have you know it all. So you can be so sure I'll *know* you are."

And now she said, "I'll have to act surprised when we get here with the kids on Thursday." We'd finished up with Rennie's dad by then. "Oooh, my!" She rolled her eyes and bent her wrist and put a finger on her breastbone. "Why, what a lovely pool!"

"I keep forgetting that's this week," I said. I had to grin. Her gesture and her face were so demure, for an actress sitting on a beach towel with her legs apart, without an ounce of costume on. I was lying on my back beside her, dressed from that same period.

"Oh, it's this week, all right," she said. "Tina's and mine are the last two cabins to go out. I kept hoping we could bag it altogether, but the kids are really eager. I guess it *could* be fun. That's what you said, right? So how about you roll yourself real tight inside a sleeping bag"—she flopped down on her side and tucked her knees way up, and wrapped her arms around them—"like this. And then when I unroll it, after Taps . . . TA-tata-TA!" she sang, and sprang up to her feet, a Venus-from-the-half-shell-in-the-box. "Instant entertainment! Just add a pinch of love," she cried, and went into a little dance, raising one foot then the other, slapping at the outside of her ankles as she switched her hips around. Then she dropped beside me on her knees.

"I want to tell you something, Dook," she said. "If I didn't know that I was going to see you after"—she wiggled her fingers in the air—"after all this is done, I wouldn't go. I kid you not. I simply wouldn't go. But now . . . oh, God, I can't believe it . . . now I see that what we've got here isn't just some carnival, or summer stock." She turned one hand into a megaphone and raised her voice, sounding like a barker on the midway. "It's not a show at all, my friends. A hit, but not a show. A little classic on the stage of life, and starring, here he is, folks . . ." She switched onto her hip and threw her arm across my chest and leaned on it. Looking down at me, she smiled and took her fingertip and ran it all around my face, sketching in my eyebrows, eyes, and nose, my cheekbones, mouth, and jawline.

"There," she said, her voice much softer. "My own true love. Am I ridiculous?" She chuckled. "You'd think that I was sweet sixteen, in cutoffs and a tube-top. I swear I *do* know better. Part of it must be I want it so. The perpetual puppy, always wagging her tail." She laughed again. "But I didn't just follow you home, did I, Randy? You had to offer me some treats to get me in your car. And you know the one that worked the best? Your trusting me so much. Telling me . . . well, all that stuff, and what you felt, and all. And not expecting anything from me. I didn't have to show you mine until I felt like it. You know why you and David get along so well? Because you're lots like him. A little innocent." Her fingers traced a heart on the surface of my chest.

"Well," I said, "it's hard to see yourself the same as someone else does. But part of what you say I know is true. Telling you the truth was always easy. I wanted to, but not for any reason. I just wanted to. When I first saw you, I realized you looked like a person already. Do you know what I mean? You didn't look older, but you didn't look like a college kid either. And when I started to watch you with the kids, I realized you were like a lot of them, just so un-full-of-shit. No matter what you'd been through, or how cynical you may have got, you never covered over your self. *You're* the one who seems a lot like David to me. I wish you could have been there when we talked the other night. He loves the both of us the same as we love him." I laughed. "We must be all meant for each other."

She smiled. "I'm starting to believe it. Him and you and me. We *are* a lot alike. It's pretty amazing to meet a certain part of yourself in someone else. I feel as if I've finally found my tribe, you know?" She shook her head. "I realized the other day. The last thing I ever thought I'd feel again is just exactly what I'm feeling now: *lucky!* Can you believe it? Just think, I tell myself—if this and that had not occurred, there would have been no way I'd ever have heard of Camp Raylene, and Randy Duke Red Ryder, with his handy-dandy, rootin'-tootin' . . ."

She grabbed ahold of me; and me, I knocked her arm prop out and took some handfuls of her, here and there. We laughed.

My God, I thought, if I could still throw left, and hard, why that's what I'd be doing, maybe in Cape Cod, two hundred miles and more away. I thought that in one flash, and then I simply breathed, and breathed in Kelly, touched the sunshine on the towel and let myself be all the places that felt good.

That was Monday of the seventh week of camp. We saw each other once again that night, and at her class on Tuesday, and also Tuesday night, and at her class on Wednesday. Wednesday night, she said, she'd have to stay in camp and talk with Tina and the kids awhile, about the hike that they'd begin on Thursday. She said she'd meet me down at Emil's, late, for just five minutes, maybe. She wanted to get lots of sleep before the hike, she said.

Well, that would be okay. Harlan took that evening off and went on into Wellington to see a show. I lay down on my bunk and dozed, and when he came back in, he woke me up. It was later than I'd planned for it to be. I hurried over to the parking lot and raced straight down to Emil's.

The place was pretty empty. Two groups of five or six: one playing Buzz (with the serio-sloppy faces of the semi-smashed) and the other alternating droning talk with gusty bursts of laughter. And at one end of one long table, Running Bear and Kelly.

I hurried over, tossing "Hi's" and "Sorry, but 's . . ." before me. Running Bear leaped up, but then he didn't move or speak. I looked at him more closely. His knees were locked, and he was swaying slightly; he held a glass over his heart, as if he were waiting for the first notes of some alcoholic's anthem.

"Hey, Bear," someone hollered from the Buzz game. "You had your injury time out. Now get back over here and meet your masters." And then to me: "Old Bear is getting Buzzed but good."

"So I can see," I said, at which point Running Bear turned quickly on his heel and walked, not over to the Buzz game, but straight on out the door. He wasn't tottering, or anything like that, but still it made me glad when someone from the game pushed back his chair and rose, and followed him.

I shrugged and sat; Kel was staring at her glass. "What got into him?" I asked her.

"A lot of gin-and-tonics, that's for sure," she said. "And he's always had a sort of a thing for me—*you* know—and now the summer's almost over, and it's like he's getting sad, or pissed, or something."

"What?" I said. "At what?"

"Oh, I don't know," she said. She was twirling her glass around in its same wet ring, and talking in a soft and tired voice. "Himself. Me. You. Opportunity. Time. I don't know. There *is* something sad about the end of the season. He's hard to figure out. I guess he's really envious of you." She smiled a little short one. "He really thinks you're something. That he'd give anything to be, of course."

"Good Lord," I said. "He *must* be crazy. I can't blame

him for wanting to be me as far as *you're* concerned. But otherwise? Could it be my car? My cowlick? My avocado leisure suit? Being Head of Baseball isn't *that* important. And he was drafted—what?—two rounds ahead of me. Envious of *me?* He must be nuts.'' I found that as I talked, I actually began to get a little angry. I'm always grouchy when I wake up from a nap. ''What the hell. It *must* be you. Unless he's always wished he were adopted. Maybe Papa Bear's an asshole.''

Kelly shook her head and smiled down at her glass again.

''I don't think it's that,'' she said, ''exactly.'' She made a little mouth. ''But who knows? Maybe it is your parents; you never can tell. It seems as if the Dukes are pretty social people. From all I hear.'' She stood up then, and raised her glass and drained it. ''I've *got* to get some sleep. I guess I'll see that for myself, before too long. About the Dukes, I mean. You are planning to introduce us, aren't you?''

She had to be putting me on.

''Oh, hell, yes,'' I said. ''First chance we get. You've got to come and stay. They'll eat you up. My God, my mother will adore you. And Tish . . . she's always said she wished she had an older sister, too.''

We were walking toward the door.

''I wonder what they'll want me to call them,'' Kelly said, still in that funny, teasing tone. ''Mr. and Mrs. Duke? Mom and Dad? Ugh to both of those. What are their first names, anyway?''

''Weldon and Anita,'' I said, glad to tell her another part of the truth, but still discomforted. This conversation was not the one I wanted to be having just now. In the morning, Kelly would be leaving on that three-day hike—on a two-*night* hike.

We got into our separate cars and drove on back to camp. I suggested that I walk her back across the playing fields, and even reached inside the Squareback for our blanket. But she said no, she thought she'd better get on to her bunk the short way, straight along the lake shore.

I trudged along beside her, through the quiet boys' camp to the fine arts building boundary. She kissed me in an absentminded way, and only nodded when I said I'd see her Saturday. I'd made the dinner reservations, and I told her so, for her and me and David.

She said, "That's nice," and wiggled her fingers at me, turned and took a step, then broke into a run.

It was hard to believe that anyone could be in such a hurry to get to bed. I stood there feeling weird, until I couldn't hear her footsteps anymore.

# CHAPTER 10

When I was little, and our family used to go driving off on vacation together, my father liked to sing in the car. Maybe he still does, I wouldn't really know. He had a hat, back then, that my mother used to hate—a sort of yellow porkpie with a multi-colored band ("my driving hat," he called it)—and he'd settle it just above his nose to shade his eyes. And pretty soon, when we were on the "open highway" (as he liked to call it), he would start to sing. "Please Don't Talk About Me When I'm Gone" was one of his favorite numbers, and though I can hardly remember any of the rest of the words in it, the title's never left me for a moment. Perhaps because I've never much liked the idea of people talking about me behind my back.

I realize that's a pretty irrational feeling. *I* talk about people all the time, and so does everyone else, starting in about fifth grade or whenever it is that you and your best friend start to make lists of who you like and who you don't like and who's "sort of in-between." I would guess that people talk about other people more than they talk about anything else, including sex, crime, religion, records, dope, parents, and how much things cost.

As soon as I realized Kelly was gone, I wanted to talk about her constantly. At first I didn't know why, and it just seemed like a natural thing to want to do, sort of cozy and affectionate. But by Thursday afternoon I faced what seemed to me to be the fact: that I was scared to death I'd lose her.

I can't be too specific about this. But you must have had

these kinds of vague and terrifying feelings. Part of me was almost sure she'd be killed somehow, an accident. I'd heard that there are limestone faults, bottomless crevasses, in those hills: holes that went way deep, with brush right to their edges, that anyone could fall in unawares. Another part of me was panicked that she'd change her mind, "come to her senses," as my mother liked to say. She hadn't really had much time, the last two weeks, to catch her breath and think. People did have second thoughts a lot; if they didn't, you wouldn't hear so much about them, right? Kelly'd acted strange the night before she left; perhaps the doubts had hit her even then.

I told myself to stop that crazy thinking and put my mind on other things. "Oh, sure, yeah, uh-huh, right away," it said. I offered it diversion: staying in that night to talk with Harlan after Taps. We sat out on the dock and listened to the night sounds on the lake, and one another: soft talk, back and forth, of Kelly, magic, life, of Mary Jean and love and Kelly. That made things somewhat better. Harlan is an optimist, a kid, a true believer, and I was not about to pick at him. Dunny had been right to say that there was magic in the summertime, at camp. But magic, as I saw it now, was not outside of life but part of it, and summer gave us time to notice that and go with it. I'd always sort of itched to know the magic words, the final Open Sesame's. And now it seemed to me that you can't ever learn them after all, but have to keep on trying, hanging in there, as they say. And *that's* what makes you a magician, being part of stuff you don't control.

When I got into bed, I pulled my extra blanket over me; the wind had changed, down on the lakefront, and gotten kind of cool and damp. Weather in Vermont was changeable, all right. I thought of Kelly at our campsite, and the last time we'd been there, just four days ago. I guessed she'd be asleep already, and tried to send her happy dreams.

And then, a moment later, my head was full of fears again. What was going on, I asked myself? I was imagining too stupidly, too much. Maybe if I wasn't so *imaginative* . . . I had to smile. I also could imagine happy things, and often did—ridiculously optimistic outcomes. I couldn't blame this whole thing on my mind—it seemed to throw with either hand as well as I could. Who *was* responsible? I fell asleep before I figured that one out—a lucky thing, you might say.

By Friday afternoon, I'd reached a different state (of mind?); I'd turned myself into a numb, dumb Pollyanna. Kelly would come back on Saturday, all right; the three of us would have our dinner up in Manchester, with revelations and mementos for dessert. End of all my problems, whoopee. But, first . . .

That afternoon there was a Bobcat baseball game—the ten-year-olds—their last one of the season. I can't speak for other summers, but the Bobcats had a lot of talent this year. Those little kids could really play, and being cute and real intense, they drew a color-patriotic crowd of older kids and counsellors. The game was something of a classic. Red edged out the Blue by 2 to 1, scoring on a Freddie Williams' homer, following a walk, in the bottom of the fourth. Freddie, weighing eighty pounds with both his t-shirt sleeves cut off, got both the Red team's hits ("That kid is instant offense," Rennie Watson said), the Blues made only three themselves, all singles. The greatest thing about the game was hardly any walks or errors, which also meant the players didn't throw their gloves or whine at one another. I'd like to say the coaching was responsible, the *standards* that we set all summer long. But modesty forbids. *You* know.

So anyway, they played six innings in an hour, gave each other cheers, and left the field. With lots of "extra" time before free swim, Amos, Running Bear, and I were soon surrounded by a band of eager Bucks who clamored for some extra batting practice. "BP! BP! BP!" they shouted. "Please, dear handsome, noble, perfect coaches, give us some BP!" When he saw that most of them were Reds, Blue-blood Amos would have none of it, but Running Bear and I (sweethearts, both, in victory) agreed to hang around.

"How about I pitch, you catch?" I said to him. That

would make things move along. I can throw a lot of fat ones nowadays, in very little time; "the thirteen year old's friend," they call my fastball. And having Bear to catch would speed the process up still further. BP's awful boring when there isn't lots of action, with the hitters changing fast.

I'd never thrown to Running Bear all summer. I think I mentioned this before: we spread the coaches out on practice days, so kids would all stay busy doing different things. That's the way it seemed to work out best. Now I warmed up quickly near the bench with Simon; Bear got the full-sized catcher's stuff from the equipment shed: the shin guards and the mask and chest protector. By the time that he came back and put them on, my arm was loose enough.

"Let's go," I said, and hustled to the mound. Gerry Ramos had his bat already. Running Bear bent over in the catcher's crouch and showed me his big glove.

I wound and fired (*sic*); Gerry let it go. "Tha's not my peetch," he hollered. Running Bear whipped back the ball.

I don't know. It could have been the way he moved the glove and hid his throwing hand, or shifted weight to stay behind the pitch. It *could* have been the way he cocked his wrist, released the ball, and followed through. It could have been the sum of all of these, or something different altogether.

In any case, I knew beyond a doubt: I'd pitched to Running Bear before.

At first, that fact was just a baseball fact, a more or less impersonal abstraction, surprising but that's all. Like, "Holy Cow. Somewhere, sometime, I pitched to this same catcher." Catchers are all different, see. Counting only high school, summer Legion ball, tryout camps, and college, I'll bet I've pitched to more than fifty catchers. Closer to a hundred, probably. And all of them are different.

I'm not talking about looks, as I'm sure you understand. I couldn't say hello to some of those catchers if I saw them on the street, having never seen their faces, except behind a mask and more than sixty feet away. And there are others whose faces I've forgotten, never mind their names. But if I had a chance to pitch to them again, I'd know it. Know that we had been a team before, one time, however briefly.

Most pitchers have amazing memories. Not for French or physics, maybe, but for little things connected to their craft. I can tell you what I threw to Willie Bogan at the NCA's, and what he hit and what he missed, as well. And if you put a paper bag on twenty people's heads and made them crouch and give me finger signs—like, fastball: one; and curve ball: two; and slider: three; and so on—I'd tell you which of them was Al Camargo. Some things you just remember, without trying.

But now I had to try a little. I knew that Running Bear had been my catcher once. But where? Not in high school or in Legion—neither one of those, for sure. I'd known the people who tried out for baseball back in high school, and our Legion team was also local guys, guys from my own school and one opponent, plus a few from private schools. That meant . . . let's see, it *could* be college. My second year, there'd been a bunch of freshman catchers, and Salty'd moved them in and out of there quite rapidly. Some of them were cut right off the bat (I'd *wondered* where that saying came from!), and others stayed around for just a day or two. But if it had been college, I might have seen the guy around the campus, or maybe Dunny might have. No, chances were (it didn't take me more than thirty seconds to come to this conclusion) I'd seen him at a Phillies tryout camp.

I'd continued right on throwing while I had these thoughts: automatic, like you get out there. Gerry got his "peetch" a bunch of times and hit some pretty fair line drives. My mind was at that Phillies tryout camp.

And then—as surely you'd expect—it bounced back to the present. Fact: if I had pitched to Running Bear before, that meant that he had known, for almost seven weeks, that "Randy Duke" was not, in fact, my name. "Eureka," Archimedes said. Gulp, thought Randy Duke.

" 'Ey, Randy, cut the stalling, man." Gerry Ramos pounded on the plate. "You can' throw nothing I can' hit, today!"

I got myself in gear and kept on throwing strikes. I had to

concentrate when I was *pitching*, but I can throw BP for kids and think about (forgive me, Billy Martin, Gerry Ramos, and the like) the more important things in life.

An hour later we were done: two rounds, a dozen swings per kid per round. A good BP. Don't think we weren't sweating.

I told the kids to hustle down to swim, that Running Bear and I would put the stuff away today, and follow. When they'd disappeared, I said to him, "I just now realized we've met before."

He was sitting on the bench, unbuckling his shin guards. He stopped and then looked up, as if to check me out; his cheeks were streaked with catcher's warpaint: the paste of dust and sweat that forms inside the masks they wear. "Oh, yeah?" he said.

"Yeah," I said. "The Phillies tryout, wasn't it?" I named the place and year, and grinned. "I threw a little different, then."

He made a kind of grunting noise and finished with the shin guards. "I guess," he said. "You could really bring it, Jonny-Jet. My hand was sore three days."

"How come you never said something?" I asked.

He did the sound again. "How come *I* never did? How come *you* didn't? You can speak, the same as me." He shrugged. "First time I saw you, I said, 'Shit.' Just my luck to have a guy who knows me come to camp—there goes the noble redskin shtick. And then I see you're not reacting any way at all. First off, I say, maybe I'm wrong. Then I get a look at your hand." He nodded at my left one. "I'm sure you're Jonny ______________, but you—you're telling everyone your name is Randy Duke. I wonder: what's this bullshit, anyway?" He rubbed a backhand all along his forehead, snapped it to one side. "My real name's Richie Behr. B - E - H - R." He spelled it out, accenting the "H." "Fisher knows it. In fact, he thought of 'Running Bear' himself. I've been into nature and canoeing—all that stuff—for years, so when I asked to work in that up here, old Fisher, he said, 'Why not be an Indian? The kids'd go for that.' And I said sure, okay. I go to ______________." He named a college in my state. "We never get to play you guys in baseball. We play Division Two schools, mostly."

"I see," I said. "You never would have said a thing to me . . ."

"Sure." And then he said, "Why should I? You don't remember me, I don't remember you. To hell with it. I've got a reason why I use a different name: it's kind of, like, my *job.* What's your excuse? I figure you're just playing games up here. And if you can't bother to remember *me*"

"Wait a minute, Bear," I said. "That wasn't any college mixer we were at. You know how it was. They said, 'Throw to that guy,' and you threw. I didn't even see your face down there."

"Maybe so," he said. "But other guys still introduced themselves. . . ." He looked away.

I shook my head. My God, the guy was pissed I hadn't gone around to every catcher in the place and asked them home to dinner. "I don't see what that's got to do with now," I said. "Six weeks we've worked together. I thought we got along . . ." I really couldn't believe this yet.

"Oh, sure," he said. "We get along all right." He'd rolled the shin guards up inside the chest protector and put the mask on top of them. "You even seem more friendly, like, up here. But why should I trust *you?* You could really mess up my whole deal. All I know for sure is, one, you're not the guy you say you are and, two, you don't remember me and, three, the one time that we met before, you're up so high you wouldn't say hello. How do I know you wouldn't tell the kids I'm not an Indian?" He put on a real affected tone of voice. " 'Hey, everyone, guess what? Running Bear is really *Richie* Behr. He's just a lousy Jersey half-breed's all he is.' " He went back to his normal way of speaking. "How'd I know you wouldn't be that kind of prick—maybe even think it's funny? This may be one big joke to you, a place where you can come and kid around, and then take off, and people don't even know who you are . . . but me, I like this job. I like this *place.* In lots of ways, I feel much better here than anywhere. You could really fuck it up for me."

I heard him; he was angry. Someone else's anger almost always finds the place where I keep mine, and gets it to come out and play, all hot and huge and wriggly.

But this time it got blocked by something else. I saw just how this whole thing looked to him. Why *should* a person trust a Randy Duke?

"You told her, didn't you?" I said to him.

He shifted on the bench, leaned over, picked the mask up by the face bar.

"Yeah," he said. And then, a good deal louder, higher: "I should have done it sooner. It may not matter that you fuck around with Fisher, or Martin Raycroft, or the kids, or me even. But Kelly's something different. It isn't right to treat a girl like her that way. She may be just another groupie to the great Jet-fire Jon, but as far as I'm concerned, she's—"

"You *are* a sorry bastard, Bear," I said, instead of screaming. I turned and walked away from him. There wasn't any point in punching at his face, or talking to him, either. Neither would have helped my program much. He wanted to believe I was a prick. Well, same to him.

Oh, God, I should have told her long ago.

I also should have gone right out there, Friday afternoon, I guess. Just driven down Clinch Hollow Road and parked right by the trail, then marched right up and talked to her.

I didn't, for two quite monumental reasons. That sounds good and grownup, doesn't it? Wait until you hear the reasons.

First of all, I was . . . embarrassed. How totally uncool. But no matter how I tried, I couldn't see myself sashaying up that trail and entering a campsite full of barely teenaged girls. Suppose they were changing clothes, or skinny-dipping? Not that I wouldn't like to be invisible, and watch. But can you imagine what a scene there'd be, assuming that I wasn't? I know how Tish's friends go on, and they're like ten, eleven. I mean, even if I called ahead, shouting something idiotic up the trail, before I came in sight: "Yo, better cover up there, girls. Here comes Burt Reynolds and the BeeGees." That wouldn't be much better. Kelly'd be embarrassed, too. And then she'd have to talk to me, and if she was upset—which, naturally, she was—that wouldn't take five minutes, either.

Which, mostly, was my second reason. Now that Running Bear had done her this big favor, there'd be a different atmosphere between us for a while. She was upset I hadn't told her first, as well as being pissed, or mystified, in general. That was understandable, for sure. If I went charging into the campsite now, we couldn't just sit down and take our time with it. She'd have her kids to think of, deal with; it wouldn't be relaxed at all. Better, every way, to wait for Saturday, when she got back.

If you're thinking that there just might be another reason, still, a thing that Jon and Randy haven't mentioned . . . well, maybe you'd be right. Dunny wouldn't fumble for the words that would identify it, either.

"Fraidy cat," he'd say.

Friday night I stayed right in the cabin and felt weird. Harlan took the Taps and read a little scene out of a book, about two brothers, younger kids, the two of them in bed and talking in the dark. The title of the book was *Dandelion Wine*. The reading got to me; I couldn't say a word. Other people talked all right. It seemed that no one looked at me; ridiculous, I told myself. I went around and said good night, and things seemed fairly normal. I wouldn't look for trouble. I fell asleep and woke up much too hot; the wind had changed again, and there was thunder in the distance. Rennie made a little whimper in his sleep.

Saturday I had the Bears for basketball, the first thing after cabin cleanup. It looked like it would surely rain but didn't; I was glad. Time was heavy-legged anyway. Rog and Hillside, both, were just the same as usual. After basketball, I had a blank till lunch. I figured Kel and Tina would get back by then; I'd try to leave a message at the girls' camp office.

I hung around the courts to pass the time. David happened by and joined me; on other Saturdays, he'd had a dance class then, with Kel. We shot some fouls, and then played one-on-one awhile. David had been showing up a lot, wherever I was. He seemed to want to spend as much time as he could with me; I thought that he'd been looking sad, a little. Maybe it was just the end of camp. As Kelly'd said, it got to people, knowing that they'd have to say good-bye to friends and summertime: the non-world had an end, amen. I knew I'd keep ahold of Kel and David, that was sure, but what about old Hillside, Roger, Bilgy, Amos? Not to mention Simon, Rennie and the rest. Some of them (of us) would not be back. Would I be? Possibly. I doubted it. Mitch and Tiny never saw each other in the wintertime; you couldn't say the things at P.J. Clarke's you used to say at Emil's Rustic Inn. Maybe David wondered what'd happen in New York.

"Hey, *Randy!*" I'd been in daydream-land again, just catching, shooting up the ball. What the hell was Tina doing here?

Clearly she was just back from the hike. She had on sturdy boots and red wool socks, and short white gym shorts, and a big blue football Giants' jersey, number 85, a wide receiver's number. She'd rolled her blonde hair up behind her neck, but some of it was wisping out, and she wore a sooty smudge above one eyebrow. It made no sense at all for her to be there.

"I've got to talk to you," is what she said, of course. She sounded either scared or angry.

"What?" I said. I sounded much the same, I guess.

"Kelly's disappeared," she said. "Some time last night she just took off, don't ask me where. No one heard her go. I lied and told the kids that I knew she was planning to—that she wanted just a little time alone. I got her stuff together and left it at the campsite—said that she'd be back for it some time today. What I didn't tell them was: she has her nightgown and her sneakers on. I checked." She took her lower lip between her teeth and put her head down. "I don't know what to do," she said.

I swear that it was almost like The Accident. My head got

full of sound and colors: a great red roaring rumble in my ears. I made myself suck in a big deep breath, and swallow, and then I got real cold and calm. Did you ever see the Dallas Cowboys on TV? The football team? They have a coach who never raves or smiles or sweats; he always looks the same, all sharp and clean and concentrated. You'd never know, from seeing him, if he is mad or glad, winning by a ton or way behind. From time to time a former player with a grudge will tell the press, "The man's not human." That's the way I felt, I swear. It was like I'd been short-circuited somewhere, or *disconnected,* better, from the stuff that made *me.* My mind was clear, perhaps its clearest ever, but clear is empty, in a way. If I could feel, I might feel dead, I thought. And like they say: it didn't seem to matter much.

"Come here with me." I led her to a bench beside the court, and we sat down. "She didn't leave a note?" Tina shook her head. "She didn't give you any hints that she was planning this? Or where she might be going?" Tina sort of shrugged and shook her head to both of these. "What do *you* think she's doing?"

"Wait. You tell me something, first," said Tina. She got herself to look at me. "Is your right name Randy Duke?"

"No," I said, "it's not. Goddam it. It's just a name I picked out for the summer. And I found out yesterday that that bastard Running Bear told her it's not my name. My right one. I was going to tell her tonight, but of course she's got no way of knowing that."

"No, she doesn't," Tina said. "She sure as hell does not." She'd laced her hands together and put them on her knees. "Even when we started out, she didn't seem quite right. She said she had a headache." Tina sat there rigid, staring at her hands. "Thursday, when we got there, she said she had a headache. But she had a thing of aspirin in her pack. She took some after lunch; by suppertime, she said that she was better. You know the way she is; she didn't want to spoil it for the kids. That night, we made our plans for Friday by the fire, then we toasted marshmallows. Everyone had gone to bed by ten.

"Well, sometime later, I woke up. And heard some

noises by the fire. I figured it couldn't be a bear, I *hoped*, and lifted up my head, real slow, and looked outside the lean-to.

"Kelly's sitting by the fire with her back to me, so I go, 'Kel, are you all right?' She doesn't answer me, so I get up and stagger out. She's sitting staring at the fire. I go, 'Kel?' again, and she goes, 'Randy isn't Randy, Tina. His name is something else, Jon Something. He's been lying to me all this time.'

"And I go, 'What? He wouldn't do a thing like that. Where'd you get this load of crap from, anyway?' and she said Running Bear, and I said Running Bear is full of shit, and she said no, he's not, and he can prove it . . . da-da-da and so on. Something all about your being such a big athletic star at college, and how you're used to having lots of different girls down there, and that you've kept that up, up here. And how, sometimes, you don't even bother to say hello to people—"

"And she believed all that?" I had to interrupt.

Tina nodded slowly, up and down. "Uh-huh. I guess she did," she said. "What do you expect? It's true. You said you weren't Randy Duke yourself. Why shouldn't she, or me, or anyone believe all that?" She turned and looked me in the face again. "You know what Kelly said to me? Smiling like it was a big huge joke, except you know she isn't joking? She said, 'This time they cut my heart out, Tina. There isn't just a whole lot left in good old Blaze.' "

And Tina began to cry, looking down at her folded hands and rocking slightly back and forth. Some tears ran down her face and landed on her wrists.

"I told her"—Tina took a breath—"not to talk that way. I said . . . I said she didn't know for sure. An' she, she shook her head. 'Oh, God, I wish I didn't,' she kept saying."

"Okay," I said. "But finally she went back to bed? And yesterday—what happened yesterday?"

Tina rubbed her face on one blue sleeve and shook her head. "Yeah, I'm sorry." Her voice was hoarse, but she'd stopped crying. "Yeah, I talked her back to bed, after a while. She seemed to feel a little better. Yesterday we hiked straight up the Hollow. We'd decided we'd go along the creek, upstream, and keep on going to its source. We thought we'd like to find that. Well—maybe you know this—you follow it a real long ways, and then it splits. Like, what I mean is that there're two much smaller brooks that come together and make one. So half of us went up the left-hand fork, and half of us went up the right; that way, we'd find *two* sources, so we thought. Kelly got the best of that deal, let me tell you. Our fork went through . . . oh, I don't know, a mile of swamp, at least. And brambles—berry bushes, Susan said. And on the other side of *that*, it was just a kind of trickle. We followed it up to some slimy rocks, and that was it. Some source. Really. Kel and *her* girls took the right-hand fork and went straight up the mountain there, and found a real neat bunch of little waterfalls and stuff. And way up near the top there was a spring, I'd guess you'd call it, where the water bubbles up from underground. They all said it was neat, and although Kel was sort of quiet, I could tell she liked it, too. I figured she was tired, missing all the sleep she did.

"Anyway, we had a really super meal, and later on a real warm wind came up, and most of us decided on a midnight swim, so what if it was only ten o'clock, or something? And then we toasted up some marshmallows again and dipped them in this chocolate sauce we'd made. And *then* we went to bed, at maybe twelve, or quarter of. I went off in the woods with Kel, before we went to bed—*you* know—and asked her how she was. She said, 'Okay, I guess. I'm working on it.' And then she put her arm around me and gave me a hug and a big loud kiss on the cheek. And then we walked back. In the morning, she was gone."

I straightened up a bit, and took another big deep breath, and rubbed my hands along my thighs. "What do you think happened?" I asked Tina.

"I don't know," she said. She shook her head and bent a little farther forward. I knew that she would start to cry again. "I tell myself that maybe she woke up real early, and knew she needed time to think before she came back here. How she'd . . . deal with you and all. She wouldn't want to wake up anybody else, and have to start explaining, so she just picked up her sneakers and took off. She'd know *I* knew she did some things like that . . . *impulsively,* you might say.'' She nodded, trying to be convinced. ''Probably, by now, she's gone back to the campsite, found her stuff, and gotten dressed and started back to camp. But . . . but I don't know . . . I really don't.'' She took her hands apart at last and let her face come down in them. I watched her body shake and got the feeling that she thought her friend was dead.

I didn't want to touch her. ''Tina, listen to me. Are you listening?'' I said. Her body kept on shaking, but she nodded, too. ''I'm going to drive on down there, now, and see if she's come back. If she hasn't . . . well, I'm going to look for her and find her. Everything is going to be all right,'' I said, in that same careful, even voice. I wonder how many times that sentence turns out to be true, when people say it: everything will be all right. Three times out of ten? That many?

''Don't you . . . don't you think I ought to . . . oh, dear God . . .''—she took a deep, wet sniffle through her nose and started to sit up—''don't you think I ought to tell the Raycrofts''—she ran the sleeve across her eyes again—''so, if in case she isn't back, maybe there could be a lot of people looking? In all those woods, the chances are you'd never—''

I didn't want to hear it. It wasn't as if she was *lost,* for God's sake.

''Kelly wouldn't want that.'' I really did believe that, too. ''Look. She's probably gone back. And if she hasn't, she'll be somewhere in the woods close by still—*you* know—just getting it together. The last thing she'd want would be a hundred locals tromping through the woods with dogs and whistles, and a helicopter overhead. You *know* that, Tina. Right?''

She thought that over. ''I guess you're right,'' she said, but sounded like she meant, ''It doesn't matter.''

''Why don't you go on back to camp and be as cool as possible,'' I said. ''And better tell Raylene exactly what you told the kids. She thinks all artists are a little nuts, so I'm sure she'll believe you. Then if Kel's not back in camp by later on this afternoon, you can sign out for dinner and drive down to the campsite and meet us—Kel and me. I'll want a little time to talk to her down there anyway. How's that sound—okay?" I sounded like a Moonie, or a used-car salesman.

She nodded still another time. "Yes. Okay, I guess," she said. You always hear about people wanting to know the worst, but sometimes they'd rather put it off. And you know when that is? When they think they already know it.

She looked at her round-faced wrist watch. Tina wore a wrist watch that looked like one a nurse would wear, with a plain round face, and a black leather strap. "Suppose I meet you there at five. Unless, of course, I see Kel back before then. She'll know where to find me, up at camp." She tried to smile a cheerful one. Now we were both doing it. "Thinking of the children," that's called, when you're a grownup.

We said, "Okay, then. See you later," and we both got up and went in opposite directions, still not having touched.

I was walking swiftly toward the parking lot when he fell in step beside me.

"I heard the first thing Tina said," he said. "Are you going to go look for her?"

"Yes," I said.

"I'm coming with you," David said. Not "Can I?", "Would you mind?", or anything like that. "In case she's hurt herself, one of us can stay with her."

I looked at him. What did he mean by "hurt herself"? Kids aren't much for euphemisms, unless they have the Larrabees for parents, or the bathroom is involved. David just looked serious.

"Okay," I said. "But first, do me a favor, okay? Run back to the cabin and tell Harlan what we're doing—no, tell him that we're *meeting* Kel and going out, and won't be back till real, real late. That way they won't worry that we're gone."

"Right," he said, and turned and ran off toward the cabin. I considered getting in the car and leaving him.

"Thinking of the child." Then I thought how that would feel to him. I waited in the car.

He came back out of breath. "I had to go find Harlan. He was up at Fossel for rehearsal. I had to wait until they had a break." He buckled up his seat belt, and when I looked at him, he smiled. What a kid. Maybe taking him was the worst thing I could ever do to him. Maybe I was taking him for my sake, not for his at all. Shades of Mr. Watson. I started up the car.

Driving down Clinch Hollow Road, I started telling David my whole story—all the parts he hadn't heard, that is, the baseball parts, the names. I still was telling it when we pulled off the road and parked, and took the trail up to the campsite.

Before I started, though, I babbled nervously awhile: that I'd *wanted* to tell him all this for a long time, but because I *knew* I was going to tell him eventually, it hadn't seemed to me that *when* was too important. I said I hoped he'd realize I never had set out to lie to him, or trick him. He'd nodded when I said all that, and instead of looking puzzled, he'd looked pleased.

"So that's the story," I concluded finally. We were almost at the campsite. "In certain ways, I feel more like a Randy than a Jon, or Jonathan, so if you want to go on using Randy . . . well, feel free. But, of course, my parents call me Jon, and everyone at college does."

"And Mr. Watson," David said, and smiled a small, apologetic one.

"What?" I said. And something like that *does* stop you in your tracks.

"Rennie's dad told Rennie who you are. He said he knew you from some country club that you belonged to. Or at least your parents did. He said your accident had made the papers—when you lost your fingers? He said you were a big-league prospect. I guess he had it all down pat, except for why you changed your name."

"What did *he* say?" I asked.

"He said that accidents like the one you had sent people

into shock sometimes. And even when they're over that, they're kind of . . . funny in the head? He told Rennie he shouldn't *ever* bring it up to you. That you had to be real, real careful with . . . 'shock victims,' he called them. Like you.'' He smiled again. ''He said he was going to write Fisher after camp was out and tell him all about you. Warn him, you might say.''

''Is that why Rennie didn't tell . . . well, *everybody?* He was afraid I'd go berserk or something?''

''I doubt it. I don't know. He might have told lots of other people besides me. I just don't know,'' David said. ''But *he* didn't believe his father. His father'd told him other stuff about people that he liked—about his mother's boy friend—that turned out to be big lies. So he didn't believe him at all. Rennie really hates his father.'' David shook his head.

''Yeah,'' I said. ''I kind of do myself. But how about you? Did you believe his story?''

''You know,'' he said, ''I guess I really did. I liked it that you'd been great at something, Randy. Jon, I mean. Boy, I don't know if I can remember . . .'' We'd started walking up again. ''And that you wouldn't want to talk about it, be reminded all the time. *I* sure wouldn't, if it was me.''

''But weren't you also a little—*I* don't know—*hurt* I hadn't told you? That I'd gone on letting you think I was someone else all this time?''

He seemed to think about that for a couple of steps. ''Yes,'' he said, ''I guess I was, a little. And scared, you know?'' He took a sideways glance at me, then dropped his eyes. ''But, I don't know, it seemed as if you had a reason that I understood. It's sort of like my voice, you know? Now that . . . well, I'm losing it, I kind of try to get away from that whole part of me. That's why I wouldn't sing for Kelly. If you all hadn't known I was a singer, from my scholarship, I guess, I never would have mentioned it. Anyway, besides, I know the stuff you've said to me that *really* matters, I know that stuff's the truth. It has to be.''

I turned and looked at him. ''It has to be,'' he'd said. I got his meaning and felt awed by it. It touched my calm, my clarity, and blurred it. That wasn't good. I had to have control today; this was bigger than the NC double A's.

We reached the campsite. Kelly's pack was still inside a lean-to, looking undisturbed and left behind. I told myself I shouldn't think of it as hers.

"Well." I took a major breath. "She hasn't come on back yet, so maybe what we ought to do is . . ."

I'd thought about this waiting in the car for him. I figured Kelly wouldn't cross the road; she wouldn't want to take the chance of being seen, for one. Also, from the hike, she knew that on this side, the campsite side, was all the empty wilderness that anyone could ask for. Whatever Kelly had in mind, it wasn't meeting people, I was sure.

The plan I offered David was: we'd start down on Clinch Hollow Road, and walk in, roughly, semicircles, arcing round the campsite and returning to the road beyond it. Each lap would take us farther from the campsite, and a greater distance up and down the road. Periodically we'd call for her.

Who knows what David thought about this scheme? In actual fact it was, as my father likes to say, neither fish, nor flesh, nor fowl. The routes we took were ridiculously close to each other, in terms of Kelly being able to hear us, but also much too far apart for us to see every place she might be hidden in. The way I figured it was: if she was willing to be found, she would be. If the whole thing was out of her control, it'd be a matter of luck. I kept David pretty close to me, and hoped he wouldn't be the lucky one, if it came to spotting her.

Those were strange hours that we spent. At first, David expected to find her quickly, I am sure. "*Kell-eeee,*" we'd call, first my foghorn of a baritone and then his husky, sweet soprano. We'd stay stock-still and listen for a bit, and then we'd trudge along a hundred steps or so and try again. A new breeze had sprung up; that complicated things. It tossed the maple and the aspen and the birch leaves back and forth so that they made an intermittent rushing sound. Our voices sounded insignificant below them. Wind is an unsettler; I feel a little crazy in the wind. Above the trees, the broken clouds stampeded through the sky, trying to reach some calmer place by sundown maybe. The biggest, oldest trees let out some cracks and groans.

The ground we crossed was hardly ever level: glaciers cut it up and smoothed the edges, umpty-hundred-thousand years ago, and rain and melting snow kept washing down the soil that tried to pad those rocky bones. All this made for pretty forest, though: here a stretch of paper birch with big ferns underneath, slowly swallowed up by one strong stand of spruce, which then gave way to mostly maple, fine young trees and nicely spaced, and old decaying stumps among them. From time to time we'd come upon an opening, a little glade without a leafy canopy. In one of these, we both called *''Kell-eeee''* twice, and then I added, *''Kel.* I love you''—that old vow.

About the only place the ground was flat was down there near the creek; sometimes that was spongy, too. The visibility was at its worst in swampy places, with lots of silver willow thickets, and other junky little trees and bushes. That didn't seem like Kelly's kind of country, but we surprised two white-tailed deer, who'd probably been napping on a broad and grassy hummock. They bounded through the swamp away from us, not moving very fast or far before they stopped and stood and twitched their ears and looked in our direction. More in irritation than in panic, so it seemed. We got our feet a little wet, of course, and scratches on our legs from berry bushes.

David thought we'd find her right away, I've said that. Or she'd find us, more likely—answer when we called. But bit by bit, he settled down, not losing hope, as far as I could tell, but just not feeling, ''. . . any second now.'' He was kind of like a fisherman who knows the fish are there and still expects to catch one, but has to tell himself he must be patient. I think he was convinced that Kel would come to him if she could hear him—that when a fish comes by, he'll take the bait. I had no such certainties. Kids are more self-centered, I suppose, or possibly more willful. They sometimes can't believe that if they want something, grownups won't provide it, if they can. The old ''But Mommie, I *need* it'' thing. Or it may just be that kids are more hopeful, faithful (why not throw in charitable, too?). Early on, he thought he'd heard her answer once or twice. ''Randy, wait, what's that?'' he'd say, his hand laid on my forearm, almost trembling. And then we'd listen to the wind and have to shake our heads and keep on walking.

At one point in the afternoon, he asked me why I thought she'd done it—''gone off in the woods alone'' is what he said. I told him that I thought one reason was she'd heard (''somehow,'' I said) that I was Jon ______________, not Randy Duke. That made her real upset, I said, ''partly because of something that happened to her before we even met,'' I said. David nodded. That was enough for him. Kids don't always want to know it all.

He did decide I needed this, though: ''I'm sure that Kelly knows you're really Randy, even if you're Jon to other people. I'll bet you anything she knows that, Randy, even if she's, like you say, upset. My mother told me that even when she's really sore at me, she loves me underneath. I bet it's just the same with Kel and you.'' I nodded when he said that. ''You do believe that, Randy, don't you?'' he insisted. ''Sure,'' I said, figuring he ought to feel he'd helped.

We kept on walking; our arcs got longer, deeper. When it got close to five o'clock, I realized he must be getting tired. Then I thought he hadn't had his lunch. He hadn't asked what time it was or when we'd eat, or anything. He'd come to look for Kelly; what a kid.

''We've got to go meet Tina now,'' I said, as we finished off a sweep. I tore a thin strip from my handkerchief to mark the place along the road where we came out—that looked real professional, I thought—and then we hiked on down the road back to the campsite.

Tina wasn't there, and didn't come until five-thirty. By then the sky was almost clear, and the wind, though dying down, was chilly. I would have made a fire, but I didn't have a match. We sat inside a lean-to to escape the wind.

Tina didn't see us right away. She came up at a trot, wearing jeans and jacket and carrying a day-pack. She dropped her pack and looked for Kelly's—saw it, and her shoulders slumped. We stood up and came on out.

"Oh, hi," she said. She smiled at the boy and touched him. "David. I guess you haven't . . . ? No. Okay. I'm late because I realized you hadn't eaten, Randy. Kelly, either," she added. It didn't look like all that much food. "Jean-François let me make sandwiches, and I brought some milk and coffee. I had something back at camp, David. Really. So when you're ready, help yourself. I brought some flashlights, just in case." Sure, Tina. "Christ, it's getting colder, isn't it? I should have brought some extra clothes. David, you could wear a shirt of Kel's." He and I were dressed almost the same: t-shirts, cutoff blue-jean shorts, and sneakers.

I asked, and she had matches in her jacket pocket. "I think we ought to make a fire," I suggested, "just in case she comes here when we're gone. We can even leave a note so she'll know that we're the ones who made it. She's got her clothes and sleeping bag inside her pack, so she can get real warm, real quick, beside the fire. Dave and I can get the blanket and the poncho from my car, and carry them along with us. It isn't all *that* cold; I imagine when we're moving we'll stay warm enough." I could make a fire for Kelly, if Tina could make her sandwiches. Sure, Randy. David, are you listening?

We gathered wood—that took a little while—but when we came to write the note and lay the fire, we realized we hadn't any paper.

Tina said, "You don't need much; I learned that on our hike. We forgot the paper, too. All we had was toilet paper. Don't bother with the note for now. We can always write right on her pack; I've got a felt-tip here. Did you guys check your pockets? How about some Kleenex, maybe? It doesn't have to be real clean. . . ." Tina babbled on; she had a bunch of little sticks and birch bark set off to one side. Chances were that those would do it fine.

"Wait," I said. I almost laughed. "I guess I have some." And indeed I did. I'm the big-fat-wallet type; we aren't that uncommon. Every odd-and-end goes into the thing: ticket stubs, directions to some person's house, the terms of some fool bet you've made, receipts from every store that offers one, and so on so forth, fifty or a hundred times. Everything but condoms; only kids in junior high keep condoms in their wallets.

I pulled mine out and fished around in it: sufficient trash for fifteen fire-starts, at least—plus scraps enough for Rilke's correspondence. And two small red and golden running *R*'s.

Tina saw them fall and picked one up.

"What's this?" she asked, and turned it over. She read the backs of them out loud.

"K.C., D.T., Randy, Jon," she said, and stopped, and did a number with her almost nonexistent eyebrows. "Wait. You couldn't have gotten . . .," she began, and then broke off. She looked at me with brimming eyes. "Oh, Randy, you *were* going to tell her, weren't you? Why couldn't she have known that—yesterday? Oh, God, if she had only known you had these things. . . ."

David didn't get it right away; Tina's crying threw him off, I guess. He picked up the pins and read their backs, and put it all together.

"You got these made for *us*," he said. "And they've got *both* your names on them. . . . I *knew* that you were going to tell us. I knew it all along. I *knew* you were. Oh, Randy, wait'll Kel sees these. . . ." He kept on looking at the pins, first one and then the other, and smiling and repeating, "I *just* knew it."

*I* knew that he was lying. Who was that, Shakespeare? "The kiddy doth protest too much, methinks"? Oh, sure, he knew it now, but not before. Before he'd thought the same thing Kelly had: that I was going to walk away and leave them.

Exit Randy Duke, the nonexistent man;
go ahead and find him if you can.

Pianola music furnished on request. *Semper Fidelis*, I don't think.

* * *

We started up a roaring fire, using mostly slips from Campus Store cash registers. We also munched on sandwiches and sipped down milk and coffee. "Hey," said David, "don't forget to save some food for Kelly." Tina's eyes met mine and bounced away. We put a half a sandwich in her pack, and took the other half, and coffee, with us.

Tina thought we should go where Kelly went the day before. "I don't know," she said, "but that's what I'd do. I'd take a route I knew, at first, and maybe then go off it later. Besides, she said it was so beautiful up there."

And so we started, following the brook that people named White Creek, perhaps two hundred years ago. It's hardly what you'd call a major waterway. Where we picked it up, it's maybe twenty feet across, in August, and not particularly swift, and never deep. Brooks like this become real fierce in springtime, when it's snow-melt on the hillsides and their ice is breaking up. Then they run all muddy-brown and foaming, and over four feet deep in spots, and strong enough to sweep a pig away, I'll bet. But August is the slow time of the year; they just meander during August, and the brook trout have no trouble lying still in little pools, pointed straight upstream. Like hungry students waiting on the porch of the fraternity, they know which way their pizza comes from.

You don't walk fast along the banks of brooks like this—or don't for long, in any case. The swampy patches and the vegetation see to that. We were slowed some more by stopping to call out. Every quarter mile, or less, we'd walk a short way from the brook and call to her. I noticed Tina doing just what I did on these pauses: strolling to a spot where she could see a little distance every way. I'd asked her, out of David's hearing, what color Kelly's nightgown was; she said that it was white, and long. If we came upon her, it'd just be luck, of course, but if she'd kept the nightgown on, she would be extra visible. After we'd called, and waited, we'd cross the stream and do the same thing on the other side.

The fork that Tina'd told me of was more than three miles

in. By the time we got to it, the woods were good and shadowy. It might not be quite sunset out at sea, but in these quick and frequent hills, you lose the source of light much sooner than the almanac suggests. We took the right-hand tributary—the one that Kelly'd taken on the day before—and started up the mountainside.

This brook was easier to walk beside. In lots of places it ran right on ledge rock, skipping down from step to step to step, like lengths of spangled silver ribbon. The scrubby growth of lower down gave way to trees that kept their distance from the flowing water, mostly; in places where the brook made curves, it carved steep banks into the mountainside. Soon it was no wider than a standing jump, and we kept crossing it, as we went up, keeping to whichever bank was easier to walk on. But by the time we reached the source, the spring, it was gray dusk.

We kneeled beside the spring and drank the water. It was very cold and didn't taste at all like city water, which tastes like people manufactured it. I wondered if spring water's very old, the way it looks, or new, the way it tastes. I wondered that, but I didn't bother to ask.

I looked at Tina, seated in the gloaming, and saw that she'd begun to cry again. She'd dropped her chin and crossed her arms below her breasts, as if to try to hold herself together. It almost worked; her rounded shoulders only shook a little, and she didn't make a sound. I didn't try to comfort her. There wasn't anything to say, and we were out of things to do, and day to do them in, let's face it. I'd invented Randy Duke for fun, to save myself a little hassle, maybe, and he had just, like, killed a person that I loved. So now try facing that one, Randy.

I heard a noise and turned away from Tina. David had gotten up, and now began to walk across the little clearing that the spring was in. Probably he had to piss, I thought; I hoped he'd watch his step. Then I saw him looking backward, toward where we were sitting, but also up, a ways above our heads. I craned my neck and realized he'd moved to watch the moonrise better: a brilliant, silver-yellow but imperfect disc was floating up from just behind the ridge.

He waited for the moon to make it all the way, till it was running free and clear above the ridge, rising like a scarred and pitted streetlight in the sky. Then he turned away from it and, facing down the slope, began to sing.

I've simply no idea how great a boy soprano gets. I've never heard the name of one, or seen a record: Little Claude Lambrusco's Greatest Hits, or something. And maybe David wasn't totally as good as Kel had said.

But then, that night, he sang more beautifully than anyone has ever sung. Ask Tina, she will tell you. It's just not possible that anyone has sung so beautifully before or since.

There wasn't any wind to ruffle up the song; the night was calm as it was clear and cool. Forest birds keep early hours, and no coyote yet had seen the moon, so other than his voice there wasn't any sound at all, except a little whisper from the spring. His voice was colored like the moonlight; it was soft and high and silver and so very, very pure it made you ache all down your chest.

"And now she's gone, like a dream that fades into dawn.
But the words stay, locked in my heartstrings,
'My love loves me.' "

That's what the last verse said. He paused. The moon rose higher in the sky, but still there wasn't any other sound.

"The joy of love . . ."

He started at the top again, or maybe that's the way to end the song—repeating its first stanza. In any case, he got four words along, and then his voice just fell apart. Prepare to mock me, but: it made you think he'd had that one song left in him, and had saved it for a time he really needed it, and when he'd sung it through, well, that was it.

He didn't stop, though; he kept on going to the end of it.

". . . the pain of love endures the whole life long."

And, awful as it was as singing, it was also very wonderful. I closed my eyes to keep it all inside me for a minute.

I opened them in time to see her coming. She'd been above him somewhere, farther up along the ridge. She sort of floated down the slope toward where he was, not going fast, but lightly like a dancer, holding up her nightie's hem, as if it was a wedding gown.

JULIAN THOMPSON helped a group of teenaged people start their own high school in New Jersey, in the early Seventies, and he worked there for a few years doing teaching, counselling, college admissions, and the bathrooms. Now, though still devoted to the academic calendar, he writes novels and lives with his wife in Vermont.

# Flare Romance Novels

**LOVECRAZY Judy Feiffer** 84160-6/$2.25
When two Manhattan teenage temptresses decide that their divorced mothers are weak in matters of the heart—they decide to learn from the best role models for romance—each other's fathers!

**ROMANCE IS A WONDERFUL THING** 83907-5/$2.25
**Ellen Emerson White**
Trish Masters, honor student, tennis player and all-around preppy is surprised when she falls in love with handsome Colin McNamara—the class clown.

**I LOVE YOU, STUPID! Harry Mazer** 61432-4/$2.50
Marcus Rosenbloom, an irresistible high school senior whose main problem is being a virgin, learns that neither sex, nor friendship—nor love—is ever very simple.

**RECKLESS Jeanette Mines Ryan** 83717-X/$2.25
Fourteen-year-old Jeannie Tanger discovers the pain and bittersweetness of first love when her romance with school troublemaker Sam Bensen alienates her from her friends and family.

**SOONER OR LATER** 61275-5/$2.25
**Bruce and Carole Hart**
When 13-year-old Jessie falls for Michael Skye, the handsome, 17-year-old leader of The Skye Band, she's sure he'll never be interested in her if he knows her true age.

**WAITING GAMES** 79012-2/$2.50
**Bruce and Carole Hart**
Although Jessie loves Michael more than ever, he wants more from her. Jessie must make a decision. How much is she willing to share with Michael—the man she's sure she'll love forever?

**FLARE Paperbacks**

Available wherever paperbacks are sold or directly from the publisher. Include $1.00 per copy for postage and handling: allow 6-8 weeks for delivery. Avon Books, Dept BP, Box 767, Rte 2, Dresden, TN 38225.